INFERNO!

"If you bastards know how to pray," Bogner muttered, "you better start praying I can get us out of here before this place blows apart at the seams."

Bogner jerked the aging Ristovok into gear, slammed his foot down on the accelerator, and plowed through the door of the building. Wood splintered and there was a rain of glass as the windshield disintegrated and one of the headlights shattered. He careened several hundred yards between two rows of buildings and headed for the main gate. Behind him there was a chain of violent explosions as one arsenal building after another began detonating in a succession of volcanic eruptions. Zeverin Arsenal had become flaming rubble.

At that point he was no longer driving, he was aiming. The gates were closed and he saw one of the guards step from the building, drop to one knee, shoulder his SMG, and start to aim.

"Hang on," Bogner screamed as the Ristovok rocketed toward the gate. "Head for cover, we're going through!"

RED SAND

R. KARL LARGENT

LEISURE BOOKS   NEW YORK CITY

To all my heroes

A LEISURE BOOK®

September 1997

Published by

Dorchester Publishing Co., Inc.
276 Fifth Avenue
New York, NY 10001

RED SAND

PART ONE

Chapter One

It was raining hard again as Homicide Inspector Yuri Illich's Zaporozhet inched its way through the clutter of obsolete props in the back lot of the Odessa Film Studio.

After twenty years on the Odessa Constabulary, Illich knew what to expect. The monotone voice of the dispatcher at Police Metro had termed it a 77-50. That was the code for an unidentified body when foul play was suspected.

By so designating it, the dispatcher had deprived Illich of the opportunity to linger over a cherished cup of *kofi pavastochnamu*. Yuri Illich viewed a cup of Turkish coffee as the only civilized way to top off his favorite meal, *varyoniy yasik*, boiled tongue. Now he was disgruntled; not only had he already put in a twelve-hour shift, he had been called away from dinner, he was wet, and he was cold. He searched the shadows for the waiting studio security officer.

When Illich finally found the man, he was still grousing. He pulled over, turned off the ignition, fumbled around for his flashlight and raincoat, and sloshed his way through the darkness to the abandoned building and the waiting officer. Twice he stepped in deep puddles that sent water cascading over the top of his shoes, intensifying the late-night chill and accentuating the sensation of fatigue.

One damn shift was enough. The word "damn" seemed wholly inadequate.

The officer motioned him toward a partially opened door in a darkened building halfway across a rutted, muddy lot littered with parts of airplanes, a small roach wagon, and an assortment of mock military equipment—all studio props.

Fedorovich was waiting just inside the door, out of the rain. Like Illich, he was irritable. He too had already put in a full day. Central had called them both in because of the nature of the crime.

Illich picked his way through the bowels of the building, following the younger man, until they came to a service elevator. To the veteran inspector's surprise, the lift worked. They descended one level to where two additional officers were working.

Illich had worked with one of the men before; the other was unfamiliar.

He nodded to the former and glanced around what appeared to be a deserted maintenance area; pipes were leaking, the glass in the transom-style windows was broken, and there was no electricity. Backdrop illumination came from a bank of battery-driven crime lights erected by the investigation team, and augmented by the officers' flashlights playing back and forth across and over several inches of standing water.

"All right," Illich said with a sigh, "what have we got?"

Fedorovich dragged the beam of his flashlight back and forth over what Illich had first assumed to be a pile of rags and debris. "Hope we caught you before you had your supper, Inspector," the man muttered.

Yuri Illich circled the body, kicked away some of the clutter, lifted the poplin sheet, and felt his stomach revolt. The skin had been peeled off the woman's face, the eyes gouged out, and the ears cut off. Only the brown, blood-soaked hair remained. Yuri studied the familiar mutilation pattern for several moments, then played the beam of his flashlight down the length of the victim's body, making note of the woman's clothing. For the most part, it was intact. He doubted that the woman had been violated.

The woman was wearing what appeared to have been at one time an off-white blouse. He couldn't be sure without further investigation because it was saturated with blood and dirty water. Her suit was either navy blue or black, standard attire for most of the young women who had joined the Odessa post-Soviet Union workforce. There were no shoes and no hose. Finally, Illich trailed the beam of light down the length of the woman's sleeves to check the hands. The assailant had been thorough. The woman's hands, not just the fingers, had been amputated.

Illich closed his eyes while he regained his equilibrium. When he was confident he had everything under control, he looked at Fedorovich. "How long have you been here?"

"Long enough to find this," the man said. "It's her purse."

Illich took the leather bag, made a mental note of the quality of the leather, opened it, and began rummaging through the contents. The wallet had been stripped of identification documents, but still contained one hundred and thirty rubles.

"Among the papers we found a Metro ticket dated two days ago," Fedorovich informed him, "and an appointment card to the Odessa Medical Center across the street from the Krasnaya. Note the name on the card, Rubana Cheslov. It may be a piece of identification her assailants overlooked."

"Check it out," Illich ordered.

Fedorovich nodded. "I will call the medical center in the morning and get a copy of her file—if she has one."

Red Sand

"If she was going there for the first time, it could be a dead end," Illich reminded him.

Fedorovich shrugged. It was that particular and all-too-frequent phlegmatic gesture that made Illich doubt whether his young associate would ever be a good homicide investigator. Fedorovich had a habit of considering "close" good enough.

Illich paused long enough to light a cigarette before he began sloshing around in the water again. He continually probed the beam of his flashlight into the shadows. "Who discovered the body?" he finally asked.

Fedorovich leafed through his notebook. "One of the studio's security people, name of Bosninov."

Illich looked around. "When?"

"Around eight o'clock. We received the call at eight forty-two." Fedorovich anticipated the senior investigator's next question. "From what I've been able to determine, this old building hasn't been used in years, and they were planning to shoot some film of it burning down tomorrow morning. The State Film Officer instructed a couple of men to go through the building and make certain nothing of value was still stored here. That's when they found her."

Illich put his cigarette out. His expression was one of puzzlement. "Curious," he said . . . and paused. "Ten years ago, this kind of scene was not uncommon. When the State wanted to dispose of someone and send a message, this is what the victim looked like. Ten years ago I would have said the GRU had a hand in this."

"The GRU has been disbanded," Fedorovich reminded him.

"Have they?" Illich mused.

Fedorovich followed the inspector back to the lift, comparing notes. "The lab people are on the way," Fedorovich informed him, "and I'll check with the Citizens Affairs people to see if anyone's filed a report on a missing Rubana Cheslov. Anything else?"

Illich handed the purse back to the young officer and got on the elevator. It creaked its way back to the surface. "Order an autopsy," he said. "Two things disturb me. Why did the assailant go to such extremes to conceal the woman's identity and then overlook something as obvious as a medical card? That, my young friend, reeks of planned carelessness. It may well be that the assailant left the card in her purse on purpose—to make us think that body down there is Rubana Cheslov. If we're supposed to think that—odds are it's not Citizen Cheslov. And, if it's not Rubana Cheslov, then who is it?"

Datum: One-Two: Washington International: 14:20 LT

The gleaming blue-over-white Tupolev Tu-204 taxied up the ramp and came to a halt less than thirty yards from the waiting entourage.

Fifteen minutes earlier, three Lincoln limousines

had rolled onto the wet tarmac and began disgorging a welcoming committee. The dignitaries included the Vice President of the United States, Christopher Markland, the Secretary of State, C. Cyrus Fleming, and a host of other officials including the new Ukrainian Ambassador, Moshe Paliy, and his staff. Behind them were members of the Secret Service and the predictable battery of Washington media types. Flashbulbs popped against the gray October day and TV cameras rolled.

For the moment, the daylong rains had stopped.

For the moment, there was nothing to do except wait.

A tow vehicle maneuvered the boarding ramp into place while in the distance there was a long, throaty peel of thunder. Moments later the door opened and the President of the Ukrainian Republic, Uri Yefimov, stepped out. Flanked by members of his delegation, he began to descend the stairs to the waiting welcoming committee.

There was a round of polite applause and Markland's wife stepped forward to present Ruta Yefimov, the Ukrainian President's wife, with a bouquet of long-stemmed roses.

With all eyes fixed on the proceedings taking place at the bottom of the ramp, no one noticed a small, nervous-looking man wearing a chauffeur's uniform step from the third of the three limousines. He worked his way to the front of the car without calling attention to himself, and slipped a .45-

caliber military-issue automatic from under his black raincoat.

From a distance of less than ninety feet, he extended his arm, sighted—and squeezed off three quick rounds.

Uri Yefimov, the first President of a Ukrainian republic formed after the collapse of the Soviet Union, on his way to a podium to receive his official welcome to the United States, staggered, clutched his chest, and pitched forward.

The gunman, amidst a cacophony of screams and shouts, turned the weapon on himself, stuck the barrel in his mouth, and fired again.

Datum: One-Three: NBS Studios, Washington: 15:33 LT

The screen went blank.

Then the words News Bulletin appeared on the screen.

A sober voice, pregnant with what viewers have come to recognize as a kind of "official" urgency, announced that regular programming was being interrupted. At the same time, Joy Carpenter slipped into the anchor chair at the news desk and began to read.

"We have just received this word from Washington General Hospital. The Associated Press confirms that at 2:31 P.M. Washington time, Uri Yefimov, President of the Ukrainian Republic,

*was shot while deplaning at Washington Inter-
national.*

*"A spokesperson at Washington General con-
firmed that the Ukrainian President was taken
by ambulance to Washington General and at this
hour is being attended by doctors at that facility.*

*"For further word on what happened, we
switch you now to our correspondent, Bill Hancock, who is still on the scene at Washington
International. . . . "*

The scene shifted to a rain-swept view of the airport
tarmac. People were still milling around and the
NBS reporter hunched his shoulders to ward off a
driving rain.

"Right, Joy . . .

*"Behind me you still see the confusion sur-
rounding what transpired here a little over an
hour ago when President Uri Yefimov of the
Ukrainian Republic was shot by an as yet unidentified gunman as he was greeted by Vice President Markland. Immediately afterward, the
gunman apparently turned the gun on himself,
killing himself instantly. In the background, you
can still see Secret Service agents combing the
area, questioning witnesses, and trying to determine the exact sequence of events.*

*"So far we have been able to learn that the gun-
man carried no identification and that he somehow managed to replace the driver of the third
vehicle in the Vice President's official entourage.*

"Both the Vice President and the Secretary of State were standing within a few feet of the Ukrainian President when he was shot. Neither was injured. I might also mention, Joy, that the Ukrainian Deputy Prime Minister, Josef Berzin, who was accompanying President Yefimov, also escaped uninjured. As you would expect, all of the officials, of both countries, were immediately ushered from the scene by Secret Service personnel. . . . "

The camera went to split-screen again, showing Joy in the studio and Hancock at the airport. "Bill," Joy cut in, "is there any indication that the gunman attempted to shoot anyone else?"

Hancock shook his head. "No, Joy. In fact, two witnesses the Secret Service has since questioned indicated that he fired at President Yefimov, saw the President fall, and immediately turned the gun upon himself."

The camera revealed a man moving into the anchor desk beside Joy.

"I'm joined now by Barry Chambers, NBS analyst, who has been following this story and has some background for us."

Chambers, gray haired and paternal looking, was still shuffling papers.

"Joy, President Yefimov's reason for coming to the United States has been the subject of a great deal of conversation here in the Capital for the last several weeks. As you well know, when the

Red Sand

*Soviet Union disbanded, the Ukraine found itself
in the rather dubious position of housing almost
one fifth of the former Soviet nuclear arsenal.*

*"Uri Yefimov succeeded Vladimir Schcherbit-
sky just one year ago when the latter stepped
down because of ill health. Yefimov's first order
of business when he took office was to get the
long-stalled Forty-Second Amendment back on
track and proceed with the disarmament of a
wide range of sophisticated nuclear warheads.
That plan called for the French to do the disarm-
ing and have the United States foot the bill. Yefimov and President Colchin had previously
arrived at what could be termed a partial agreement and Yefimov's visit was to be used to iron
out the final details."*

"I know it's early, Barry," Joy asked, "but do we
have any clue as to who might be behind this assassination attempt?"

Chambers nodded.

*"When the finger-pointing starts, in all probabil-
ity, the name you are going to hear most frequently is Aleksei Savin. We don't know a great
deal about him, but what we do know is that he
is a member of the Ukrainian Cabinet of Ministers and is known to be violently opposed to
the disarmament agreement."*

A photograph of Savin appeared on the screen. He
was a mild-looking man, nearly bald, and wore rim-

less glasses. On the surface at least, he appeared to have few distinguishing characteristics. Chambers cleared his throat before continuing.

"Savin seems to be wearing several hats. He is an acknowledged former Communist Party hard-liner, a former member of the Politburo, and is said to have been instrumental in getting his country's leaders to sign the Minsk Agreement. That agreement ties the Republic of Ukraine to the Commonwealth of Independent States.

"Despite all of this, he has been singularly unsuccessful in persuading President Yefimov to turn the arms back over to the Russians."

From off-camera Joy Carpenter was handed a piece of paper, and she interrupted her colleague. "I've just been handed this statement from a spokesperson for Washington General Hospital." She began to read.

"President Uri Yefimov of the Ukrainian Republic of the Commonwealth of Independent States was pronounced dead at 3:05 P.M. Washington time. No further information is available at this time."

Then she turned to her colleague. "Well, Barry, we feared the worst when this story broke—and it's happened."

"I'm afraid so, Joy. Needless to say, our deepest sympathy and condolences to Mrs. Yefimov and the citizens of the Ukraine."

Datum: One-Four: Ploschad Potemkinsev, Odessa: 22:57 LT

The offices of Leonid Grechko were, even by opulent Czarist standards, ostentatious.

An oversized oval desk fashioned of black walnut, trimmed in teak, with gold inlay, dominated the center of the room. It was, he had been told when he purchased it, over four hundred years old.

For Grechko, the desk was the crown jewel in a room otherwise dominated by the enchanting beauty of a blue-green, woven wool and silk mid-eighteenth century Iranian rug that covered the entire floor.

The lamps, made of crafted brass, had been purchased in Portugal, and the two mirrors, both elaborately framed and trimmed in gold leaf, had come from Sweden. Only the origin of the crystal chandelier that hung from the fifteen-foot ceiling was unknown. When people asked, however, he told them it came from Germany.

Leonid Grechko, it was said, had parlayed a handful of counterfeit rubles into one of the city's most notorious money exchanges. Now he was one of the richest and most powerful figures in Odessa, if not the entire Ukraine. He was a member of the Cabinet of Ministers, a former member of the Supreme Council, and espoused capitalism while secretly endorsing, even funding, activities of the former Party.

What the citizens of the new Ukrainian Republic did not know was that he had become a power behind the power. His contacts stretched far beyond the new republic and his own agenda was far different from that of his contemporaries.

Now he watched from his office window as the black four-door Moskvitch slowly worked its way across the rain-slicked parking lot and came to a halt near the building's south entrance. The driver got out, produced an umbrella, and opened the rear door on the passenger's side, and Aralov Lavrenti emerged. From the way the senior cabinet official carried himself, Grechko knew he had been successful.

Leonid Grechko walked back to his desk and looked for the pouch containing Yefimov's itinerary. Surely Lavrenti knew, but details were important.

He waited for the sound of the lift to come to a halt and the door to open. When it did, Lavrenti was smiling—a good sign; Grechko knew Aralov Lavrenti seldom smiled.

"You have heard the news?" Grechko asked.

The aging, still slender Lavrenti nodded. "I heard the initial announcement before I left Kiev. Needless to say, our capital is in shock."

Grechko walked across the room to an ornate sideboard, opened it, and took out the silvery bottle of Kuban. "Then a toast is appropriate," he announced. "Chaos is our ally."

Both men bolted their drinks, and Aralov Lavrenti walked to the window and looked out at the rain with his hands folded behind his back. "We are a new country with old ways," he mused. "Now the power struggle begins."

"And the plan with Savin?" Grechko said. There was an element of concern in his voice.

Lavrenti was still looking out the window. "It proceeds. The time is right. We are a country of factions. Soon we will be a country united. There are those who believe our future is with the Commonwealth—but there are even more who are bitterly opposed to it. Savin's leadership in the KON has made him unpopular in many quarters. Many refer to the KON as merely a modern-day version of the KGB or the GRU. The KON is more feared than respected. We are wise to have planned to take steps to distance ourselves."

"You will proceed then?"

"It has already begun," Lavrenti admitted.

"Then on to other matters," Grechko said, smiling and changing the subject. "You have word of the missile shipment?"

"Three days ago. The shipment left the Balnecha Arsenal exactly as planned."

"And the arrangements—they will come off as planned?"

"Dubchek assures me that the switch will be made when the shipment arrives in Odessa. The

SS-28s will be replaced with older units in the rail-yards. He has indicated the conversion of the flat-cars is likewise complete and that the train will leave sometime Monday."

"Excellent," Grechko replied, again smiling. "Success makes me hungry. Even at this late hour we can enjoy a repast. Will you join me for dinner?"

Lavrenti held up his hand. "Will it seem strange that we are not joining others in grieving for our fallen President?"

Grechko laughed. "Only a few moments ago you were telling me how our country was divided. If that is the case, some are grieving—and some re-joice. We will join those that rejoice."

Datum: One-Five: Odessa Shipyards: 01:32 LT

Mikos Komenich cautiously made his way through the darkened warehouse, pausing from time to time to seek shelter amidst a confusion of containers and crates staged at the end of overhang near the cargo pier. Thus far, his task had been eas-ier than anticipated, explained in part by the fact that there were too many distractions for the man who was supposed to be guarding the shipment.

First there was the ancient smoke-belching switch engine in the rail yards adjacent to the docks. Then there was the rattle and clamor of a ponderous freight train, pulled along by diesels, clawing its way from the Black Sea to Kiev. Finally, there was the tumult resulting from the loading of an aged Cypriot cargo ship at Pier C3. Men struggled, yelling and cursing, as the crane hoisted container after container from the pier to the deck of the creaking vessel.

It had occurred to Komenich that the guard might be a young man, and that it might well be his first duty assignment—but he had already decided not to dwell on that thought. He moved in behind the guard, slipped the garrote wire out of his coat pocket, and wrapped it around the man's throat. Two twists and it was over—with only a minimum of protest. Komenich would allow that perhaps—just perhaps—there had been a slight gurgle or some other audible manifestation of dying, but he would swear he did not hear it. Garroting, after all, was a very efficient way to kill a man. More important, it was the KON way. And that's what he wanted the ones who found the body to think.

Now Komenich searched the railyards, looking for the three long shrouded flatcars Kochinski assured him would be there. According to Kochinski, the warheads, staged, paired, and inventoried in three groups of two, had been transferred from the arsenal inventory and loaded on flatcars at the Balnecha Arsenal depot in Kiev for transfer to the shipyards at Odessa. They were not, as the government had been informed, leaving from Ilichyovsk, the newer Ukrainian port eighteen miles to the south. That would be too inconvenient—and too inaccessible for the press. Leaving from Ilichyovsk would not enable the authorities to make a show of turning over the warheads to the French.

Komenich laughed. He had heard that the press had been invited to watch the ceremonial loading of the first two warheads at Balnecha. But what now? What if they wanted to see them again? What would they be shown? Freedom of the press was still new in the Ukraine—men had to learn to be free. The press had not learned that yet. They did not know what questions to ask.

Using the darkness to his advantage, Komenich pulled the guard's body over to the edge of the pier and dropped it over the side. The splash was lost in the ceaseless din of commerce sounds, and Komenich waited, watching until his kill slipped beneath the surface of the black waters. It occurred to him that on such occasions, night was an ally.

Now he headed for the flatcars, wearing the guard's hat and tunic. If he was discovered, he was confident he would be mistaken for a member in good standing of the Ukrainian Restructuring Force, more commonly known as the KON.

It did not take long for Mikos Komenich to locate the three flatcars built specifically to transport the once-formidable arsenal of former Soviet missiles. The cars were one hundred and two feet long, ten feet longer than the conventional Russian flatbed railcar. Even so, it had been necessary to install additional spacers between couplers to accommodate the gigantic SS-28s, which exceeded thirty meters in length.

Red Sand

To Komenich, the configuration of the shrouds covering the rolling stock easily betrayed the nature of each car's individual cargo. Kochinski had been right; to someone familiar with the missiles, the ruse was obvious. Nevertheless, thus far no one had noticed—or if they had, they kept their observations to themselves.

The cars with the missiles bundled and covered were exactly where he was told they would be.

Checking one more time to make sure he had not been spotted, he climbed up on the bed of the first flatcar, peeled back the rain-retardant canopy, and examined the cone-shaped head protruding from the wooden cradle. He knew what it was, but took out his flashlight and verified the nomenclature. SRF-Dc: 55-lm. It was an obsolete SS-19 Stiletto, probably from the Strategic Rocket Force inventory, and in all likelihood, the even-less-desirable silo-deployed version. If, as reported, Savin was behind this, he had indeed found a way of trading old for gold.

Mikos Komenich was well aware that his country still had a sizable inventory of obsolete Soviet ICBMs, Stilettos as well as SS-11s and SS-17s. It was said that a fifth of the Russian arsenal was located in the Ukraine when Gorbachev pulled the plug.

The missile Komenich was looking at now had been replaced six years earlier by the SS-24; same range, approximately ten thousand kilometers, but carrying ten warheads as opposed to the earlier model's six. He smiled; what was it the Americans called it, "more bang for the buck?"

He pulled the canopy down, relaced it, and checked the second unit. It too was a Stiletto. The inventory code indicated it was even older than the first.

On the second flatbed he uncovered more of the same, and the third rail car was no different from the first two. If the D-A committee of the Cabinet of Ministers thought they were carrying out the wishes of the Supreme Council, they were wrong— very wrong. Savin had been successful in pulling his switch. Not one of the units in the so-called first missile-compliance shipment contained anything other than obsolete, and for the most part, non-operational hardware. The rumor was probably right; the good stuff was probably on its way to China.

Komenich had seen enough. He checked his watch and jumped down from the flatcar. No doubt the guard was expected to report in; likely, on the hour. When he didn't, and someone came to check on the reason for his failure to do so, Mikos Komenich intended to be a long way away.

Datum: One-Six: Faculty Housing, Odessa University: 19:40 LT

Dmitri and Elana Tairov were longtime friends of Polce Berzin's family, and her father had once commented that he regarded the scholarly Dmitri as his most trusted friend. Now it was Dmitri Tairov's chance to prove that trust well placed.

When Dmitri contacted the young woman through his old friend Aralov Lavrenti to arrange for her to come to Odessa, he was informed by him that it would take a couple of days for her to arrange her affairs, but she would be there. Now, as the elderly couple escorted the woman they hadn't seen in over fifteen years from the dining table into the small sitting area, Elana Tairov paused long enough to pull the shades.

"You have heard from my father?" Polce asked.

"We have," Dmitri confirmed. "That is why we asked you to come. I trust you knew of his intentions when he arrived in America?"

Polce nodded as Elana poured tea and handed her a cup. What the woman did not know was how much the Deputy Prime Minister had confided in his friend. She paused, exercising caution. "I feel certain the assassination of President Yefimov has only entrenched his resolve."

Dmitri Tairov sighed and settled back in his favorite chair. "I do not question your father's wisdom," he said, "nor his timing. Unfortunately, the element of time is dictated by events and not your safety. Now that Yefimov is dead, your father has decided to reveal the full details of his arrangement with the Chinese."

"You seem certain," the young woman observed.

"He informed me he intends to talk to the American authorities tomorrow. When that happens, he believes the KON will be looking for you in a matter of hours. Even in a country preoccupied with mourning the loss of their President, they will waste no time."

"Not all mourn," the young woman reminded him.

Dmitri Tairov leaned forward. "Before we go further, I must ask you some questions. The first, of course, is whether or not anyone knew you were coming here."

Polce shook her head. "I merely informed my superiors that I was going to Moscow to visit relatives. They do not expect me to return to work until Monday."

"Excellent," Dmitri said. Still, his expression was grim. He had the curious habit of speaking with minimal lip movement. The young woman suspected his condition had been caused by a mild stroke. Throughout the evening his voice had seldom revealed emotion, but now his unusual speech mannerism had a decidedly clandestine dimension to it.

"You were saying my father intends to reveal—"

Dmitri responded before she finished. "When the train arrived from the Belnecha Arsenal three days ago, we were scheduled to receive the first shipment of missiles. Under the terms of our agreement with the Coalition, the initial shipment was supposed to contain a representative inventory." He paused and took a sip of tea.

"Did it?" Polce probed.

"Quite the contrary," Dmitri continued. "One of my colleagues in the Rukh, or the Ukrainian People's Movement for Restructuring, as you know it, inspected the shipment before it was shrouded. Admittedly, he is not an authority on such matters. Nevertheless, he is of the opinion that the missiles we are turning over to the French are all obsolete."

"I'm afraid I don't understand."

"Obviously, a switch has been made. The Supreme Council authorized the initial shipment of missiles. We were told the shipment would include six fifth-generation SS-28s. The missiles, of course, being of the treaty-banned configuration."

"You are claiming that none of these arrived in Odessa?"

"None," Dmitri exclaimed. "Somewhere between the Balnecha Arsenal and Odessa, the missiles were switched. Since all three configurations are a minimum of twenty meters in length, both the manner in which such a switch could be accomplished and the location of such a switch are limited."

Polce's look was penetrating. "Do you know how it was accomplished?"

Dmitri gave the young woman one of his infrequent smiles. "It had to be accomplished here, in Odessa, right under our noses. We have no alternative other than to believe that under the cover of darkness, the newer missiles were stored in three sealed container cars due to become components of a train bound for eastern Kazakhstan."

"Kazakhstan?" the young woman repeated.

"Precisely. There have long been rumors of a growing alliance between certain members of the Supreme Council and a dissident faction of the current PRC government in Beijing known as the Fifth Academy. It has even been said that your father was involved. Has your father not discussed this with you?"

"You are referring to the group headed by Mao Quan, headquartered on the island of Hainan?" Dmitri realized after Polce said this that, in a fashion, she had evaded the question.

"One and the same," Dmitri confirmed. "When our Cabinet of Ministers proposed to have the United Nations supervise the disassembly of the nuclear warheads remaining in our arsenal, former Party members viewed the action as an irreversible step away from Party control. Selling them to the Chinese, at least a *sympathetic* faction of the Red Chinese Army, made a great deal more sense. This somehow seems to be a symbol to Party hard-liners of a hope for an eventual return to control."

"Then you personally are opposed to the Party's return to power?" Polce asked.

"I believe there is no future for the Party," Dmitri said. "That is where your father and I have had our philosophical differences in the past."

"Yet you remained friends?"

"Of course." He seemed surprised by her question.

The young woman finished her tea and looked at the man's wife. She wondered how much Elana knew. Women had a way of seeing through veneers, and Polce wondered if Elana Tairov could see through hers.

"Then you believe the original shipment of designated state-of-the-art missiles is right here in Odessa and on a train bound for the east?"

"Once they cross over the border into China, the Party will have achieved a coup of significant proportions—not to mention an embarrassment to the Ukrainian people."

"Not everyone would agree with you."

"When your father left Odessa, it was only a plan. Now, with Yefimov dead, it is actually happening— a reality."

Dmitri glanced at his watch while his wife stood up, walked to the window, and peeked down at the street from behind the drawn shades. "The car is there," she said. It was the first time Polce had noticed her decidedly Moldovian accent.

"The plan is simple," Dmitri assured her. "To comply with your father's wishes, our American friends have devised a scheme to get you out of the country. This was prearranged by your father if he decided to go ahead and reveal the details of the sale of the missiles. The two men in that car will take you to Kharkiv, where a plane will take you across the border into Poland. From there you will have safe passage to the United States."

The immediacy of the plan surprised the young woman. She had been told to expect something like this, but not now, not this soon. "But I have made no provisions to leave the country," she protested.

"As we had hoped. If you traveled light leaving Kiev, there would be no reason for anyone to be suspicious. Elana and I have made provisions. You will be quite comfortable."

The young woman watched as the elderly professor and his wife put on coats, picked up a suitcase, and motioned for her to follow.

Outside the university housing unit, Dmitri and Elana escorted the young woman down the street to the waiting Moskvitch. Dmitri was surprised when he recognized the driver, a student who frequently authored essays expressing socialist views in the university newspaper. The young man was rolling the window down and smiling.

"You are right on schedule," Dmitri started to say. But his words froze in his throat as a bulky-looking man wearing a heavy coat stepped from the shadows. At the same time, the light from a nearby street lamp revealed the presence of another man sitting in the backseat of the car.

Dmitri had been informed that the driver who picked up the Berzin woman would be alone. He put his hand out to stop her, but it was too late.

"Good evening, Professor Tairov," the man said. He had a thick voice with a Belarussian accent and he was brandishing a Stechkin. Even though the man had called him by name, Tairov did not recognize him. What he did recognize was the man's demeanor—clearly that of the KON.

"What is the meaning of this?" Dmitri demanded. But he was too late; the heavy one had already circled around behind them and had Polce by the arm.

"Come, come, Professor" the man said. "There is nothing to be gained by theatrics." He took out a flashlight and shoved the beam of light into Polce's face. He studied the woman for several seconds before he turned to the man in the backseat of the car. "Is this the one?"

There was a muffled *"Da"* from the darkness, and the heavyset man forced Polce ahead of him toward the car. The rear door opened, and the man put his hand on top of Polce's head and pushed her head down as he forced her in.

For Dmitri Tairov there was a sense of helplessness. He was outnumbered and the men who had taken Polce were armed. When the fat man turned back toward them again, he motioned to Elana. "You, old woman," he said, "get in the car."

"You will not get away with this!" Dmitri shouted as his wife moved reluctantly to comply. But even he could hear the quiver in his voice.

The man walked toward him, the Stechkin still evident. "Listen carefully, Professor. We have a message for Deputy Prime Minister Berzin," he said. "If he insists on further dialogue with the Americans, he can be assured that he will never see his daughter again. And you, Professor Tairov, will never see your wife again."

"I am not in a position to advise Deputy Berzin what he can and cannot do," Dmitri protested.

The man laughed. It was an unpleasant, guttural, mocking sound. "I'm afraid you were not listening, Professor. We are not asking you to *advise* the Deputy Prime Minister. We are instructing you to *inform* him of the fact that he is in danger of never seeing his daughter again."

Dmitri Tairov stared back at the face in shadows.

"You strike me as an intelligent man, Professor. His options, as well as yours, and the ultimate consequences, seem quite clear, do they not?"

The man turned and headed back toward the car as the engine of the Moskvitch came to life. He went around to the passenger's side, opened the door, and got in. Even as the car pulled away from the curb and disappeared into the night, Dmitri Tairov knew he was powerless to stop what had already been set in motion.

Chapter Two

Robert Miller was, depending on a person's perspective, either cursed or blessed with the perpetual state of bachelorhood.

For Clancy Packer, Miller's status was a blessing because his assistant's lifestyle enabled him to devote sixty, often seventy hours a week to his first love—his position as administrative assistant to the longtime ISA bureau chief.

Others, including many of Miller's coworkers, viewed him as a workaholic and bureaucrat.

In reality, Robert Miller was a pragmatic, nondescript man in his mid-forties, with average features that complemented a frame of medium size and girth. He had discovered that the one or two hours others spent fighting Washington's traffic snarls and delays at the end of the work day could be better spent slogging his way through the volumes of paper that came across his desk. Miller reasoned that if that made him a workaholic, he was stuck with it.

It was Friday, and most of the ISA personnel had long since departed for the weekend. Henline and Oskiwicz had left early, ostensibly to catch flights back to their respective regional offices in Omaha and Minneapolis. Miller doubted that. Earlier Henline had expressed the desire to catch a pre-season NFL game between the Redskins and the Baltimore Ravens—and Oskiwicz had claimed to have a sister in Bethesda.

As far as Miller was concerned, each had reason enough to avoid a Friday afternoon in the office, but their early departure meant he and Millie had to answer the phones—and when you were responsible for the phones, not much else was accomplished.

Now, as he waited for Lattimere Spitz to return his call, he watched CNN for the latest developments on the Yefimov shooting and wished he had asked Millie to have some Chinese food sent in before she'd left. Spitz had indicated he would get back to him within the hour—but that was three hours ago, and still there was no call. Spitz, no doubt, had his hands full. The Yefimov assassination had Washington tied up in knots.

For all practical purposes, the October day was spent. There was little more than a red-yellow glow in the western sky and the traffic on Pennsylvania Avenue had thinned to a trickle when the phone finally rang. It was Spitz.

"It's on," the President's aide informed him. Spitz had a slightly nasal voice to go along with his hawkish face. Miller couldn't remember hearing the man when he didn't sound either angry or harried. Now he sounded both.

"Time and place?" Miller asked. He was entering the information in his electronic log.

"The Farm," Spitz said. "We'll get rolling as soon as David Langley of the State Department gets there. He's flying in from Boston. Berzin is already there. The Secret Service hustled him straight from the airport to The Farm. We've got him buttoned up. I sure as hell don't want to have to explain two assassinations to the head shed."

Miller always did a double take when he heard Spitz refer to the President. David Colchin's official code name was Prometheus, but Spitz seldom used it.

"Who needs to be there from our end?" Miller asked. He wanted to ask Spitz about Yefimov, but he knew Spitz didn't need the grief.

"For the time being, just you and Clancy."

* * *

Robert Miller spent the next two hours preparing for Spitz's meeting. After calling Clancy Packer and making arrangements to drive down to Colchin's farm on the Chesapeake the following morning, he pulled the X-10-A file. He poured over the reams of paper that had accumulated since Komenich had uncovered the preliminary details of the KON plot to sell missiles to the Chinese. Unfortunately, someone in the State Department had leaked the story, and T. C. Bogner's ex, Joy Carpenter, had broken it on the six o'clock network news. When the *Washington Post* ran the story the next day, the cat had been really out of the bag. As a result, too many people knew the real reason for Yefimov's visit to the United States.

Reviewing ISA files was easy; Millie used a yellow highlighter on the key points of anything important that came across her desk.

At the bottom of the pile of papers was a copy of the preliminary report from Mikos Komenich. In an area where there had previously been little activity, Komenich had suddenly become a key ISA operative. He had infiltrated the KON and worked his way up the ladder to become a Unit Leader. As such he was privy to most of the organization's sensitive information.

Miller had been through the entire file once when he leaned back in his chair and reviewed Millie's highlighted excerpts from Komenich's report a second time.

. . . first shipment from the Balnecha Arsenal scheduled to leave Cerkassy by rail 27/10. Stop scheduled in Kirovograd for change of crew. Consignment includes six SS-28s. French representatives will meet train in Odessa and missiles will be handed over to them on 29/10. Kochinski advises unable to accompany shipment from Cerkassy to destination. . . .

Miller skipped the next several paragraphs of the report, most of which were devoted to a lengthy description of the model's hard-target-kill capability, all based on Komenich's recently acquired information on improved accuracy and mobility factors. The latter part of the report referred mostly to the vastly improved deployment systems and Komenich, always thorough, gave several examples. Even for the man from Georgetown, it was ponderous reading.

Thirty minutes later, Miller stood up, stretched, went down the hall to the vending area, and bought a cup of coffee. He was still reflecting on Komenich's report. Komenich was now ISA's only mole in the Ukraine, and Miller decided the man would make an excellent aerospace professor if he ever grew tired of the spy business. Komenich actually understood the performance parameters of the hardware he was describing.

The coffee did the job, and alert again, Miller went back to his office and continued with the report.

. . . rumors persist from reliable sources inside the Rukh that Aleksei Savin, the leader of the KON, held meetings in Hainan with Mao Quan, head of the Fifth Academy. These meetings were held two months ago when Savin agreed to ship only those units that Mao Quan felt met 5A demands for survivability, responsiveness, and accuracy parameters.

Based on such required performance criteria, anything lower in nomenclature than the SS-25 and the two variations in that series would be unacceptable to 5A. . . .

Miller was nearing the end of the report when the blue phone rang. There was a saying around the office, "If it's blue, it's Packer." The ISA chief was the only one who used the blue line.

"Yeah, Chief, I'm still here," he said, picking up the receiver. A telephone call from Packer never included an exchange of pleasantries.

"Any new developments on Yefimov?"

"Hell, Pack, I'm watching CNN. They're getting info faster than we are. Nothing official in the last hour or so, though."

"Then go home," Packer said. "You just cost me five bucks. Sara bet me you were still at the office prepping for the meeting tomorrow and I said you had enough sense to go home and get a good night's sleep. Obviously, I was wrong. Now go home and pick me up at six."

Miller heard the *click* in his ear, put the receiver

back in the cradle, and started to laugh. If there had been a Mrs. Miller, he doubted that she would have been as concerned for his welfare as Clancy and Sara Packer. If anyone had asked, Robert Miller would have told them he considered himself more fortunate than most bachelors. In his case, someone actually did care about his welfare.

Minutes later he picked up his coat, turned off the lights, said good night to the two men working the ISA night desk, and headed for the parking lot.

It had been a long day. Worse yet, it had all the earmarks of deteriorating further. It was raining again and there were times when it sounded like freezing rain. Even so, Robert felt adventurous. He decided to stop at Hargers for the vegetarian special; then it was home to watch the news.

Datum: Two-Two: Faculty Housing, Odessa University: 02:51 LT

Dmitri Tairov sat waiting in his darkened apartment. He had checked twice in the last hour and although he could see nothing, there was little doubt in his mind that they were still out there. If the kidnapping of Elana and Berzin's daughter was the work of the KON, and he was certain it was, they would surely have someone watching him and the apartment.

If he tried to leave the university complex, they were certain to follow. If someone came to his apartment, they would know. There was even the possibility his phone had been bugged. He had checked his phone twice and as near as he could determine, there was nothing in the receiver or the housing that would indicate his phone had been bugged. As Elana often said, nothing looked "foreign." "Foreign" was a word Elana used to describe everything from an insect to something that suddenly turned up in a place where it didn't belong.

Still, there was no way to be certain. He was well aware that his phone calls could be monitored just as easily from a location off-site, close by, far away—anywhere—even in the dark van he could see from his window.

Dmitri was angry. Angry for being old—angry for being helpless. What did they think he would do? They had brazenly abducted his wife—not to mention the daughter of the Deputy Prime Minister. Did they expect him to stand idly by, doing nothing?

For Dmitri there was another frustration. It came from the fact that the abduction was the old way of the GRU and the KGB. The promise of a different way of life in his country was fading fast.

When the phone finally did ring, he was relieved. Mikos Komenich's husky voice was reassuring.

"Sepana said you called."

"They have abducted Elana and the young Berzin woman," Dmitri whispered.

There was a pause on Komenich's end of the line. "When and how did it happen?" The question was designed more to give Tairov a chance to talk. Komenich already knew who the abductors were. What surprised him was that he had not heard of the plan in any of the KON sessions.

Tairov launched into a lengthy explanation of how he had established contact with the Deputy Prime Minister's daughter and asked her to come to Odessa after learning of her father's plan. He went on to explain that there was a growing fear among members of the Rukh that the KON had organized a death squad and there would be reprisals against the lives of anyone who attempted to stop the sale of the missiles to the Chinese—all of which Komenich knew.

"There were arrangements for her to be taken to Kharkiv," Tairov continued. "From there, the Americans were arranging her passage to the United States."

"How many kidnappers were there?"

"Three, maybe more. For certain, three. One was a student here at the university. I recognized him. He shares a room with two other students in the central housing unit. I had university security go to his room. His roommates said he moved out earlier this afternoon."

"Did you recognize the others?" Komenich pressed.

"No. But the one that forced Elana and the Berzin woman into the car was a big man, very heavy, with a curious laugh. The others remained in the car."

"There is nothing we can do tonight," Komenich said after a pause. His voice was steady. "If I begin making inquiries at this hour they will become suspicious."

"It had to be the KON," Dmitri said. "Even though I did not recognize them, I recognized their ways."

Again Komenich paused. "There will be a Unit briefing in the morning. All KON Unit Leaders have been instructed to be there. The Directorate will be there as well. If the Deputy Prime Minister's daughter was abducted under orders from Savin, I will hear about it."

"In the meantime do I contact the Odessa police?"

Komenich thought for a minute. "Perhaps it is best if you do not contact them tonight. Contact them in the morning. Tell them that Elana did not return from last night's performance at the Odessa State Academic Opera. Say you went to bed early and woke up to discover that she never came home. Whatever you do, say nothing about the Berzin girl."

Dmitri Tairov started to object, stopped, and considered his options.

"Can you do that? Can you wait?" Komenich demanded. He could sense that Dmitri's composure was eroding. When the old man finally agreed to Komenich's plan, he sounded less than committed. His voice quaked. He could no longer hold back the tears.

Datum: Two-Three: ISA Offices, Washington: 04:15 LT

Kent Peters had recently transferred from the ISA bureau in Los Angeles, and at four o'clock in the morning he was still poring over the rental ads in the classified section of the *Post*. There was a sense of urgency in his search because his wife, Kim, still living in southern California, was expecting their first child. Her due date was less than two weeks away. Kent Peters was growing more anxious by the day.

"Hey, Gordo," he said, "here's a two-bedroom in Naper. What do you know about Naper?"

"Pricey. Cost you an arm and leg," Gordon Hatton, an eleven-year-veteran of the ISA, said. He started to say more, but saw Peters pointing at his telephone.

"Red Line Two, Gordo, they probably want a routine security check. Want me to get it?"

Hatton waved him off and snatched up the receiver. The voice on the other end of the line sounded familiar as it gave the code.

"Universal here," Hatton confirmed. "Sunrise 2. Which line are you transmitting on?"

"Hey Gordo, it's me, Presley. We've picked up a Code T for ISA. Open for business?"

"Yes, indeedy," Hatton answered. "How have you been, Pres?"

"Busier than hell since that Yefimov thing. Ready to receive?"

Hatton leaned back in his chair and opened the line, and the words began stringing across the monitor.

> XXX-33-Ai-Snowman—29/08 Code 3. [confirmed] 0610Z
> Tiger Lily abducted . . .
> whereabouts unknown . . . Harris a no-show

Hatton leaned forward and read the transmission a second time, then checked the code book, then the day log. Peters heard him mutter and reach for the telephone. He was hitting the automatic dial button for Miller.

When Miller answered, his voice was heavy with sleep.

"Roberto, old buddy, we've got a hot one. Just logged it. Snowman reports someone kidnapped Berzin's daughter. . . ."

Datum: Two-Four: The Farm: 09:32 LT

The Farm, as it was known, had been purchased as a weekend refuge by David Colchin during his first term as President. North of Lexington Park and west of Cambridge, it embraced several hundred rolling acres of grasslands and wetlands along the shores of the Chesapeake.

To the casual observer, only superficial changes

had been made to the charming old Maryland farm, but insiders, particularly those responsible for Colchin's safety, knew better. The Secret Service had installed a twelve-foot chain-link fence around the perimeter, and relied on an elaborate series of audio sensors and video cameras to monitor everything from curious tourists and would-be intruders to poachers.

Other changes included the fact that Rose Colchin, famous for her Tex-Mex brand of cooking, no longer prepared the President's meals. That task was left to a full-time kitchen staff who fed the First Family, a legion of Secret Service personnel, and the Colchins' frequent guests—both official and otherwise.

A security system had been installed, and the old round barn now served as quarters for the Secret Service men on duty.

But the biggest change for the President, who'd had his favorite quarter horse gelding shipped north, a grulla with bloodlines stretching back to The Old Man, was that the horses now shared their barn with two jeeps. The jeeps were used by the Secret Service to insure Colchin's safety when he went for one of his infrequent weekend trail rides— all too infrequent as far as he was concerned.

It was the third time Robert Miller had been to The Farm and the third time he'd attended a meeting held in the sprawling open room, an addition to the original structure, that looked out over the horse paddocks and, behind them, the bay. Miller, who knew nothing about horses and even less about the Chesapeake, admitted it was an enchanting setting.

When they arrived, Colchin's two top aides, Lattimere Spitz and Chester Hurley, often referred to as "the mind" and "the mouth" by members of Colchin's cabinet, were already there. They had arrived early and already had a two-hour meeting with Berzin under their belt.

Miller and Packer, discussing Yefimov's assassination, had driven down from Washington, and were greeted by a cold, depressing rain. They were followed into the meeting by Cecil Mower, Oscar Jaffe's right-hand man at the CIA, and Peter Langley of the State Department.

Hurley, who had spent most of the morning briefing the President after his conversation with Berzin, was the one who got the session rolling. He looked down the table and began with Miller. "Robert, I think we better start by having you let everyone know what happened last night."

Miller's reputation preceded him. He was respected for his attention to detail.

"At 04:16 LT this morning, we received a report that Dr. Berzin's daughter had been abducted as she attempted to make contact with our agent in Odessa. Unfortunately, that's all we know. Anything beyond that is pure conjecture."

"What about all this talk about a so-called KON death squad?" Langley asked. "Any connection?"

Miller shrugged. "There's no way of telling, Peter. But it's a distinct possibility."

Hurley looked around the table again. "Anything else before we get started? If there isn't, I think that little bit of sobering news from Miller should give you some idea of what we're up against."

Mower leaned forward with his arms on the table and took off his glasses. "Before we get too far into this, I want to ask Peter Langley a question."

Langley, the State Department man, spoke up. "I think I know what you're getting at, Cecil. Yes, I'm the one who instructed the Secret Service to bring Berzin here. If there is some kind of KON death squad operating out there, at least we know he's safe here at The Farm. Unfortunately, getting his daughter out of Odessa was part of the deal—and we blew it."

"I think we're getting a bit ahead of ourselves," Hurley said. "I want to make sure everyone is singing from the same song sheet, so I've ask George Triton of MSTI, the Miniature Seeker Technology Program, to bring us up to speed on what they've come up with."

Triton, ever professorial, put on his glasses, stood up, turned off the lights, and lowered the projector screen. It occurred to Miller that Triton looked like someone ought to look if they were representing MSTI. He was a young man with a narrow face, was prematurely bald, wore horn-rimmed glasses, and had a heavy British accent.

"Good morning, gentlemen," he began. "When

Mr. Hurley asked me to attend the meeting today, he suggested that I start with some background info. Therefore, the first satellite photo I'm going to show you was taken from a third-generation KH-11. This particular satellite is equipped with adaptive optics that compensate for atmospheric blurring.

"The image you are looking at in this photo is the Balnecha Arsenal in the Ukraine on the morning of September 15, last year. In the lower right corner of the photograph you can see a series of elongated objects that may appear to you to be nothing more than trucks in a parking lot. What you are looking at, however, is a cluster of six SS-28s. The SS-28s, as you well know, carry a multiple warhead with ground-penetrating capability. These, then, are land-based ICBMs, either launched from silos or from mobile units, employing a lethal penetration component. Four years ago, the President referred to the SS-28s-2a as 'probably the dirtiest warhead outside of those being produced by the Libyans.' "

Packer watched Langley lean forward and squint. He remembered a time when the former NI officer could have seen the details in the Balnecha Arsenal photo from a photo-reconnaissance plane at 40,000 feet without all the high-tech visual aid.

Spitz, who had been unusually quiet up until that point, spoke up. "Explain what we're using here, George."

"This particular satellite and camera is in a sun-synchronous orbit, so we're seeing the same thing from the same angle every time. In other words, we're over the target area at the same time every day. What you see is what you get."

A second photo appeared on the screen and the missile count was the same.

"I can show you gentlemen a sequence of photos over the next twelve months and the SS-28 count remains consistent. Then, exactly one month after discussions opened on the RIMROD agreement to have the French disassemble these warheads, we see evidence of them being relocated to the rail yards ostensibly to ship to Odessa and the French inspection team."

Triton turned off the projector and looked around the room. "Let me add, if these pictures were our only evidence, we would assume that the Ukrainians were in compliance."

Hurley looked across the table at Mower, then down at Packer and Miller. "Be patient, gentlemen, this thing fits together like an intricate puzzle. All right, Cecil, your turn; take it from there."

Packer had attended meetings with Mower before. Jaffe's man had a flair for the dramatic. He stood up and cleared his throat. "This is what we've been able to confirm so far. We know that six days ago, six SS-28s were loaded on flatcars at Balnecha Arsenal. Our agent witnessed the loading. And under the guise of visiting his elderly mother, he witnessed the train when it pulled into the freight yards at Odessa. The train stopped only once, to change crews. When it arrived in Odessa, the flatcars containing the missiles were moved to a secured area in the freight yards to await the arrival of the French technical delegation."

Clancy Packer began to smile. "Enter KON. Right?"

"Exactly." Mower said, looking at Triton. "Show them the satellite photos of the rail yards."

The recon photo that appeared on the screen showed three empty flatbed rail cars parked parallel to the ones containing the SS-28s.

"Early yesterday morning, a switch engine moved the Balnecha shipment down to the docks. Guess what?"

"No SS-28s." Packer smiled. "The old switcheroo, right?"

Mower nodded. "Here's the way we think it plays out. Our man Kochinski believes the French will go waltzing out of there with a bunch of obsolete warheads missiles in configurations that Gorbachev discarded eight to ten years ago. Odds are the French will never know the difference until they start to disassemble them. Bottom line, the government in Kiev, formerly headed by Yefimov, thinks they've complied with the terms of RIMROD, turned over the first of the SS-28s—but in reality someone, more than likely Savin and his cohorts in KON, are getting ready to route them to points east."

"I follow your logic," Langley said, "but how does Dr. Berzin fit into all of this?"

"He was part of the negotiations with Mao Quan and the Five A," Hurley said.

"Then he knows what's supposed to happen with the missing SS-28s," Packer guessed. "Right?"

Spitz stood up and walked down to the end of the table. "Berzin claims he's had a change of heart. He also claims Yefimov knew nothing about the deal with Mao Quan. Berzin is blowing the whistle now because he thinks giving the Chinese the SS-28 capability is too risky. Because of that, he's willing to tell us everything we want to know about the deal with the Fifth Academy—predicated on two conditions. One, that we guarantee political asylum for him and his wife, and two, we help him get his daughter out of the Ukraine."

Packer pushed himself away from the table and went to the window. He stood there for several minutes staring out at the fog rolling in off the bay.

"Okay, so what do we tell Berzin? Do we tell him our shot at getting his daughter out of Odessa went sour? Do we tell him we don't know where she is? Do we tell him we're still trying . . . or what?"

Langley held up his hand. "One thing at a time. From our perspective the political asylum part is doable, but legally we can only offer it to his daughter if she requests it."

Mower shook his head. "Hell, we don't even know if she's alive. Miller said she was abducted last night."

Packer tamped his pipe and lit it. The smoke curled over his head. "She's alive all right, Cecil.

You can bet your last kopeck on that. She doesn't do them a bit of good if she's dead. If she's dead, they don't have an ace to play as far as Berzin is concerned."

"Makes sense," Langley admitted.

Hurley looked around the table. He was smiling. "I get the feeling Clancy hasn't shown us all his cards. What have you got up your sleeve, Pack?"

"Nothing," Packer admitted, "at least nothing to go to the bank on—but our man in Odessa is a Unit Leader, an officer in KON. Let's give him twenty-four hours to see what he can come up with."

"That's risky, Pack. We haven't got a hell of a lot of time," Spitz reminded them all. "Berzin is waiting down in the guest house. Any minute now, he's expecting us to march down there and tell him whether or not we pulled his daughter out of there last night."

"Tell him it's a deal," Mower said. "We don't have to tell him about his daughter."

Miller had been quiet for several minutes. "Risky, Cecil. We can't stop him from establishing contact with members of the Rukh back in Kiev. When he does, sooner or later he's going to find out we screwed it up. If he finds out we lied to him, he's going to clam up."

"How soon do you expect to hear from your man, Pack?" Spitz asked.

"Within the next few hours. He's been instructed

to get back to us as soon as he has something concrete."

"I still say we stall Berzin until we know more,"
Mower suggested.

Chapter Three

**Datum: Three-One: Treyakov Warehouse
District, Odessa: 17:39 LT**

Mikos Komenich went directly from the KON Unit
Leader briefing to the warehouse district to find Nikolai Sukharev. Komenich was playing a dangerous game—and under the circumstances, Sukharev
was the only man he knew he could trust.

Nikolai Sukharev, a one-time minor official with
the former Soviet Rail Ministry, now held a position as a supervisor in the new amalgamation
known as the Commonwealth Rail Authority. If Komenich had guessed right, Sukharev would know
when the missile shipment was scheduled to leave
Odessa.

He located Sukharev exactly where he expected to find him, in a card game at the Treyakov Warehouse. Cards and women were Sukharev's passions. But at age sixty, the cards held more allure than the women.

"I must talk to you," Komenich said, eyeing the other four men in the room. He did not recognize them—and none fit Tairov's description of the men who'd abducted Polce Berzin.

Sukharev laid down his cards, stood up, and left the room, and the two men walked the length of the darkened warehouse until Komenich was satisfied they were alone.

"It's too bad about the President," Sukharev said, "but in turbulent times, a man in his position has many enemies. Is that not true, citizen?"

"Regrettable," Komenich acknowledged. "He was a good man."

Physically, Nikolai Sukharev was the antithesis of Mikos Komenich. He was short, soft from his thirty-five years of being a member of the Politburo and a section leader in the Radio-Technical Intelligence Regiment. A former avowed Party member, he, like so many others since the fall of the Union, now claimed to have seen the error of his ways. As evidence of his new perspective, he pointed to the 180-degree turn in political philosophy that had allowed him to be instrumental in the formation of a new rail shipping enterprise. Mikos Komenich had no way of knowing for certain, but he suspected the old Bolshevik's actions were motivated more by newly discovered economic opportunities than any disillusion with the Party.

Sukharev's transformation even included wearing a dark three-piece suit and an expensive silk tie. To Westerners, he looked like countless other Ukrainians who enjoyed the advantages of embracing capitalism.

"This better be important, my friend," Sukharev said. "My cards have been running well today."

Komenich frowned. "I just came from a meeting of Unit Leaders."

Sukharev shrugged and shook his head. "Based on what happened in Washington, it would appear that the KON has finally launched its scourge. I guess my only question is, who will be next?"

Komenich didn't know. At the same time he knew better than to reveal anything even if he did know, particularly if it was information Sukharev could sell. Instead, he treated Sukharev's question as rhetorical, avoided speculation, and leaned against a small table. "Is it safe to talk here?"

Sukharev knocked the dust off of a nearby chair, pulled it up to the table, and sat down. "It depends on what we are going to talk about."

"What do you know about a shipment of highly classified missiles that arrived in Odessa two days ago from the Balnecha Arsenal?"

Sukharev's eyes darted in both directions. He lowered his voice. "I see why you wanted to know if this was a good place to talk. Do I need to remind you that you are playing with fire, my friend?"

"Yesterday you would have called me 'comrade,' " Komenich reminded him. "We were playing with fire then as well."

"Even an old dog can learn a new vocabulary," the round man said with a smile.

"Kochinski inventoried the Balnecha shipment prior to leaving Kiev. There is no similarity in what he claims was shipped and what I saw being readied for turning over to the French inspection delegation."

Sukharev laughed. "Of course not. Does that surprise you? As a member of KON you surely knew that."

"I did not expect them to divert the first shipment," Komenich admitted. "The French are fools. They are accepting nothing more than a series of obsolete missiles, most of which have been non-operational for several years."

Sukharev took out his handkerchief and dusted off a small area on the table. Then he reached in his pocket and extracted a small black notebook.

"So it is you who visited the shipyards last night. That explains the body of the young security guard we found floating in the pilings this morning."

Komenich ignored the comment; he admitted nothing. Sukharev knew what kind of man Komenich was—and he knew he did what he had to do. Verifying the switch of flatcars obviously had to be done by someone. Finally Komenich said, "The SS-28s Kochinski described are merely the first of the units to be shipped to the Chinese."

"I know nothing of that," Sukharev said. "I no longer engage in the dirty laundry of politics. I can only tell you what I know about rail matters." He was smiling.

"Which is?"

"You have heard of the American satellites that are capable of tracking our every move?"

"Of course."

Sukharev lit a cigarette and exhaled. "The Americans are a suspicious lot. Is there any reason to believe that they no longer employ this method of monitoring what goes on in our beloved country?"

Komenich shifted his weight. "You are saying that KON cannot move the missiles for fear of detection?"

"Quite the contrary. Flatcars that carry the missiles are being camouflaged to look as though they are carrying materials for the hydroelectric projects in the east. If, by chance, the Americans become suspicious, and begin to monitor what is going on, it will appear that we are merely taking the southern route with intentions of shipping materials and supplies to the hydroelectric projects east of Alma-Ata."

"Is that the route?"

"Perhaps."

Komenich slumped down in his chair. There was an insidious element operating inside the bowels of the KON that was in many ways more cunning and more dangerous than the organization itself. Whoever they were, they were being clever, far more clever than he was prone to give them credit for.

"The southern route," Komenich repeated. "Impossible. The tracks are old and in disrepair, the equipment is outdated."

"There are times when cunning and deceit outpace technology." Sukharev laughed. "As a businessman, I have learned that."

"Deceit?"

"From one hundred and forty miles in the sky, it will appear to be nothing more than an outdated steam engine struggling with our newfound zest for commerce. In reality, it is a unit from which we have removed the firebox, the boilers, as well as other nonessential parts, to be replaced with powerful diesels. We have even devised a way to make smoke belch from the old chimney. Clever?"

Komenich was beginning to fit the pieces together. "Go on."

"Once we pass over the border, we have even devised a plan to make it look like the Chinese are taking over this rather pedestrian-appearing shipment of materials. Then, our marvel of deceit will chug back to Odessa for a second shipment. Ponderous? Yes, but workable—and effective. Even more important, we feel quite certain it is unlikely to be discovered by the Americans, regardless of their satellites."

"You are more cooperative than usual, my friend. Why are you telling me all of this?"

Sukharev laughed again. "There is a word in the American vocabulary, my friend. That word is 'investors.' True, I no longer espouse the doctrines of Lenin, but that doesn't necessarily mean I embrace democracy. I prefer to think of myself as an investor. There may be certain financial rewards for cooperating with the KON in this venture, correct?"

Komenich stood up and began to pace back and forth. "There is a young woman. . . ."

Sukharev laughed. "Mikos, my dear Mikos, don't tell me you are involved with an affair of the heart?"

"She is the daughter of Josef Berzin. She was abducted last night. Do you know anything about it?"

Sukharev shook his head. "Should I? Is it railroad business?"

"We were attempting to arrange safe passage to Warsaw."

The little man began to shake his head again, but suddenly stopped. "Wait a minute," he said, holding up his hand. "Perhaps I do know something. I was contacted early this morning. An inquiry was made as to whether or not it would be feasible to attach an additional sleeping car to the train leaving for the resorts north of the Caspian. I asked why they would need such a unit since the security forces on the train will all be disguised as Kazakh militia."

"And the answer?"

"I was told it was not my concern."

Komenich scowled. "As long as they have the girl, they can be reasonably confident that the Deputy Prime Minister will not divulge all of the details of the missile sale to the Chinese. If Berzin does not reveal what is happening for fear of his daughter's life, then the Americans will be unable to do anything to stop it."

"What is your concern in this?" Sukharev pressed.

Komenich stood up. "I will tell you when I know," he said.

Datum: Three-Two. The Farm: 15:15 LT

By mid-afternoon, Lattimere Spitz had assembled the group around a large oval oak table in the dining room. That table was one of the President's few concessions to such occasions.

The gathering included most of the people who had attended the earlier meeting that morning: Cecil Mower of the CIA, Peter Langley of the State Department, Lattimere Spitz, Colchin's aide, along with Miller and Packer.

Hurley, Colchin's senior aide, had been summoned back to Washington, while George Triton, who'd represented the Air Force's MSTI program in the morning session, had likewise departed. The only new face was the Deputy Prime Minister of the new Republic of Ukraine, Dr. Josef Berzin.

Berzin was a nervous little man with hooded, close-set eyes that seemed to regard everyone with an air of suspicion. He had an unlikely head of thick gray hair, was slightly chicken chested, and walked with a cane. Miller decided that if anyone asked him, he could think of no better word than "suspicious" to describe the man.

It wasn't until Berzin spoke that the image changed. His voice was charged with passion augmented by eloquence. It was easy to see now why the Deputy Prime Minister had become a spokesmen for his country and the one to negotiate the sale of the missiles to the Fifth Academy leader, Mao Quan.

Spitz went around the table introducing each of the men and explaining the reasons for each man's presence. Then he summarized what had transpired since Yefimov's assassination. Finally he turned his attention to the Deputy Prime Minister. "Doctor . . . earlier today we received word from a representative of one of our agencies who confirmed the information you had previously revealed regarding the initial shipment of ICBMs to the PRC. However, we still have questions."

Berzin appeared to be ready to cooperate. He opened his briefcase and removed several files. "Hopefully, gentlemen," he said in a halting English, "I will be able to answer them."

Mower turned out to be the most aggressive; he leaned forward, eyes fixed on the Deputy Prime Minister. "Perhaps you would be willing to tell us just exactly how many variations of the SS-28 there are. Then my second question would have to be, how many of these various configurations have you agreed to sell to the PRC?"

Josef Berzin took time to light a cigarette. He paused to weigh his answer. "The present plan calls for us to ship six fourth-generation boosters in an eight-week cycle."

"Over how long a period?"

"At present there are plans to ship in concert with the completion of launch facilities. We have been informed they are constructing eighteen such silos."

"And how many missiles in all?" Mower pressed.

Berzin hesitated again. "First, you must understand the situation as it exists in my country today. At the time of the collapse of the Soviet Union, there were perhaps ten thousand operational missiles, many of them with nuclear implications. It has been estimated that perhaps as much as twenty percent of that capability was located in my country. The inventory included ICBMs, SLBMs, LRINFs, and SRBMs. None of the inventory was returned."

"Concerning the ICBMs . . ." Mower prodded.

"We differentiate between short-range and long-range capability."

"How?"

"If you are referring to range," Berzin replied, "anything over six hundred kilometers in my country is considered long range."

It was Packer's turn. The ISA chief studied the man before he began. "As you are no doubt aware, Dr. Berzin, we have maintained a constant surveillance of the area since we learned of the negotiations between the KON and the forces of Mao Quan. Our best guess is that the most feasible way of transporting the missiles would be by rail—and that the most direct route would be to utilize the rail system of the Trans-Siberian Express. Is that correct?"

Berzin hesitated. "There are other ways," he said.

"We realize they could, of course, be completely disassembled, and flown to Hainan—but thus far we have not been able to uncover any silo construction activity on the island," Spitz said.

Berzin looked around the table. "That is because there is none. It is the intention of Colonel Mao Quan to deploy the missiles from launch sites in what you refer to as Lower Mongolia. The Fifth Academy has, in recent months, been very active in the northern regions of China—particularly the area known as the Gobi Desert."

Packer glanced at Miller. The Ukrainian Deputy Prime Minister had just dropped his first bomb. "Then you are confirming that the shipments will be by rail?"

Berzin scowled. He closed his file and folded his hands on the table. "Let me assure you, gentlemen, you could monitor the progress of shipments along the trans-Siberian route and never uncover the presence of the missiles. Not only have they been cleverly concealed, they will travel by a southern route, along the steppes adjacent to the Caucasus. The line my country has selected is a seldom-used route. It was chosen because of the low density of population and the remote likelihood of discovery."

Suddenly the room had grown quiet. Berzin's surprising revelation had caught the interrogators off guard. Mower's face was red. Both Langley and Spitz appeared to be completely taken aback, and Clancy Packer knew what each of them was thinking: A country with the world's most sophisticated system of photo-reconnaissance and intelligence satellites had been caught with its pants down. The twenty-five-year-old Corona program was capable of giving them resolution sharpened to six feet, but all that resolution didn't mean much if they were taking pictures of the wrong thing. Packer now realized they had been watching the front door when the back door was where everything was happening.

"If what you say is true, Dr. Berzin, that would necessitate building a railroad through the Caspian depression clean across the Kyzyl Kum Desert," Langley speculated.

"As I said before, the line has been in existence for some time. Only its use has been minimal. Besides, do you not have rail lines across vast expanses of your American West?"

Langley laughed. "You've got us there, Doctor."

Berzin held up his hand. "Forgive me, gentleman, but I must ask. Do you have word on my daughter?"

Mower leaned forward. "We are expecting word from our contact in Odessa any minute now."

"Something has gone wrong?" Berzin asked.

"Just a communications glitch," Mower lied.

Datum: Three-Three: Odessa Champagne Factory: 21:21 LT

Mikos Komenich never ceased to be amazed at the sites Yuri Illich selected for their meetings, places Komenich would never have thought of—and he would have readily admitted that he did not think like a police officer under any circumstances.

On this occasion, Illich indicated they would meet at the Odessa Champagne Factory on Proletarsky Boulevard—a six-lane boulevard that even at night revealed the distressing fact that the trees had already shed their leaves and the summer street vendors had sought warmer venues. As he passed the Filatov Scientific Institute, Komenich realized he was again entertaining his annual dread of the impending winter.

Komenich pulled into the empty parking lot across the street from the factory, crossed over, and entered the building. Illich, chatting with one of the security guards, was waiting in the vestibule. There was no exchange of greetings; Illich merely nodded and Komenich followed as the homicide detective led the way up a marble staircase to a second-floor alcove used during the day to accommodate tourists waiting to tour the champagne factory. It had been a wise choice; they were the only ones there.

As there had been no greeting, nor was there an exchange of pleasantries. As Komenich knew all too well from their previous meetings, Yuri Illich was seldom prone to more than a curt exchanges of information—always face-to-face—never over the telephone.

Telephone conversations, Yuri Illich liked to point out, were either monitored or taped or both. That was seldom the case when a man was forced to exchange information face-to-face. Illich put a great deal of stock in his ability to read facial expressions and body language.

The inspector unbuttoned his coat and dropped into a chair. Komenich sat down across from him.

"How have you been?" Illich inquired. The question was completely out of character.

"Busy," Komenich answered. He tried a smile to see if the inspector would respond. Illich's expression didn't change, so Komenich continued. "I assume there is a reason for this meeting?"

Illich reached in his pocket, extracted a length of stainless-steel wire, and began winding and unwinding it. "How shall I say this, Citizen Komenich? Shall I say your colleagues in the KON are getting careless and, even more important, predictable? When people get careless and predictable, I usually catch up with them."

"I assume you are getting ready to tell me what this is all about?" Komenich said. Then he had to wait while Illich fumbled through his pockets for a cigarette. When he found one, he did not light it; he simply held it as if he planned to—at any minute.

When he finally decided to speak, Illich's voice was tired. "We discovered a young man floating in

71

the water down at the docks this morning. In and of itself, not terribly significant, except to his parents or perhaps some girl someplace."

"Let me guess." Komenich said. "That wire you are holding has something to do with your discovery?"

The inspector frowned. "No, not really. It has something to do with another equally obvious homicide we discovered later in the day."

"Am I to assume you think I know something about one or both of these incidents?"

"In your capacity with the Trade Bureau you often have contact with foreigners," Illich began. Komenich knew it was not like the man to play cat and mouse, but he waited anyway. "Does the name Roger Harris mean anything to you?"

"Sounds British," Komenich stalled. "Why?"

"An American, obviously a businessman; I thought perhaps his name might have come across your desk—perhaps one of the trade missions."

Komenich had stiffened when he heard Harris's name, and there was little doubt in his mind that Illich had noticed. He also knew that the small delay in his response would simply inspire the inspector to ask more questions.

"We found Harris's body in the alley behind the shops on Shevchenko. Normally we would assume such a man, well dressed and apparently prosperous, was the victim of hooligans bent on robbery." Illich finally lit his cigarette. "But two things about this case have piqued my curiosity. One, the man was not robbed. Hence, no obvious motive. Second, we don't usually see Americans in that section of town—at least not of their own volition."

"Crime is everywhere," Komenich reminded him. "I read about it every day." He was smiling when he said it. The conversation was settling into its usual pattern. With a minimum of fanfare, Komenich realized that the detective had just given him valuable information. Now he knew how the KON had figured out where to intercept Polce Berzin. Everyone sold information. It had a low cost—and profits were high. Someone had obviously informed someone in the KON of Harris's purpose for being in Odessa. The rest was easy. Follow him to the contact point, get rid of him, and wait.

"I think it is only fair to ask what you want in return," Komenich finally said.

If possible, Illich's face sobered and sagged even further. He measured his words. "I want you to deliver a message," he said. "The body we found floating down at the docks this morning was the son of a colleague—not a political adversary, not even a hooligan. Perhaps you should remind your citizen friends that many of the activities of the KON are tolerated because they have sympathizers in the ranks of the Odessa Police. But even that will not protect them from—"

"Perhaps you should be talking to Aleksei Savin," Komenich suggested. He knew Illich understood.

"If it were me, citizen, I would choose my words even more carefully. I would suggest the use of the word 'warn' instead of 'talk to.'" With that, Illich fell silent.

Komenich got up to leave, but Illich stopped him. "There is talk that the assassination of President Yefimov is but the first of a purge of KON's opposition. I was wondering if perhaps you knew anything about it?"

Komenich shook his head. He knew that as far as Illich was concerned, it was even more important that he hadn't denied it.

Illich stood up, picked up his hat, and paused momentarily to look at a display of the champagne products. "Do you have time for a small libation?" he asked.

At that point, Komenich knew the rest of their conversation would be off the record.

Datum: Three-Four: ISA Offices, Washington: 21:10 LT

Kent Peters glanced at the clock over the door to the computer room and compared it to his watch. It was ten minutes after nine. Three hours to go. Gordon Hatton referred to it as the "shit shift." It was his contention that working from four o'clock in the afternoon until midnight either one or both days of the weekend qualified a man to "feel shit upon."

Peters walked around the office checking the nine o'clock transmissions on the E-mail pool, the report distribution bulletins, the two fax machines, and the two dedicated printers for inter-agency exchanges. Everything was in the receive mode.

"All right," he muttered, "Kent baby is bored. Someone out there do something. Let's get a chess game going or someone tell a dirty joke."

He was still contemplating trying to drum up a conversation with someone at TAC COM, PRe-EMP, or Jaffe's night man over at the CIA board when he heard the bell ring. By the time he got to his desk, the red light was blinking. He snapped up the receiver.

"Universal here," he said. "This is Sunset."

"Code T, ISA. T-time :08, no code. I'm giving it to you just like we picked it up, straight out of the bottle. Ready to receive?"

Peters double-checked his receiver, hit the power switch, and pressed the "receive mode" key. "Start talking," he confirmed.

There was a momentary delay before the laser printer leaped to action.

XXX-33-Ai—Deception—30/08
Code 57. [confirmed] 0317Z

Peters scrambled to check the code designator; on 31/10 it was Snowman, on 01/11 it was Deception. He glanced back at the printer. It was cleared and printing.

. . . Odessa Police have confirmed finding body of Roger Harris in Schevchenko section of city.

Police reports indicate cause of death strangulation.

For the second time in as many days, Peters searched the keyboard to call up the electronic dossier on Roger Harris. He began scanning, looking for PI.

. . . forty-four years old. Wife: Virginia. Two children: boy-ten, girl-eight. Northeastern University: BA-Criminal Justice, 1972 . . .

He went back to the open line.

. . . all indications daughter Deputy Prime Minister Berzin now being detained by KON with preparations being made to take her out of the country . . .

The transmission still wasn't complete when Peters reached for the telephone to inform Miller.

Datum: Three-Five: Falls Church, Virginia: 07:11 LT

Sara Packer had a habit of getting up early on Sunday morning. The ritual included making coffee and orange juice and reading the paper before she woke up her husband, after which they attended the early service at the Ravana Presbyterian Church. Clancy was still asleep and Sara had just sat down with her first cup of coffee when the phone rang. It was Robert Miller.

To Sara Packer, her husband's administrative assistant sounded less chipper than usual.

"I always wondered how a bachelor spent his Sunday mornings," she teased, "and Clancy told me they did the same thing their married counterparts did except there was no one to tell them when they had to get up. Is that true?"

Miller chuckled. "Normally I'd get up at seven or so, shower, shave, and jog down to Rudy's on Hawthorne for a toasted bagel, half a grapefruit, and apple juice. After which, if I felt terribly Catholic, I would go to Mass."

"Sounds disgustingly health conscious," Sara said.

"Or, I'd sit by the phone and pray Sara Packer would happen to think of me and invite me over for breakfast. Rudy's seafood omelette can't begin to compare with yours."

"That's exactly what we're having this morning," Sara Packer admitted. "Would you care to join us?"

"Sounds appealing," Miller said, "but something has come up. Actually, I'm down at the bureau. Is the main man up?"

Sara Packer was already on her way to the bedroom to wake up her husband. She handed him the phone. "It's Robert. I can tell it's important. He asked to speak to you. Normally he just asks me to relay a message. He's down at the office."

Clancy Packer came out of a good night's sleep

like a bear comes out of hibernation. The transition between sleep and being awake was a plodding process. By the time he picked up the phone, Sara Packer had already returned to the kitchen and started her first cup of coffee.

"Yes, Robert." Packer was giving it his best shot even though his eyes were barely open. "Sara says you're down at the office. What's up?"

"Peters logged 'deception' early last evening."

Packer had to think a minute. The transmission code word "deception" was the date code for the first two days of the new month. He looked out the window and his mind drifted away from the conversation.

"Komenich has learned that they found the body of Roger Harris in the Odessa warehouse district."

Packer swallowed hard. Harris was one of Jaffe's men at the CIA. Packer didn't know him, but he knew Oscar Jaffe had personally selected Harris because of his high regard for the man's abilities. He tried to pull himself together while Miller continued.

"Komenich believes the KON have Berzin's daughter."

"Does he know where?"

"He hasn't been able to confirm it, but he believes Aleksei Savin has put some kind of Machiavellian spin on all of this. He thinks Savin is holding Berzin's daughter on the same train that's moving the missiles east. Komenich also cautions us that Berzin won't be so damned cooperative if he knows his daughter's life is in jeopardy."

Packer was silent for a moment. "Who else knows this?"

"You're the first, but I think we better be letting Lattimere Spitz and Oscar Jaffe know what's coming down as soon as possible. Spitz has a briefing scheduled with the President when he returns to the White House this morning. You know Lattimere; even if he decides not to get Colchin involved, he'll be damned unhappy if he thinks we haven't kept him up to speed."

"Okay, start running with it. If anyone asks, I'm on my way."

Datum: Three-Five: Odessa Rail Yards: 04: 17 LT

The woman known to her abductors only as "the Berzin woman" had spent most of her captivity blindfolded and being shuttled from one location to another. The first stop had been a small room in what she'd believed was originally intended to be a holding area for freight. It had had no windows, no toilet facilities, and no heat. That was also the last time she saw Elana Tairov.

Later, long after she had lost track of time, she was led through a maze of passageways and the blindfold was again taken off. That time she was detained in a room that had windows. The problem was, the windows were covered with sheets of plywood. It was drafty and damp, and even though she was exhausted, there was little opportunity for sleep.

That second room also gave the woman her first opportunity to see what at least one of her captors looked like. The woman, like her, was tall and somewhat slender, but that was where the similarity ended.

She introduced herself as Olga Serova and to the abducted woman's amazement, she did not seem to be reluctant to discuss what was happening.

On closer inspection, Olga Serova turned out to be an angular woman with a narrow face and high forehead accentuated by the way she wore her dun-brown hair, combed straight back and parted in the middle. Every feature seemed disproportionate to her size. Her eyes were large, her nose small, and her neck and chin unusually long. She wore a plain, heavy wool blue suit and a turtleneck sweater. Her hands were large and she wore no makeup. It was as if she wanted to look plain.

Everything about the Serova woman pointed to a peasant heritage until she spoke. When she did, Olga Serova was both educated and articulate. It was Olga Serova who in only their second meeting accused her charge of being taciturn and noncommunicative. "We will be together for some time," she said. "We may as well learn to get along."

All of the abducted woman's impressions of Olga Serova had come from two brief meetings when the two women sat in a dimly lit room and waited for the man who seemed to be in charge of her fate, a man Olga referred to only as "the general." Olga's charge had seen the general only once. On that occasion he'd ignored her and spoken only to Olga.

The most recent move had taken her to a third location. She had walked much of the way, and made note of the fact that it was either a gravel or stone path. After walking some distance, she had been assisted up a narrow, difficult set of steps not unlike climbing a ladder. Finally she was led down a narrow corridor, told to wait while someone opened a door, and ushered into a room, only to have the blindfold removed and the door closed and locked behind her.

She was not surprised that she was in a sleeping compartment. She had assumed that would happen, but she was surprised that they had put her in a compartment without lights. It was obvious now that even Olga Serova had not been told. Nevertheless, the Serova woman left her in the darkness, and locked the door behind her.

She went to the window of her compartment and peered out into darkness. From the minimal light outside her window, she was able to determine that her view consisted of nothing more than a wall—a wall of rust-colored steel—part of what she surmised to be the side of a boxcar on a parallel track only a few feet from her window. After that, she spent several minutes groping around in the darkness trying to determine the nature and scope of her new world.

The compartment contained a bed. The linens smelled surprisingly fresh, with two blankets, both folded neatly on the end of the bunk, and a harsh pillow. The pillow slip, however, could not conceal the fact that the pillow itself was old with traces of mildew.

Across the compartment from the bed was a bench seat with a minimum of padding and a small reading light projecting from the wall near the window. The light did not work.

The compartment's other feature was a small personal toilet. Both the commode and the tiny basin were made of stainless steel.

Finally she found a light that worked, but it was barely adequate—serving as little more than a night security lamp. When she looked in the small mirror over the basin, she realized just how much of a toll what she had been through had taken on her.

In the darkness she allowed herself to reflect upon what was happening. He had warned her there would be difficult times, times when uncertainties prevailed—when she would wonder if she had the strength to do what she knew was expected of her. She found strength in remembering the education at the Central Commerce Institute in Kiev where she'd achieved early, middle, and advanced certificates. Then there was the important post she'd held; the respected position of advisor at the prestigious Dnepro Economic Models Academy. She dared not forget that. Nor should she forget other small details; that she was never a member of the Party, that she had been awarded the Dnepro post in spite of the fact that she was the daughter of Josef Berzin, and that she did not necessarily share the political views of her father.

All of this made little difference now. It was only important to remember if they asked. It was important to remember that she had a job to do.

The ravages of her recent hardship had been costly in other ways as well. There were hollows around her hazel eyes, her complexion was sallow looking, and her face was drawn and tired. More than anything, she would have liked to have paid attention to her brown-blond hair and luxuriated in a long steamy bath. Neither of which was possible in a darkened sleeping compartment. Besides, under the circumstances, they were not the behavior patterns people were trained to expect of Polce Berzin.

Instead, she turned her attention to her second most pressing need, the need for sleep. After that, she would be able to think more clearly.

She was still contemplating her situation when there was a knock on the door of her compartment. She heard someone insert a key in the lock and heard the door open. In the half-light that filtered in from the passageway, she recognized Olga. The woman used the same key to open the switches in the compartment, and the tiny room was suddenly bathed in harsh light. Olga was holding a stack of utilitarian clothing.

"You will need these," she said. "The days will grow cold."

As Olga Serova reached out to hand them to her, Polce Berzin felt the sleeping car lurch and begin to move.

Chapter Four

Log: Four-One: The White House: 15:37 LT

During the Colchin Administration, Washington insiders had learned that any meeting at the White House was scheduled in deference to the President. When David Colchin was in the Capital, he stayed close to home. Lattimere Spitz's spur-of-the-moment three o'clock briefing on a Sunday afternoon was no exception. If the meeting was held in the White House, there was always the possibility the President would attend.

The briefing was scheduled in a small conference room adjacent to the Map Room on the White House's lower level. Earlier that day, the President had indicated he intended to join them if he could break away from a State Department reception for a group of visiting British industrialists.

"All right, gentlemen," Spitz began, "in the interest of expediency, we'll dispense with the formalities and get down to business." He turned the projector on and looked around the table. "We've got a lot of ground to cover and not a helluva lot of time to do it. We need to get through as much of it as possible before the head shed gets here. He's bound to have questions and we better have answers."

Spitz pressed a button on the audio-visual control panel, the screen descended, and the room darkened.

Packer took one last look around the room as the lights went out. There was a new face in addition to the people who had attended the Saturday meetings at The Farm. The newcomer was David Harper, a senior program manager from the Miniature Seeker Technology Labs. Spitz motioned him to the lectern as two satellite photos flashed on the screen side by side.

"Gentlemen," Harper said, "map number one, the map with the yellowish tint, is a baseline reference photo of the Soviet Union prior to the breakup. This is one of the earliest recon refs made by a certified MST mission. This picture was taken in early 1990. I ask you to pay special attention to the railroad, marked in red, that runs from Guryev at the north end of the Caspian south and east to Urgench." Harper was tracing the line with a pointer. "Finally, if you look carefully, you can trace it due east then to Alma-Ata."

Then Harper turned to the second photo.

"At MI's request, we were able to divert one of the MSTI units to a more southerly orbit during the last eighteen hours—and this is what we came up with. Notice the very definite line north of Shymkent through Zhambyl to Alma-Ata."

Miller caught Langley leaning forward again, squinting.

"Every bit of what you see," Harper continued, "is new rail construction, new tracks laid in the last three years. I hasten to point out, however, that even if we had been aware of this activity, we probably would not have considered it to be significantly strategic, if for no other reason than we have long known this part of Kazakhstan plays a vital role in the area's economic survival. A new railroad, therefore, would have seemed to our analysts to be a logical step on their part to insure progress in their restructuring plan for economic revival— mining, some timber, and a great deal of light manufacturing."

"Pay special attention to this next overlay," Spitz cautioned.

Harper replaced the first two maps with a third. "Now we see the results of The Peoples' Joint Economic Development Endeavor, up until now a rather lightly regarded Sino-Soviet agreement signed back in the early eighties. If you look closely, you can now trace the rail line across the border into Urumqi, the capital of the province of Sinkiang. From there on, the route generally follows the basin of the Kerulen River until it reaches Ulan Bator in Mongolia."

Harper heard the people mutter as he turned off the projector and Spitz stood up.

"All right, now we've got some hard information," Spitz said. "Our weapons analysis people over at NI assure me that Dr. Berzin was giving us good information yesterday. In essence, they verified everything he said. What it boils down to, gentlemen, is this. Sometime within the next few hours or days, a handful of Ukrainian ex-Party dissidents are going to start shipping ICBMs armed with, fortunately for us, what appear to be outdated nuclear warheads. That's the good news. The bad news is they're shipping them to a very querulous group in China known as the Fifth Academy. And as you've no doubt figured out by now, while it isn't exactly the global threat we were led to believe it might be in the beginning, we cannot allow it to happen."

"I'm curious, Lattimere," Mower said. "If all of this is taking place on either former Soviet or Chinese soil, just exactly how does the Administration figure they're going to stop it? The last time I looked, Ulan Bator wasn't exactly in our backyard."

Spitz hesitated, choosing his words carefully. He had a peculiar habit of spacing his words when he was discussing sensitive information.

"I don't suppose it will surprise any of you to learn we're addressing that issue as well. Less than two hours ago, the President called a meeting of his national security advisors for seven o'clock this evening. And he has requested the presence of Generals Kramer and Abrams at that meeting."

"I still don't see how we fit into all of this, Lattimere." Packer said.

"We'll be relying on each of you for some kind of support. As soon as we get our ducks lined up, we'll know where, when, and how. For the time being, it's the old army game. Your job is to hurry up, get your shit together, and wait."

Spitz was beginning his wrap-up when Miller saw the President slip into the room. Colchin's collar was unbuttoned and he had loosened his tie.

"Mr. President," Miller said, standing up.

Colchin held up his hand. "Keep your seats, gentlemen. I'm here primarily because Lattimere was telling me in our briefing earlier that we've had some difficulties getting Dr. Berzin's daughter out of Odessa. Any late word?"

"Matter of fact we have, Mr. President," Packer said. "Our contact in the region now believes that the KON has her in custody. He also believes that the KON intends to use her as a pawn in our talks with Dr. Berzin—a kind of hostage situation—maybe even putting her on the same train with those missiles. Our man in Odessa seems to think their thinking goes something like this; If they do have Berzin's daughter and Berzin knows her life is in jeopardy, that may keep him from offering any further cooperation."

"It also keeps us from taking any kind of overt action against that train," Miller reminded them.

"Will it?" Colchin asked, looking around the room.

"It could be a real stumbling block to further progress," Spitz admitted.

Colchin eased himself into a chair across the table from Peter Langley. "Peter and I talked earlier today, so he already knows most of what I'm about to tell you. But for the record, late last night I had a chance to sit down and talk to Dr. Berzin. Hurley and I went to his cottage at the Farm to express my condolences for the death of President Yefimov. During the course of that conversation I got to know him better. What it boils down to is this. As Deputy Prime Minister, he may be one of the two or three most powerful men in the Ukraine. According to the best thinking of our State Department, this missile thing with the Chinese notwithstanding, he stands a good chance of becoming the next President of his country—if he chooses to run. Our view of all of this is that Berzin appeals to us more than the other candidates. Why? Because if we can believe what he's telling us, he's already seen the error of his ways. He realizes making a deal with Mao Quan and the Fifth Academy was a step in the wrong direction—and we don't think he's likely to let his country start drifting back into Party control." Colchin paused for a drink of water. "For the record, I believe him when he tells us he's trying to rectify the situation, but he needs our help. And he believes he has to get his daughter out of the country so that she doesn't become a pawn in this whole affair."

"That may already be the case," Spitz interjected.

"I assume you have been informed about the death of CIA Agent Harris in Odessa, Mr. President," Mowers said.

Colchin nodded. "I heard early this morning, Cecil. In fact, I talked to Roger Harris's wife earlier today. She said she had a premonition something bad was going to happen."

Packer cleared his throat. "That's our other problem, Mr. President. At the moment we don't have anything concrete on the whereabouts of Dr. Berzin's daughter. With Jaffe's man, Harris, out of the loop, we're down to one source, our ISA contact, a KON mole by the name of Mikos Komenich."

"How about Borodin?" Langley asked.

Packer shrugged. "We don't know. He's disappeared. Either he lost his cover or he's gone into hiding. We've had no contact for over a year."

"How well do you know this man Komenich?" Colchin pressed. "Or let me put it another way. Do you think he's resourceful enough to get Berzin's daughter out of there in one piece?"

Packer thought for a moment, and looked at Miller before he answered. "I'm afraid he may be too well recognized. If he starts asking questions of the wrong people, he's going to arouse suspicion. If he arouses suspicion, he loses his effectiveness. It has taken us a long time to get him positioned."

Colchin was working up to a smile. "You other gentleman are about to become privy to a long-standing inside joke between Lattimere, Clancy, and me. Whenever we seem to run into a rather knotty problem that requires a bit of resourcefulness, I usually suggest what, Mr. Packer?"

"You usually recommend that we make Captain Bogner available, Mr. President."

"And why is that, Mr. Packer?" Both men were enjoying the exchange.

Packer was laughing. "I've never been quite certain, Mr. President, but I rather suspect it's because he's a Texan."

"Damn fine qualifications if you ask me, Pack, glad you suggested him." Colchin winked as he stood up. "See if you can round Toby up. When you do, tell him I 'suggested' his involvement. He'll get the drift." Colchin's smile faded. "Don't let me down, gentlemen. I gave Berzin my word. I promised him we'd get his daughter out of there. If Langley is right and Berzin ends up as the next President over there, I want that bridge of credibility."

Spitz waited until the President left the room. "We've still got a lot of ground to cover." Then, almost as afterthought, he turned back to Packer again. "If we're going to get your people involved, Clancy, you better attend the session with General Kramer and General Abrams later today."

Red Sand

If it had not been for the assassination of Ukrainian President Yefimov, Tobias Carrington Bogner would have spent much of the day doing what most visitors do in Key West, fighting his way through hordes of crowded tourists, paying the obligatory homage to the Key's famous watering holes, and idling away time watching the fishing boats.

The events of the previous Friday had changed all that. Instead of enjoying his days off, Bogner had spent most of the weekend surfing back and forth between CNN and C-SPAN, trying to stay abreast of the latest developments in the Ukraine and resisting the urge to check in with Roger Miller.

Kim had informed him that morning that she wouldn't be home until six, and Bogner had planned to make the most of it. But the day hadn't turned out quite the way he had planned. Now, sitting on Kim's veranda overlooking Powell's Marina, he sought refuge in a scotch and water and waited for her to return.

They had plans for dinner at a small Cuban restaurant on the waterfront and he was looking forward to it. It wasn't often that he had Kim all to himself. His daughter usually had some adoring swain hanging on her arm.

Bogner was still indulging his reflective frame of mind when the phone rang.

Robert Miller's voice was easy to recognize. He was abrupt without being unpleasant, and had the annoying habit of forgetting where he was in a given conversation—which often introduced long pauses into the conversation. Bogner had once remarked that he understood why Miller was still a bachelor; Packer's assistant had never learned the art of putting people at ease when he was speaking to them. By the same token, he had the ability to wrap up and capsulize a convoluted situation better than anyone Bogner knew.

With Miller there was never any "How's the weather down there?" or "How's the weekend going?" Miller simply launched into whatever was on his mind.

"So, where are you?" Bogner asked.

"In the office," Miller replied. "Where else?"

"Well, for starters, why not here? Beautiful sunset, pleasant breeze off the gulf, a little scotch—and in a couple of hours I'll be dining with one of the most beautiful women in Key West."

"Go ahead, twist the knife," Miller said, "and while you're at it, tell Kim I said hello. But just in case it hadn't occurred to you, someone has to watch the phones at this pop stand. With this Yefimov thing it's been a long weekend."

"I've been trying to keep abreast," Bogner admitted. "Anything later than what I'm picking up on the news channels?"

Miller laughed. "If this had happened in the Middle East we would have had two or three different militant groups taking credit for Yefimov's assassination by now. Not these guys; other than a stiffly worded, predictable protest about our lack of security and a rambling 'loss of a great leader' diatribe, we've heard nothing. Langley tells me we're not even sure what they want done with Yefimov's body. The boys over at the State Department figure there's been a whole lot of behind-the-scenes maneuvering going on in Kiev in the last few hours. Yefimov is dead. Berzin has sought political asylum here in the States. And there's been nary a word from Lavrenti in the Cabinet of Ministers."

"What about Savin?" Bogner asked.

"Equally conspicuous by his silence is General Aleksei Savin—but KON's hand in all this seems fairly obvious."

Bogner knew Miller could go on for hours; the ISA was his life. Still, he tried to steer the conversation away from Yefimov. "How the hell did you find me?" he asked. "I purposely left a vague message on my answering machine."

"You're easy, T.C. You're becoming a creature of habit in your old age. You're either laying low down at La Chamanade in Negril or hiding out in Kim's apartment in Key West."

"Ahhh, Jamaica, lovely Jamaica," Bogner sighed. "Haven't been there in over a year. Maybe that's where I go from here, huh?"

"I don't think so."

"Which is the reason I'm sitting here listening to your dulcet tones on a Sunday night, I'll bet."

"We've got a situation developing," Miller revealed.

Bogner had heard Miller's lead-in before. "What kind of *situation*?"

"How much do you know about Berzin?"

"Deputy PM from the Ukraine. Wasn't he a member of Yefimov's entourage?"

"You got it. Spent the day with him yesterday. He's in the process of blowing the whistle on a deal between some Party hard-liners in his country and the Mao Quan faction in China. Seems the Deputy Prime Minister was involved in the original negotiations to ship some long-range missiles to Mao Quan—and now he's having second thoughts."

"So what's the problem?"

"By now Berzin has figured out that we're the only ones with the resources to stiff the deal and he's willing to give us all the particulars with one not-so-small caveat. His daughter is still over there—and he wants us to get her out."

"So, get her out." Bogner took a sip of his drink. "Doesn't sound like a deal breaker to me."

"We've already tried once. We're going to have to try again."

"I don't like the sound of this."

"I didn't figure you would. I'll cut to the bottom line; Colchin wants you to go in and get her." Miller put special emphasis on the word "you." "It's that simple."

"Go in where?" Bogner blustered.

"Last time we heard, she was in Odessa."

"Odessa? Hell, Roger, I don't know anything about Odessa."

Miller ignored the protest. "I just came from Spitz's briefing at the White House. Prometheus asked the old man if you were available."

Bogner sighed. Packer had promised him two weeks. He was in the third day. "I don't suppose you'd be willing to tell Pack you couldn't locate me?"

"Packer knows better. As we speak, Spitz has him tied up in a session with Generals Abrams and Kramer. The President made it pretty clear. He wants the Berzin woman out of there before we take any action."

Bogner recognized the inevitable. "So when am I supposed to be back there?"

Miller laughed. "If you don't make it back until tomorrow morning, you're the one who'll have to come up with some believable reasons for being late."

Bogner stalled as long as possible before he relented. "All right, let me make a couple of calls and see what kind of flights I can get out of here."

"I've already checked. There's a flight from Key West to Miami at eight-thirty. Space available. There's another at eleven. Same story, space available."

"Suppose I waited until tomorrow morning."

"Hey, it's your career. If you think you can piss off the President and get away with it, more power to you."

Bogner gave him the usual assurances that he would be there as soon as possible, and Miller hung up. It wasn't until later that night, after dinner, that Bogner informed his daughter he was cutting his stay short.

Datum: Four-Three: Taganrog: 05:13 LT

At first, Polce Berzin tried to sleep. But though she was exhausted, sleep did not come. Finally she decided to get up and sit by the window. Her compartment was dark and chilled and she wrapped herself in a blanket.

The train, it seemed, moved slowly. Still, there was an steadiness about its progress. The grimy rail yards of Odessa eventually disappeared behind her, and they were followed by long periods of dark emptiness beyond her compartment window.

As the train gained elevation, climbing into the grassland steppes east of the city, the cold autumn drizzle became a wet snow. She shivered and stared out at the nothingness, wondering how the plan would evolve. From time to time her eyes grew heavy and she dozed, but each time the lurching motion of the sleeping car brought her back to awareness.

Finally, they stopped at a remote station where, for the first time, she could see lights. A single incandescent lamp struggled to illuminate a deserted station platform, and she could see another cluster of lights in the distance. It was obviously a village, and there were two men huddled under a small overhang, out of the weather. They appeared to be wearing some kind of uniforms—uniforms she didn't recognize.

While she watched, a *provodnik* stepped down from the train, his collar buttoned against the cold, and the two men handed him a small bundle. There was an animated conversation among the men that lasted for several minutes. When they finished, the aging conductor got back on the train.

Several minutes later, the train had still not pulled away from the station and she heard muted conversations in the corridor outside her compartment. Finally there was a knock on her door. She heard the key being inserted in the lock, watched the door open, and saw Olga Serova silhouetted against the light filtering in from the passageway.

"You are awake?" Olga asked.

"I am, but it is cold," she complained.

"Do you know where we are?"

Polce shook her head.

"Tanganrog. We will cross over into Rostov-on-Don as soon as the bridges clear."

"Why did we stop?"

Olga Serova went back to the door and checked up and down the corridor. Then she closed the door. "Those men were militia. The Odessa police had asked them to make inquiries."

"About what?" Polce demanded.

"They wanted to know if the train had stopped and taken on any passengers after it left the rail yards in Odessa. The *provodnik* informed them that no one had boarded since our departure."

Polce turned back to the window and stared out. If the woman was prone to conversation, she would share her information. If she wasn't, Polce was confident no amount of cajoling would induce her to reveal what she knew. Finally Olga sat down on the narrow bench across from her. Her question surprised Polce. "Who are you?"

Polce looked at her. "You do not know?"

"I know only that it is most unusual to have someone like you aboard this train. You must be very important. You are being treated like a prisoner. At the same time I have been instructed to see that you are comfortable until we reach our destination."

"And where is that? How long am I to be held a prisoner like this?" The lines came easy—just as she had rehearsed them.

Olga Serova shrugged her shoulders. "I am never informed of our destination. I know only what I have been told—that the journey would take the better part of a week. In the past, before the dismantling of the Party, I was called upon to serve as attendant to those who were being sent to the camps at Nyuba or Oleminsk. Therefore I assume that you are being sent to a camp. Is that correct?"

"If we were going to Nyuba or Oleminsk, would we not be taking the northern route, the route of the Trans-Siberian Express?"

"That's the way it was done in the past," Olga admitted. "When I came aboard, I talked to the *provodnik*. He is an old man and he has traveled this route for many years. He knows nothing of your situation, only that you are to be watched closely and not allowed out of your compartment until he is informed otherwise."

"Then you know nothing of the KON? You are not affiliated with them?"

Olga Serova lowered her voice. *"Nyet,"* she said cautiously. "The KON is very dangerous, they are not to be trusted. There are rumors that say they are responsible for the assassination of President Yefimov. I fear we are returning to the ways of the KGB. Now we have learned of the deaths of the Tairovs."

"The Tairovs?"

"The bodies of Dmitri Tairov, the chairman of the Ukrainian People's Movement for Restructuring, and his wife were discovered in a remote woods near Odessa last evening. They were murdered."

"How do you know this?" Polce demanded.

"At our last stop, those two men, they were listening to the radio. They informed the *provodnik* when they provided the transfer papers for our train to go into Kazakhstan."

Datum: Four-Four: A Wooded Area Near Berezovka: 05:56 LT

Homicide Inspector Yuri Illich took time to light a cigarette and check his watch. It was almost six o'clock. In another hour or so it would be dawn and if the sun dissipated the thick blanket of fog, he would be able to get a better look at the site where the bodies were found.

The initial report of the discovery of the two bodies by rural militia personnel had been phoned in to the Odessa Police shortly before ten o'clock the previous evening. Illich was off duty at the time and Fedorovich had conducted the preliminary investigation. Most of the mundane details had been taken care of by the time Illich arrived.

"I think we're ready now, Inspector," Fedorovich called out, motioning Illich to the shallow drainage ditch where the bodies were located. The two militiamen who had been assisting stood back. "These men assure me nothing has been touched other than to verify identification."

Illich crawled down in the ditch and felt the water seep into his shoes. He pulled away the thin sheet of opaque plastic and studied the remains. Despite the fact that the man's face was drained of blood, Dmitri Tairov was easily recognizable. Illich had seen his picture in the newspapers and on posters too many times not to recognize him. Elana Tairov's identity, under circumstances other than these, would have been more difficult to determine. The garrote wire had been applied so tightly that a multitude of blood vessels in her face had ruptured, bloating the woman's face beyond reasonable recognition.

The ditch where the two bodies were located was adjacent to a rural road that followed the meandering Juinyi River, a river that, even though they were less than fifty feet from it, was completely hidden by the fog.

Fedorovich circled the bodies and gestured to the south, reconstructing his theory of what had happened. "About one hundred and fifty meters up that rock road is the highway. Fifty meters in the other direction is a washout, making it impassable. The bodies, quite obviously, were dumped after they were murdered." He gestured around the area. "There is very little evidence of disturbance here. It rained until midnight and the ground is wet enough that there would have been footprints. Since there are none, it would seem to indicate that the bodies were thrown into the ditch from a vehicle on the rock road where it passes over the drainage culvert."

Illich listened intently as he lit another cigarette. "How did the media learn of this so quickly?" Illich asked.

"One of the militia men that was here earlier has a brother with a radio station in Odessa. After he checked the man's papers, he called us—then he called his brother." He shrugged. "There are no laws against it."

Illich shook his head. He was surprised that, in view of Tairov's prominence, the press was not crawling all over the scene. He clawed back up the bank and worked his way up to the road. Then he stood looking down on the scene from the top of the culvert.

"You believe the bodies were dumped from the vehicle about here?"

Fedorovich nodded.

Illich began walking along the rock road toward the highway, scanning both sides of the narrow access as he went. Fedorovich scurried to catch up with him. "I would agree with you," Illich finally said. "I see nothing to indicate that there was any kind of altercation here on the road. It would have been a simple matter to drive here, dispose of the bodies, and drive away."

"The position of the bodies in the ditch would appear to support that," Fedorovich agreed. He had attended several homicides, but it was the first one where he had conducted the preliminary investigation, and he was delighted that a senior homicide inspector was validating his theory. If it had not been for the prominence of the victims, he doubted if the senior inspector would even have made the drive up from Odessa.

Yuri Illich walked all the way up to the highway and back to the culvert before he spoke again. "Have you asked yourself why they would choose to dispose of the bodies here?"

"In the hopes that they would not be found for some period of time?" Fedorovich guessed.

"Are there not dozens, perhaps hundred of similar remote places between here and Odessa where the same thing could have been accomplished?"

"Most certainly."

"Then . . . why here?"

Red Sand

Fedorovich did not have an answer.

Illich scanned the road again. "I have a different theory," he said. "There, where the road is washed out, you see repair equipment. That means there have been, and will be again, work crews in the area. Would you agree?"

Fedorovich nodded. "If it were not for the fog, they would no doubt be here today—perhaps not this early, however."

"Would they not have discovered the bodies when they came to work?"

Fedorovich frowned. "In all probability."

Illich stood at the edge of the road looking down at the bodies. "I submit that the perpetrators of this crime wanted the bodies to be found—and reasonably soon after the crime was committed—for a very obvious reason."

"I'm afraid I don't follow your reasoning."

"Dmitri Tairov was a very powerful man who many viewed as the principal voice of opposition to any discussions concerning the revalidation of the Party. He was well respected and people were listening to him. Now he is dead. Two of our country's most influential voices have been silenced within a matter of days. Is it a coincidence that both were violently opposed to the Party?"

"You believe this is the work of the KON?"

"I have no doubt. The fact that they were garroted is only a minor consideration. They were murdered, as was President Yefimov, for political expediency. Now another voice of opposition has been stilled. These bodies were put here so that they would be found, and their murderers planned on having the road repair crew find them. It is difficult to send a message to your adversaries if they have not yet comprehended the strength of your resolve. Something like this is graphic proof."

Fedorovich wondered if he would ever have the inspector's insight.

Yuri Illich turned away and began walking back to his car, but he stopped when he had gone little more than halfway. "Of course," he said, almost as an afterthought, "all of this is only a theory."

Fedorovich smiled, turned, and went back to the drainage ditch to assist the others with recovering the bodies. At the same time he was wondering how much of Yuri Illich's theory to include in his report.

Chapter Five

Datum: Five-One: ISA Headquarters, Washington: 08:10 LT

Bogner kept his word. He caught the last shuttle out of Key West and the red-eye from Miami to Washington. When most of Washington was just scratching its belly, getting ready to start the day, Bogner had already logged eight hours in the new week.

He circled by his apartment, grabbed a quick shower, an even quicker shave, and a change of clothes that made him presentable, and hustled into the ISA offices at ten minutes past eight. Millie Ploughman pointed to the coffee, winked, smiled, and gestured in the direction of Packer's office.

"They're just getting started. You haven't missed anything yet."

"What's up? Are we dodging bullets?"

Millie laughed. "I don't think anyone knows who to shoot yet."

When Bogner opened the door, Packer was briefing the staff on the previous evening's meeting with Abrams and Kramer. "Ah, Toby," he said, looking up, "glad you're here. We're just getting rolling."

It was the usual Monday morning cast: Miller, Peters, and Oskiwicz sitting on one side of the conference table, with Henline, Hatton, and Bartel on the other. Bogner knew some better than others. Oskiwicz and Henline, both *field* men, were waiting for reassignment following a department restructuring, budget cutbacks, and the closing of their regional offices. They were good men and Clancy had been able to salvage both of them. Some of the others, Bogner knew, had been less fortunate.

Millie Ploughman was an ISA fixture; she had almost as much seniority as Packer and, some said, a great deal more clout. It was rumored that Millie Ploughman knew the unlisted telephone number of every mover and shaker in Washington and wasn't afraid to use it. Bogner believed it.

He slid into the first available chair, and grinned at Miller. Packer was standing in front of a computer-generated map of the Ukraine, leaning on the console.

"Before we get started," he said, "I want to pass this along. The night crew picked this up about an hour ago. It's a BBC report. Nothing in the way of official confirmation at this point, but there doesn't seem to be any reason to discount it. We'll keep monitoring.

"According to the BBC, a Kiev television station is reporting that the bodies of Dmitri and Elana Tairov were discovered in a wooded area near Berezovka late Sunday night their time." He nodded in the direction of Millie Ploughman. "I've asked Millie to check our files to see if she could come up with any background info on the Tairovs."

Millie opened her files. "Most of this you know," she began. "Tairov was chairman of the Ukrainian People's Movement for Restructuring, also known as the Rukh. The Rukh consists mostly of Ukrainian intellectuals opposed to what's left of the Party. Over the past two years we've seen the tensions grow between the Rukh and the Party, particularly when the militant faction of the Party known as the KON was formed. We think it's likely the KON is responsible for the deaths of the Tairovs—in other words, politically motivated. And yes, what we're reading and hearing about the KON becoming more active seems to be true as well. Bottom line, no matter how you view these events, for the present Ukrainian government, this is the untimely loss of a second high-ranking official in the last seventy-two hours."

Packer waited for the news to sink in, then pointed to the screen. "All right, let's get on with our real reason for being here this morning. What you're looking at are the most recent MSTI cluster photos—and we're in luck; the resolution on these photos is excellent. Certainly they are clearer than the ones that were available for the Berzin meeting on Saturday."

"Next thing you know, T.C., they'll be peeking in your bedroom," Miller said with a laugh.

"They won't see much," Bogner said. "Clancy doesn't let me stay home often enough to get in trouble."

"So much for the social dilemmas confronting our two resident bachelors," Packer said. Then he turned back to the map. "Once again, let's start with profile information. What you're looking at is a map of the western portions of what we are now referring to as the Russian Commonwealth." Packer's finger traced along the map. "Starting here at Odessa in the Ukraine, we are following a rail line, essentially, straight east toward Alma-Ata on the Kirghiz border. I point this out because this is a decidedly different route than the one most of us think of when we think of the Trans-Siberian Express."

"Damn," Miller whispered, leaning across the table. "Almost forgot." He scratched out a quick note and handed it across the table to Bogner.

T.C. picked it up and read it. It demonstrated Miller's commitment to brevity:

Joy called, 7:30—call her ASAP.

Packer again trailed his finger along the route of the railroad. "Note that the rail line in question is visible here along the lower elevations of the Caucasus . . . and here again as it traverses the Caspian Depression. To put this in perspective, what you are viewing is almost five hundred miles of roadbed in this one photo alone."

"How'd we miss all of this when the damn thing was being built?" Henline pressed.

Packer shook his head. "First of all, we've known of its existence for years. It's an old rail line. Even at the height of the Cold War, it did not seem to be playing any kind of strategic role in their arms or supply scheme. In fact, I think it's safe to say that a casual assessment of the data we did accumulate during that period would lead most observers to believe that the rail line wasn't even complete, and for the most part, there was no work being done on it."

"Even though it doesn't show up on the MSTI shots," Miller added, "Berzin assures us it carries right on through the heart of the Kyzyl Kum Desert. The Soviets and the Red Chinese had a different view of things in those days."

Bogner cleared his throat. "Am I missing something? So far I don't see where the ISA fits into all of this, Pack."

"I'm afraid I have to agree with T.C., Pack," Henline said. "I don't know about the rest of you, but this thing looks like something way outside the ISA's bailiwick. If you're telling us this is the line where they're shipping the missiles to Mao Quan, my first reaction is how the hell are we going to stop them? Finding that train on a damn recon photo is one thing. Putting a stop to this missile business is another."

"My sentiments exactly," Oskiwicz agreed. "This doesn't look like our cup of tea."

Packer leaned against the podium. "As a matter of fact, our first concern is not the train. Stopping that train from getting through to Mao Quan is another problem. We've got a tougher task than stopping that missile shipment."

A series of photographs of Polce Berzin flashed on the screen. Then it was Ploughman's turn to speak. "You're looking at the only photographs we've been able to locate of Polce Berzin. Unless we can figure out a way to stop it, she may be on the verge of becoming a front-page story in every newspaper sold between here and Los Angeles.

"Again, as most of you know, she is the daughter of the Deputy Prime Minister, Josef Berzin. Berzin is currently in the custody of the State Department."

Bogner studied the photographs of the attractive young woman as Millie continued.

"She's thirty-one years old, five feet, seven inches tall, slender, somewhat athletic, a brunette, and has brown-green eyes—no identifying marks. She was educated at the Central Scientific Institute in Kiev and speaks four Slavic languages. Not just dialects—languages. For the last five years she has been an advisor at the Dnepro Economic Models Academy.

"Now for the kicker. The NI group claims they can supply us with photographs of Ms. Berzin in the company of Aralov Lavrenti, the current number-three man in the soon-to-be-defunct Yefimov government. Lavrenti is an ex-Party heavyweight and policy maker said to be aligned with Aleksei Savin, the man behind KON. We don't hear much about Lavrenti these days. Like most of the other ex-Party bigwigs, he claims he has seen the error of his ways. But who knows who to believe?

"Let me throw some more fuel on the fire," Millie Ploughman went on. "Nothing in the transcripts of Clancy's dialogue with Deputy Prime Minister Berzin over the past two days would indicate he knows anything about the alleged relationship, whatever kind it is, between his daughter and Lavrenti."

Millie sat down and Packer took over again.

"Actually, we know very little about Ms. Berzin's private life. We do know that, three or four days ago, she was asked to come to Odessa by Dmitri Tairov, the same Tairov whose body was discovered last night in Berezovka. We can confirm this much; Tairov was making arrangements to get Berzin's daughter out of the country when she was abducted by at least three men believed to be members of the Ukrainian KON. The KON started out to be a Ukrainian paramilitary group. It has since evolved into something quite different; a pseudo-secret police group with political clout dominated by former

Party members. Their leader, as Miller pointed out, is Aleksei Savin. According to *Newsweek*, Savin makes some of Stalin's early proclivities pale by comparison."

"Do we know where this Berzin woman is?" Bogner asked.

"We think we do," Miller said, "but as of this moment we can't be certain. Our man in that part of the world believes she's on the same train that's carrying the missiles across the border into China."

"Then the next logical question is, just how well are those missiles being guarded?" Bogner asked. "If we know that, it'll give us some indication of what we have to get past to get the girl."

"We don't know the answer to that one either," Miller admitted.

"Any idea what kind of war games Spitz has in mind or how long we've got before Kramer and Abrams get involved?"

"We don't have an answer to that one either, T.C. We'll know in the next twelve to eighteen hours, though. But I can tell you this much. They have advised the President that it's too risky for us to take any hard-line action. We do know that the missiles being shipped to Mao Quan are all models we have a fairly good dossier on—standard warheads. Abrams says we have the means to stop them if Mao Quan gets frisky—but until he does, Abrams believes a clandestine operation would be more productive."

"One girl and one train," Bogner said. "Where,

when, and how?" He was studying the map and leaning against the table. "You're talking about a lot of territory, Pack."

"We'll fly you to Odessa as soon as we have a cover and know what Abrams and Kramer are recommending to the President. By then Komenich should have a handle on where the Berzin woman is. If she's on the train, you'll have to find a way to get her off. Where and how is up to you. Suffice to say, Colchin gave her father his word, and he's dumping it in your lap."

Bogner winced, sagged back in his chair, and took a sip of his coffee. It wasn't the assignment that bothered him; it was the element of the unknown. Halfway around the world, in the middle of the Kazakh wastelands, was no place to discover your backup couldn't cut the mustard. As far as Bogner was concerned, Komenich was an unknown, a question mark in a damn risky equation. Bogner knew most of the agents within the ISA, even some of the moles. The ones he knew were battle tested. Neither Packer nor Miller had mentioned Mikos Komenich in the department's staffing or fitness reports. Bottom line: He knew nothing about the man—and that made him uneasy.

Bogner pushed himself away from the table, stood up, and walked over to the display maps. "This area through here is high country," he said, pointing to the chain of mountains along the Kazakhstan-Kyrgyzstan border. "And this is desert. By now I'd think you know I'm a resort kind of guy, Clancy, a little surf, some beach, a couple of fillies in bikinis. Why the hell can't you come up with a problem down in the Caribbean?"

Millie Ploughman laughed.

Datum: Five-Two: Near Atyrau, Kazakhstan: 11:56 LT

Prior to this, Polce Berzin had been allowed out of her sleeping compartment only once. Now she was being allowed out again. Accompanied by Olga Serova, she was permitted a brief shower in the militia car and a chance to stretch her legs outside on the ground. She used the latter as an opportunity to get a better grasp of her surroundings. The three shrouded railcars forward of the one where she had been detained appeared to be devoted to transporting some kind of cargo. The car behind her sleeping car was obviously a troop carrier.

Somewhere before the lunch hour, the train had come to a complete stop, and remained that way for the next several hours. Olga, who came and went twice during that period, informed her that they were taking on another car now that they had passed over the border into Kazakhstan and that the delay was necessary while the Kazakh border authorities in Atyrau inspected the papers.

If that was the case, Polce decided it was perfunctory inspection at best; she did not hear any voices outside her compartment during the period nor did she see any soldiers or agents moving up or down the tracks.

From the window of her compartment, Polce Berzin could see a barren stretch of lowland dotted with patches of dirty snow and an occasional birch tree. In all, she counted four peasant cottages and a few head of livestock—mostly cattle and horses. This view was decidedly different than it had been earlier in the day when the train had headed due east after passing through Ellsta and swung abruptly south. At that point, she was, for a short time, able to identify the widening Volga just before it emptied into the Caspian. For the next two hours the tracks had paralleled the great sea as the train headed east again. Now, however, the train was stopped, and there was a cold steady rain to further enhance the countryside's mood of somber austerity.

Twice during the course of the day, she heard a group of men pass in the corridor outside her compartment. She assumed they were all men because she heard only men's voices. She also assumed they were the militia Olga had described—this too because they sounded as though they had been drinking, common among citizen-soldiers, and because of what sounded like swagger in the way they walked—they had repeatedly bumped against the door to her compartment as they passed.

As the day faded into early evening, she was let out to stretch her legs again, and looked around with at first little more than passing interest. Her interest grew when two fishing trawlers maneuvered up the coast and anchored in the shallow waters not far from where the Ural River drained into the sea. The trawlers were flying the flag of the Republic of Kazakhstan, teal blue background with yellow sun. At the same time, Polce was able to get her first look at the militia accompanying the shipment. Their tunics and hats were the same, but the rest of their uniforms didn't match. From their demeanor, their overall appearance, and the way they marched, the phrase "rag tag" came to Polce's mind.

As she watched them work their way from the rail bed down to a road and ramp that ended at the water's edge, they appeared to be no more than a group of roustabouts hired from the Odessa docks more for their muscle than military skills. All in all, she counted twelve of them.

A large motorized dory was winched into the water from the bigger of the two trawlers, and a small barge from the deck of the second. After three large wooden containers were lowered onto the barge, the dory began towing its cargo toward shore.

At that point, Polce saw several of the militia wade into the water, assist in beaching the barge, and begin unloading it. They hefted the containers to safety on a narrow strip of beach gravel, pried the crates open, and began carrying the contents up the ramp to dry ground. In all there were six crates and it took four men to carry each.

One by one the crates were opened and the contents inspected. Polce saw one of the militiamen sign some papers and hand them back to the man from the ship. The dory and barge returned to the trawler as the day grew dark.

Moments later she was escorted back aboard the train and locked in her compartment. But it was several hours before the train started up again.

Datum: Five-Three: Deerfield Condos, Washington: 22:49 LT

Bogner and Colchin went back a long way. Even before Texas Governor David Colchin ascended to the Presidency of the United States, the Bogner-Colchin coalition was strong. It was a former Colchin aide, when asked about the governor's relationship with the then-young Navy pilot, who described Bogner as a "a bullheaded nomad with a penchant for getting himself in and out of sticky situations."

T.C., as most everyone called him, was prone to agree with that assessment. True, he had been promoted a couple of times since then, but he was still a nomad, still in the U.S. Navy, and as his former wife, Joy Carpenter, was quick to assure people, he was still bullheaded.

When Bogner was in Washington, he shared a two-bedroom apartment with a longtime friend, Reese Smith of the Associated Press. Few people knew that, just as even fewer knew he was still permanently assigned to the duty roster at the Naval

Air Station at Pensacola. His ISA assignments, all
TDY, were Colchin's way of keeping him handy.

The arrangement with Reese Smith worked well
too. Smith was seldom in town and Bogner, when
he did require a place to bed down, usually had the
apartment to himself. Now, with a long day behind
him, he tucked his rented Olds Aurora in the first
available parking space, took the elevator to the
third floor, and had his tie off by the time he opened
the door. When he heard the phone ringing, he realized he was already trying to conjure up an excuse
for not returning Joy's call earlier.

"Do I start with an apology?" he said after he
picked up the phone.

"How did you know it was me?" Joy asked.

"Three people have this number. I talked to
Packer less than thirty minutes ago, and Reese is
somewhere in the Orient chasing a story. That
leaves you."

"The call might have been for Reese," Joy said
teasingly.

"Reese has no friends, he's a reporter."

Joy seldom laughed at his attempts at humor.
They had both quit laughing the day a Los Angeles
County judge had called a halt to their marriage
and awarded Joy custody of their only child, their
daughter, Kim. Their sporadic attempts at recon-
ciliation since then usually ended up going nowhere, but they would have both admitted the
attraction was still there.

Their last encounter had ended up in a frantic bit

of lovemaking that went sour when Clancy Packer's early morning phone call requested Bogner's presence at "an important ISA briefing." Joy Carpenter, as they called her at NBS, stormed out of his bedroom and out of his life, and another nine months of no contact ensued.

"So why didn't you return my call?" she now asked.

Bogner shrugged. He knew that over the phone she couldn't see the gesture, but he also knew that he had no desire to tell her the real reason; stirring up old emotions served no purpose. If anything, it muddled up his life.

"How'd you know I was in town?"

"I didn't. I called the ISA office to talk to Clancy and got Miller instead. When I asked him what you were doing these days, he said you were on your way in. Good old Robert, he always tells the truth."

"I watched your report on NBS when Yefimov was assassinated," Bogner admitted.

Joy was silent for a moment. That fact that he'd been watching pleased her. "You're in town because Colchin sent for you, right?"

"No comment."

"What is it with you? Early and severe potty training? You can't keep everything to yourself."

Bogner perched himself on the corner of Reese's desk. "Packer brought everyone in," he finally admitted. "No big deal."

"When someone murders the President of the Ukraine, especially as he's stepping off the plane onto American soil for the first time, that's a big deal," Joy said.

Toby Bogner knew there were two ways to handle Joy. He could play the waiting game or ask her why she'd called. He decided on the former. Joy Carpenter was a pro; she would tell him why she'd called when the stage was set and only when she was ready.

"Aren't you going to ask me where I am, how I've been, how the job is going?" she said.

"Okay, I'll start with, where are you?"

"Downstairs. Why don't you swallow your male pride and meet me for a drink? I'll buy. NBS pays better than the Navy."

"Can I have a rain check? It's been a long day."

"Well, if my feminine charms aren't enough to get you down here, suppose I told you I just came from a department briefing and I might just have a piece of information that would interest you."

"I would like to see you," Bogner said, "and not because of any damn information. How about I meet you at Ernie's around the corner . . . in twenty minutes."

Ernie's was the kind of quiet little bistro where boys and girls did man and woman things. It had all the accoutrements required for a tryst: soft lights, candles, paintings that bordered on the erotic, soft conversation, and a piano player that knew all the right songs from the sixties, seventies, and eighties.

Red Sand

By the time Toby got there, Joy had already commandeered a table. She was wearing a trench coat with a white turtleneck, her face was flushed, and she was exhibiting just a touch of that vulnerable aura some women have when they are meeting an old flame. With her ten-minute head start, she had already downed one drink and ordered two Scorsbys, his with ice, hers with a mist, and she had freshened her makeup. As always, Bogner was appropriately impressed. Joy Carpenter was a beautiful woman—on and off camera.

She eyed him up and down as he headed for the table. "I have to admit it, Tobias, you still look good. Chasing bad guys must be agreeing with you."

"Haven't chased all that many lately," Bogner protested. "They've had me chained to my desk for the past several weeks."

"Poor baby," she cooed.

Bogner waited. It was pure Joy Carpenter theater. He had seen it before. The script included a drink with Joy, clever repartee, a devastating smile, a trip down memory lane, and, when she was inclined, an intoxicating innuendo or two—or a to-the-point question.

This time it was different. Joy opened her purse, took out an envelope, and laid it on the table.

"For me? You shouldn't have," Bogner said with a smile.

"Open it."

When he did, he was surprised to discover two reconnaissance photos. One appeared to be a pho-

123

tograph of a large open-pit mine with terraced walls. The other was obviously taken from a greater distance. "So what am I looking at?"

"Satellite imagery. The first one was taken by a low-orbit C7 satellite. I'm told it's a picture of an underground chemical and biological weapons manufacturing site near Tarhuna in Libya."

"Correct-a-mondo," Bogner confirmed. The lady knew what she was talking about. "I hate to tell you this," he said, "but we've known about it for some time now. Of course, the Libyans deny it."

"Then take a look at this one," Joy said, "and follow the line I've drawn from Tripoli . . . east on the Mediterranean up into the Aegean and on into the Black Sea."

"According to this, your line ends at Tbilisi."

"Or Baku if you draw it far enough."

Bogner laid the photos down on the table. "Outside of the obvious question concerning how you got hold of these, I'm not quite sure what you're getting at."

Joy laughed. "There's a hole in your bucket, Captain Bogner. In other words, all you big, bad clandestine types have got a serious security leak."

"And you're not about to name names, right?"

Joy leaned forward. "A fellow by the name of Jeff Rutland in NBS's counteranalysis group came to me today. We've had a drink or two and he knows you're occasionally hit with a covert assignment for the ISA. He says his source believes the Libyans have already started shipping chemical-warfare warheads from the plant at Tarhuna. He also says the same sources claim the first shipment left Tarhuna four weeks ago on a small Libyan freighter."

Bogner frowned, picked up the photos a second time, and studied them. "Are you certain you don't want to pass along any names?"

Joy shook her head. "First rule of a good journalist. Never reveal your sources. I've probably told you too much already."

"Why are you showing me these?"

"Because I want you to protect your backside, Tobias. I don't want you to get hurt. If you're back in town, that can only mean one thing. Colchin has an assignment for you. Since we're still reeling from the Yefimov assassination, I figure that has something to do with it."

Bogner winced. "Are we that transparent?"

"I was married to you," Joy reminded him. "Believe it or not, I don't want a call from Clancy telling me they're bringing you home in a box."

Bogner could feel what was happening. It always happened when Joy was around.

Joy closed her eyes and steeled her voice. "The one thing I've learned about this business is, sources are like two-headed snakes. Either end can and will bite you. Who knows, that same source may be selling information on the other side of the fence."

"I'll cover my backside," Bogner said.

"Please do. It's not your most appealing male feature, but it's one of them." Joy pushed herself away from the table, picked up her purse and her keys, blew him a kiss, and stood up. "Next time, you call me."

Bogner nodded. He was never eloquent or clever when he wanted to be. "I'll take that as a promise," Joy said.

As Bogner watched her leave, in his mind's eye he was already sketching a line from Tarhuna to a point where it would intercept the missile shipment.

Datum: Five-Four: Cabinet Building, Gidropark, Kiev: 20:40 LT

The chamber dining room of the Cabinet of Ministers was all but deserted. Two waiters hovered in the background, trying to anticipate the needs of the diners at the last two tables. On the far side of the room, two deputies from the Supreme Council were engrossed in their meal. On the near side, Grechko and Aralov Lavrenti engaged in conversation. Both men were ebullient.

"The news is excellent," Grechko said, "It is time to celebrate, comrade. Perhaps a toast is appropriate."

"A toast is appropriate," Lavrenti allowed, "but not a celebration. We will celebrate only when the task is complete. The Libyan warheads have been delivered and are being mounted on the SS-28s as we speak—but there is still the matter of Comrade Savin."

Red Sand

Grechko leaned back while the white-haired waiter cleared away the dishes. Lavrenti continued to muse. "It unfolds exactly as we have planned from the beginning," he said. "In a few days we announce to the world that we have both discovered and confirmed the identity of the man who ordered the assassination of our beloved President Yefimov. Then, as the world watches, the state funeral of our fallen leader preoccupies our nation—and our comrade General Savin joins our beloved but deceased former President in the bowels of Hell."

"It will give us great credibility with the world community," Grechko agreed.

"Quite obviously there will be no trial," Lavrenti assured his comrade. "Savin will not have the opportunity to connect us to the death of Yefimov in any kind of public forum. In a few days we will simply inform a waiting world that passions swelled and Aleksei Savin, about to be captured, was assassinated by Yefimov loyalists."

Grechko smiled. Lavrenti made it sound simple. "This will be accomplished when?" Grechko asked.

"At the appropriate time, after Savin joins the train at Alma-Ata. Everything is in place. It is simply a matter of implementation."

Grechko stood up. He was beaming. "Excellent dinner, citizen. Or should I say 'comrade'?"

Lavrenti raised his glass in a toast. "Soon, very soon, I will have a new title."

PART TWO

Chapter Six

Bogner's room at the Desna Hotel was located on the second floor. It afforded him a view overlooking a thin stream of late-night traffic on Milyutenko Street in front of the hotel, and a small park with a large monument dedicated to workers, situated directly across the street.

The park was deserted and the mixture of rain and snow kept pedestrian traffic to a minimum. In the half hour that he had been waiting for Komenich's call, Bogner had watched Metro patrons scurry in and out of the station shelter, striving to keep dry and bundle themselves against the chill night air.

His first observation had been that the atmosphere in Kiev, as well as Moscow, where he'd landed en route to the Ukrainian capital, was decidedly different since the dissolution of the former Soviet Union. Gone were the banners proclaiming Soviet sovereignty, the distressing signs of boredom with life in the State, and the omnipresence of the Party. Bogner saw fewer people in uniform and more cars, heard more music, and felt a kind of vibrancy he hadn't experienced on previous visits to this part of the world.

Even the people at the hotel's registration desk seemed happy to see him. If he needed further proof that capitalism was struggling to claw its way over the corpse of socialism, he had it when the desk clerk gladly accepted his American Express credit card instead of demanding rubles.

When the phone finally rang, it was Komenich.

"It may be a new day in our country," Komenich said, "but the arrival of an *amerikanski* still raises a bit of a stir. When I asked for your room number, they knew without looking. But the key question is, have you dined yet?"

"I could eat a horse," Bogner admitted.

Komenich laughed. "Not in *gastinitsa*."

"Yest' zdyes' karoshiy ryestaran?" Bogner asked, making an effort to speak Russian. He was rusty; he hadn't used it in a while.

Komenich laughed again. "Let's stick to English. I think we'll do better. And yes, there is a good restaurant not far from the hotel. You can walk it in less than five minutes. I'm there now. I know the manager. I'll get us a secluded table."

"Give me fifteen minutes," Bogner said. "It's been a long day."

Mikos Komenich was a big man, swarthy looking, with shocks of thick dark hair and the intense face of a gambler. His eyes were deep set, his features strong, and his movements surprisingly graceful. Bogner decided the man could have passed for a Turk . . . albeit a cultured Turk. He was wearing a heavy sweater, a bulky leather coat, and the soft-soled shoes that betrayed his former affiliation with one of the police groups. If there was anything about Komenich that surprised Bogner, it was the prominence of his brow, a brow that created the impression he was glowering even when his face softened into a smile. The mastery of English did not quite fit with his gruff exterior.

"Well, what do you think?" Komenich asked, gesturing around the restaurant. "Do you not see evidence of the first difficult steps of capitalism and progress?"

"My compliments—or should I say condolences," Bogner said. "Capitalism and progress don't always go hand in hand."

"Growth is painful," Komenich admitted. "All transitions take a while. But enough of what you already know; how was your journey? I trust your accommodations are sufficient?"

Bogner nodded, glanced at the menu, laid it

aside, and reached for his drink. "My official welcome?"

"It's Kuban," Komenich offered. "I ordered the best since I figured you would be picking up the check."

Bogner laughed, took a sip, and looked around the room. The diners consisted mostly of men involved in intense conversations. "I assume it is all right to talk here. Correct?"

Komenich had an easy smile. "This is a haven of the new way of life in my country. These are businessmen. They have their own intrigues; they are too busy for politics. Those who weep for Yefimov are home, watching the arrival of his funeral cortege on television. Those who do not weep are assembled in halls and other meeting places planning my country's new destiny."

"What's the mood of the people?"

"Some rejoice. Some weep. For the most part they are preoccupied with the more mundane aspects of their lives: inflation, getting enough to eat, the housing shortage, and how to make it through tomorrow. In my country, thinking about tomorrow is considered long-range planning."

A waiter with phlegmatic eyes approached the table and took their order. Komenich recommended the *borscht*, *baranina* or lamb, with *svyoka* and *kaputsa*, a dish consisting of beetroot and cabbage. When the waiter left, Komenich lit a cigarette. It was a Turkish brand. "One of the things that we haven't embraced is your disdain for tobacco."

Then he paused for several moments, studying the man the Americans had sent to replace Harris. "And finally, one last observation before our conversation turns serious, Captain Bogner. After meeting you, I have decided one of my concerns was unnecessary. You will not arouse much suspicion while you are in my country. Why? Because you do not look like our concept of an American. Americans are supposed to look like John Wayne or Robert Redford. Now that we have American movies on television, all our young men are wearing cowboy hats and trying to sound like the Sundance Kid."

It was Bogner's turn to laugh.

"Our young people have discovered discos and rock and roll," Komenich continued. "Our working people are obsessed with politics and our old people are afraid of winter. There is not enough housing and not enough to eat. We even have a mafia. Just like America, huh?"

"But *our* concerns are more focused, correct?"

"*Da*," Komenich said, lowering his voice, "and I have received information within the last few hours that I fear will make our task somewhat more difficult."

"Such as?"

"I am told that two Kazakh trawlers rendezvoused with the munitions train carrying the SS-28 ICBMs two days ago. It is rumored that they delivered chemical warheads—warheads that will be installed in the missiles now that they have

135

crossed the southern tip of Russia and are in more, how shall I phrase it, politically sympathetic territory."

"Kazakhstan?"

Komenich nodded. "To be precise, the train is now located in a small rail yard between Astrakhan and Atyrau. My source also informs me that the train will be delayed there some seventy-two hours while the warheads are installed by Libyan technicians."

"And all of this is happening right under the Russians' noses?"

"The Russians have their hands full, Captain. While it is true the Russians have been demanding that we return the nuclear arsenal and my country ships missiles to the Chinese, our Russian friends' attention is diverted—fighting brushfire wars all along their southern border. Azerbaijan, Georgia, Uzbekistan, and probably some we haven't heard about."

Bogner let out a low whistle. "So the train is now carrying armed bio warheads?"

"Precisely. More important, the train is also now being guarded by some twenty armed members of the KON, all disguised as members of our normally flaccid militia."

Bogner held up his hand. "Do we know for certain that Polce Berzin is on that train?"

"That has also been confirmed."

Bogner winced and searched for the waiter.

"You require something?" Komenich asked.

"A cup of coffee."

Komenich laughed. "You are in Kiev. In Kiev we top off a good meal with the delight of the Ukraine, a glass of fine cognac." He signaled for the waiter with the tired eyes.

"So when do we get started?" Bogner pressed.

"Tomorrow we will fly to Odessa to meet with Sukharev. That is the first step."

Datum: Six-Two: The Train, East of Kulsary: 10:12 LT

Again Polce Berzin was allowed out of her compartment and off the train without an escort.

The air was clean, fresh, and crisp. It was a barren, rocky area, devoid of trees, with traces of a recent snow. A river of seemingly insignificant dimensions was visible in the distance and there was a smoky haze on the western horizon, but nowhere was there evidence of a settlement or people.

A narrow dirt road paralleled the tracks, but again, she had neither seen nor heard traffic in her three-hour reprieve from the stuffiness of the railcar.

Through it all, Olga Serov maintained her vigil from a platform at the rear of the sleeping car. Polce had decided that if her activities were being monitored by someone other than the angular woman, it was being done surreptitiously.

The sun, visible at first, had disappeared behind a bank of low-hanging clouds—clouds accompanied by intensified winds from the east and the threat of still more unpleasant weather. Olga had already informed her that with the increased elevations to the east, wind and dryness, and later snow, would become the rule rather than the exception.

From where she stood, Polce could see a frenzy of activity around the three flatcars. The earlier air of secrecy around the three cars appeared to have been abandoned. The wooden structures concealing the configuration of the missiles had been disassembled, and the canvas shrouds removed. Men, wearing heavy coats and gloves, turned their collars up to ward off the chill, and scurried back and forth between flatbed cars and the crates from the trawlers. She had been watching so intently that she failed to hear Olga approaching.

"You are to come with me now," Olga said.

The young woman considered the timing. Should she refuse, or at least protest being summarily ordered before turning around and following the woman back toward the sleeping car?

"Is there a reason why I am being forced to reboard at this time?" she asked. "It does not appear that the train will be moving any time soon. The men are still working."

"The general wishes to see you," Olga said.

Polce stiffened. It had finally happened. The veneer of isolation had cracked; the fear that she would not be summoned had been groundless. They did not know. If they had, Dubchek would not have called for her. He would simply have waited and tried to dispose of her at the appropriate time. With this news there was a sense of relief; in Dubchek, she knew what to expect.

A silent Olga led her back to the sleeping car and a compartment at the far end. Polce was surprised that even here, in the middle of an unpopulated vastness, she found a heavyset militia man with a thick beard and the smell of garlic standing guard outside the general's compartment. Olga nodded and the guard instructed them to enter.

Polce had heard that Krislof Dubchek gave the impression of being detached from everything that surrounded him. Now she waited for him to look away from the window. When he did, he stood with his arms folded and his back arched. For the most part he was a homely man; bald, with a wide expanse of face, a regrettably large and bulbous nose, wide-set empty brown eyes, and a thin mouth that appeared to be cast in a perpetual scowl. More than anything else, however, there was the reputation that preceded him—a reputation for cruelty.

It was said that Dubchek's reputation was well earned, carved out of the ice and agony of the Siberian detention camp at Ekonda during the Khrushchev regime. It was also said that only a handful had survived the cruelty of the man they called the "Butcher of Ekonda" and lived to tell about it.

Now he was standing in the middle of the compartment, wearing a uniform with no apparent affiliation or rank, and motioning for Polce to take a seat across from a makeshift desk piled high with papers and technical drawings. He took out a cigarette, inserted it in a nicotine-stained ivory cigarette holder, and lit it. He studied her for a moment, then walked back to the window of his compartment and stared out at the nearly featureless landscape. He spoke with his back to her.

"It is regrettable that you are here," he finally said. His voice was flat, void of emotion. "I have better things to do than play nursemaid to a mere child with divergent political views."

Polce braced herself. She had no intention of cowering. At the same time, she knew she had to avoid arousing his suspicions. Dubchek's presence was expected, but even so, it was something for which she was not prepared. "I can assure you, General Dubchek, I have no desire to be here—regardless of our divergent political views."

Dubchek turned again and leaned up against his makeshift desk. He laid the cigarette holder in an ashtray. "You are here because your father chooses to realign his loyalties."

"I know why I am here," the young woman countered. "I am here because you and the rest of your thugs actually believe you can coerce my father into remaining silent about the details of the delivery of the missiles to the Fifth Academy." She felt good about the way she had delivered her lines.

"You are better informed than I anticipated."

"No, I am simply familiar with the ways of the KON."

"When he learns you are in our custody—"

"My father is a man of principle," she interrupted. "Unlike you, General Dubchek, he will do what is best for our country—not what is best for the Party." When she finished, she was even more pleased with herself; she was convinced she had displayed just the right touch of courage and arrogance. All the hours of practice had paid off; her carefully rehearsed lines had come off without a hitch.

Dubchek somehow managed to intensify his frown. "You would be wise to remain civil. You are still alive today, Gaspazha Berzin, because Comrade Savin wishes it so. I can assure you that when our task is finished, I do not think Comrade Savin will feel that you are such a valuable pawn in the scheme of things."

She waited. Her instincts had not failed her. She knew Dubchek had a purpose for summoning her to his compartment. It would have been just as easy for him to ignore the fact that she was on the train. He walked around to the other side of his desk, opened a drawer, extracted a pack of cigarettes, and offered her one. Even though she wanted one, she knew Polce Berzin did not smoke. She declined and waited for him to continue.

"I have heard," Dubchek began, "that you are, how shall I phrase it, a close *padruga* of Aralov Lavrenti. Is that true?"

"I do not like your insinuation, General. We are friends, nothing more." She wanted him to detect the steel in her voice. "We see each other only because my work at the Dnepro Academy brings us into frequent contact. We have mutual economic interests."

"And what is your relationship with Leonid Grechko?"

"Grechko?" Polce repeated. "Who is this Grechko?"

"Do not play games with me," Dubchek threatened.

She shrugged off the general's warning, and Dubchek walked slowly back around the desk again until he was standing in front of her. "Perhaps I should point out that there are certain advantages to cooperating with me," he said. He reached out to touch her hair and she recoiled. "And perhaps I should also mention that I have my orders. As soon as the missiles and the warheads are safely in the hands of Colonel Mao Quan, and your father has seen the wisdom in no longer throwing obstacles in the path of our endeavors—you, *maya padruga*, become expendable. Very expendable."

"Meaning what?"

"Our esteemed Director, Aleksei Savin, has made it quite clear that he has no intentions of allowing you to return to Kiev . . . alive."

Polce remained stoic. The meeting with the man reputed to be the field commander of Aleksei Savin's terror squad was not going as expected. Dubchek's revelation of Savin's intentions had taken her by surprise. The plot had suddenly taken an unexpected twist. But she knew it was still too soon to tip her hand. "Under the circumstances, what do you expect me to say?"

Dubchek folded his arms again. She could tell that he was not altogether comfortable with the conversation. "For the moment I expect you to say nothing. At the very least I expect you to reflect upon this conversation. After you have had time to reflect, we will talk again."

The man once known as the "Butcher of Ekonda" walked to the door of his compartment, opened it, and spoke briefly to the militiaman standing in the corridor.

"Escort Gaspazha Berzin to her compartment," he said.

Datum: Six-Three: The Farm, Wednesday: 14:37 LT

Clancy Packer and Robert Miller waited for the Ukrainian Deputy Prime Minister to be escorted back into the room. It was the third session of the day. To their surprise, Berzin, despite his age and the ordeal he had been through, looked surprisingly refreshed.

"You have more questions, gentlemen?" he asked with a smile.

Packer lit his pipe. "We appreciate your cooperation, Doctor. Unfortunately, yes, we do have more questions."

Berzin took a seat and glanced out the window

at the weather. There were infrequent flakes of snow and the day was dark. "For some reason I did not expect it to be so cold this time of year in your country. Here it is already the beginning of winter."

Packer laughed. "Believe me, Mr. Prime Minister, it gets much worse than this."

Berzin nodded and smiled. He seemed pleased to discover that not everything in America was better than his native Ukraine. Finally he walked back across the room and took a seat.

"Several names emerged in this morning's session that in reviewing the tapes of those conversations, we find we actually know very little about," Miller began.

Berzin urged Miller to continue.

"You mentioned the names of Leonid Grechko and Aralov Lavrenti several times this morning, and while we have files on both men, they appear to be incomplete. We know more about Lavrenti than Grechko. So we would like you to tell us just exactly how Grechko and Lavrenti fit into all of this. Our files would indicate that Lavrenti is powerful, but at best an advisor in the Yefimov government. What we know about Grechko is even less."

Berzin was amused. "Our files on the Colchin Administration are equally incomplete," Berzin admitted. "A good intelligence system is not developed overnight—and once it is developed it is difficult to keep current."

"So just exactly what role does this Lavrenti play in your current government?" Miller pressed.

Berzin reflected for several moments before he answered. "You must understand that it is currently a web of intrigue in my country," he explained. "A puzzle of new alliances, new coalitions, agreements, and understandings among men with dissimilar philosophies. Aralov Lavrenti is the equivalent of a modern-day Machiavelli. He is a manipulator of men and is generally believed to be the power behind Aleksei Savin."

"Aleksei Savin is the founder and leader of the KON, correct?"

"He is," Berzin acknowledged.

"Then it is reasonable to assume that both Lavrenti and Savin will emerge as principal players in the power struggle for political supremacy in your country."

"Savin's fortunes will carry him only as far as Lavrenti wishes. Even before I left my country, there were undercurrents that indicated Savin was exceeding his authority, and that Lavrenti was growing disenchanted."

Packer stood up and began pacing back and forth. He chose his words carefully. "In your opinion, was the assassination of President Yefimov and your longtime colleague Professor Dmitri Tairov initiated by Lavrenti?"

"The former, yes. There is little doubt in my mind. However, it is quite possible the death of my friend Tairov was an independent action engineered by Savin. It may well be that Savin now feels strong enough to disassociate himself from Lavrenti."

Miller was recording Berzin's comments. "Now, about Leonid Grechko?"

"A man who has stepped from the limelight of the Party and the Politburo into the private sector. He is said to be a very wealthy man."

"So what's his role in all of this?" Packer asked.

"An opportunist," Berzin explained. "He continues to be a member of the Cabinet of Ministers, but he is well known as a money changer. It is said that he is the man who structured the deal with Mao Quan—perhaps even financed it. There is a great deal of money being exchanged between the Fifth Academy and my government—or perhaps I should say the Party. No one knows for certain how much money will actually filter back into my country's treasury in return for the missiles."

"Now comes the big question, Dr. Berzin," Miller said. "For some time now, there have been rumors that the Libyans, who are known to have constructed the world's largest chemical weapons plant in Tarhuna near Tripoli, have been building a chemo-biological device with devastating implications."

"That is true," Berzin acknowledged. His voice was flat.

"Two weeks ago, our satellites began tracking a shipment from the plant at Tarhuna. As recently as three days ago, two small Kazakh lake vessels disguised as fishing trawlers made their way north in the Caspian Sea to Atyrau. The question, Dr. Berzin, is, were those ships carrying warheads to be mated with the SS-28s being shipped to Mao Quan?"

"You have done your homework," Berzin said. "The plan is to remove the obsolete warheads that remain from the former Soviet nuclear arsenal and replace them with the chemo-biological warheads designed by the Libyans. The missiles are of little use to our Chinese friends without the new warheads."

"What if I counter your assertion with the fact that we have known for some time that the Chinese have an entire arsenal of missiles with nuclear capability? Why would they need the SS-28?"

"They have nothing with the long-range capability of the SS-28 in their present inventory," Berzin said. "We have calculated that the range of the SS-28 and the location of their deployment silos in the Gobi Desert give them a strategic advantage of unparalleled strike capability anywhere in the world. On top of that, they now possess warheads with bio-chemical kill capability."

Packer sagged back in his chair and glanced at Miller. Berzin was confirming what until that very moment had been speculation and rumor. "Is there anything else we should know?"

Berzin hesitated. "You should know," he said evenly, "that any attempt to destroy the devices en route to the launch sites could result in a catastrophic explosion of unimaginable proportions. At

Mao Quan's insistence, the warheads are being armed as they are installed in the SS-28 missiles. This was his way of insuring that there would be no outside interference with their delivery."

Miller stopped the tape. "Who else knows this?"

"Does it matter? There is no way to stop it."

Datum: Six-Four: Treyakov Warehouse District, Odessa: 11:18 LT

Bogner eyed the little man in his too-tight three-piece suit as he counted the money. Komenich had handed the man a package containing five thousand dollars in a combination of rubles and American currency.

"I would have preferred all American dollars," Sukharev said, stuffing the money into a briefcase.

"And people in Hell want sugar-ice," Komenich reminded him. "Too many dollars would arouse suspicion."

Sukharev zipped up the briefcase and studied Bogner. "This is the *amerikanski* you spoke of? Perhaps you should introduce us."

"The less you know, the better. You are too old and too soft to withstand an interrogation by the KON."

"Perhaps you are right," Sukharev decided. He forced a smile and patted his belly, then reached inside his coat and produced a cigar and a hand-sketched map with penciled notations along the margin. He lit the cigar and spread the map on the table. "The train has been detained in Atyrau for the last two days."

Komenich frowned. "Why?"

Sukharev shrugged. "That has been the plan from the outset."

"When will it proceed?"

Sukharev checked the schedule. "It will pass by the Aral Sea and proceed to Kzyi-Orda two days from now. It is expected to arrive at Zhambyl in the foothills of the Caucasus early Friday morning. From there it will follow the Kyrgyzstan border to Alma-Alta."

"Where and how do we board the train?" Komenich asked. Most of the conversation between the two men was a rapid-fire mixture of Russian and Ukrainian, and Bogner was able to catch only fragments. He tried to listen as he studied the makeshift map.

"There will be a change of militia at Zhambyl and you will have the opportunity to board the train as replacement militia. After that it is up to you."

"Ask him if he knows for certain the Berzin woman is on the train," Bogner said after Komenich had relayed Sukharev's information in English.

Komenich translated the question and Sukharev confirmed that she was. "She is being detained in a compartment in the sleeping car. I am told that she is guarded around the clock." Komenich repeated the answer in English.

"How many guards?" Bogner asked in Russian.

"And please speak more slowly so I can understand you."

Sukharev smiled. "Many," he said, "the majority of which are KON militia; but they are mere cannon fodder—numbers assigned to assuage Mao Quan's demands for security. There are only a few trained guards to supervise them. They are the only ones who will present an obstacle. Whatever your plan is, you must accomplish your mission before the train arrives in Alma-Ata. I have been informed that Aleksei Savin plans to board the train there. At that point the security will include Savin's personal bodyguards. They are highly trained, recruited from the ranks of the former GRU and KGB."

Komenich studied the map for several minutes, then looked at Bogner. "The task appears formidable. Do you have any questions?"

"How many cars in the train?" Bogner asked Sukharev in Russian.

"Seven units including the locomotive. Three flatcars containing the missile housings, a troop car for the militia, a sleeping car to accommodate Dubchek and his entourage plus the Berzin woman, and a work car carrying tools and supplies. That car will be left in Alma-Ata."

"What about the terrain?"

"When the train passes through Chaill you will be in the foothills of the Caucasus. From there on the progress of the train will be slow and the weather will deteriorate."

"Can we count on weather delays?" Bogner pressed.

"In the vicinity of the Gregor glacier the weather is particularly cruel," Sukharev replied. "In several places tunnels have been built to insure passage."

"Tunnels," Bogner repeated. "Where?"

Sukharev pointed to the map. "There is a tunnel here, north of Kazym. There is another north of Yartsevo—and of course the great seven-mile tunnel that crosses the border into China. It is the tunnel of Jinghe. The eastern access to the tunnel is heavily guarded by the Chinese Red Army."

"And where are the missile silos located?" Bogner asked.

Sukharev shrugged. "That has not been revealed, but the Chinese have built a railroad that runs from Urumqi north to the Gobi. Perhaps there."

Datum: Six-Five: Police Offices, 610 Lenin, Odessa: 20:40 LT

Homicide Inspector Yuri Illich's supper was not setting well. The soup, a *rassol'nik*, consisting of cucumber and kidney, coupled with *sasiki* and *kapusta*, sausage and cabbage, was causing a minor turmoil in his digestive system. He had taken a stomach calmative before returning to his office but the agitation continued.

Now, as he worked his way through the autopsy report, he considered taking another antacid to try to alleviate his distress. Finally, Illich laid the file down and looked at his young assistant sitting at the desk across from him.

"Have you read this?" he asked, pointing at the report.

Fedorovich leaned back in his chair and tried to remember the details. "There have been so many lately. Is that the young woman we found in the basement of the building at the studio?"

Illich nodded, and Fedorovich admitted that thus far he had merely scanned the document. The inspector picked up the folder and began to read aloud.

"Subject: Rubana Cheslov (tentative only)
Caucasian, female, age 30; COD: asphyxiation
DON: 19 syentybar. TOD: vyechyera syem' and
dvyenatsat . . ."

Fedorovich looked puzzled. "So?" he asked. "What is wrong?"

"I find it curious that two days before, Citizens Affairs informed us, a woman by the name of Rubana Cheslov reported the theft of her purse and personal papers by hooligans in the Metro station at Varspada."

Fedorovich reached for the file, checked the dates, and rubbed his hand over his stubbled chin. He had already been reprimanded twice that day for not shaving. "Obviously, the body of the woman is not Cheslov. Either that or we are dealing with ghosts."

Red Sand

The young officer summarized his conclusion with a smile just in case the senior inspector had taken him seriously.

Illich hadn't. He was too busy fighting his stomach miseries. Instead he closed his eyes and leaned back in his chair with his hands behind his head. "All of which raises the question, why was the dead woman carrying a stolen purse and another woman's papers? Which in turn raises still another question. Why was the woman whose body we found disfigured to such an extent that her personal effects were the only way we could identify her?"

Fedorovich shrugged. "Perhaps you are seeing ghosts where there are none. The answer could be simple—as simple as the dead woman being the one who accosted the Cheslov woman on the Metro and took her purse."

Illich frowned. "*Nyet*. The answer, quite obviously, is to hide the dead woman's real identity. And, if such extreme measures were taken to hide that identity, the woman whose body we found must have been easily recognizable to many people."

"A film actress, perhaps," Fedorovich guessed. "After all, it was on the grounds of the Odessa Film Studio. I watched an American movie the other day; a film executive murdered his mistress at his wife's insistence—"

"A possibility," Illich admitted, "but we have had no reports of missing actresses."

While Fedorovich leafed through the report, Illich took another antacid, stood up, and began to pace back and forth in the small cubicle. "Why would anyone work so hard to conceal the identity of a victim?"

"As you suggested, Inspector, because they feared that the victim would be easily recognizable."

"Exactly. And if we continue that line of logic, the question arises, why hasn't someone reported this woman missing?"

"Perhaps no one noticed." Fedorovich knew his reasoning sounded feeble the moment he said it. "Perhaps the people who knew the victim have been out of touch. . . ."

Illich listened, then picked up the phone. "I am going to have the lab bring the body up to the autopsy workroom. You and I are going to take another look at—"

"What else is there to see?" Fedorovich protested.

"Perhaps we will see something we didn't see the first time around."

Chapter Seven

Datum: Seven-One: The Village of Auezov: 07:53 LT

Bogner and Komenich were aboard the Tupolev Tu-134 carrying less than thirty passengers when it lumbered into the Shymkent airport early the following morning. Sukharev's arrangements, despite Komenich's concerns, were working. He had arranged for passports and papers that introduced Bogner as a representative of a British banking consortium with interests in Kazakh petroleum reserves. Komenich, according to his new identity, was a regional representative of the Zaili Resourkas, escorting the *anglii*. The Kazakh customs agent was a tired man with numerous distractions. Only three passengers went through his cubicle/office, and he conducted his review of their papers while carrying on a conversation with an equally disinterested colleague.

"Your business in our country?" he wheezed.

"We have meetings scheduled with a series of officials of Zaili Resourkas," Komenich replied.

There were a few more questions, during which Komenich made one or two remarks that amused the customs official. Then Komenich inquired about train tickets. *"Gidya kassa?"*

The old man pointed down the corridor at a sign that said INTOURIST GIDYA KASSA, and managed a distracted smile.

"Dva bilyeta vadin kanyets kupeyniy, Zhambyl," Komenich said. Bogner realized that he had told the man that he intended to purchase two economy tickets on the train to Zhambyl. "They'll be less suspicious if we appear to be open about our itinerary," Komenich explained in a low voice to Bogner. "The Kazakhs, like everyone else in this part of the world, are still new to this 'go where you want to go and do what you want to do' routine. It wasn't that long ago that customs officials would have given one of the local KGB agents the high sign and we would have picked up a tail."

Finally the agent turned his attention to Bogner while he examined his passport. *"Vi is kakova gorada?"*

"London."

"Kyem vi rabotayetye?"

Red Sand

"Banking." When the old man appeared not to understand, Bogner clarified. *"A kamyersant."*

At that point the agent seemed to lose interest and waved them through to the baggage area.

"You require a taxi to take you to the train station?" a voice asked. Komenich slowed as the man approached. He was stout, short, wearing a cap and a heavy wool jacket. "My taxi is warm—good heater," he assured them.

"Utra?" Komenich asked, looking at his name tag.

The man nodded. He was one of those people burdened with a perpetual smile, even when it wasn't appropriate. "At your service. The name is Utra Svychi, and you've just hired yourself the finest taxi driver in all of Auezov. You will like my taxi. It is a Simca of recent vintage—practically new."

Utra Svychi took their luggage, hustled them out into the cold evening air, and into a tiny four-door Simca with the word TAKSI lettered on the side. Inside the car his smile intensified but the cherubic quality of his voice faded.

"You were fortunate," he said as he put his key in the ignition. "You got one of the older ones. The new ones are real pricks. They take this customs shit real serious."

Bogner soon learned why Sukharev had been worth the money. Utra Svychi was a treasure trove of information. He began talking when they pulled out of the airport, and the information flowed unabated until they arrived at a small roadside market on the edge of Auezov.

Svychi gave them a snapshot of his life in a rolling dialogue spiked with profanity and accented English. He was thirty-nine years old, a Kazakh by birth, educated in the Institute Karaganda, and sent to the United States as part of a study mission delegation on irrigation.

"So when I got to New York, I figured it was time to test your immigration policy. I applied for political asylum, but when some fat-ass judge found out I was a 'pinko,' my request was denied. So I did the next best thing—I took off. I headed west until I found one of your bleeding hearts, shacked up with her, got a job, and the assholes didn't find me for eleven years. When they did, I put up a helluva fight—but they shipped me back anyway.

"That was four years ago. I was still screwing around trying to figure out how I was going to put bread on the table when I met Sukharev. I had some connections, he had some connections, and things worked out. Three days ago he contacted me and said he had a couple of friends that needed a way to hop a train. I told him I was his man. I didn't ask him no questions."

Komenich and Bogner were instructed to wait while Svychi parked behind the market, went in the rear door, and emerged moments later with two bulky bundles. He handed one to each of them, jumped back in the car, and pulled into traffic.

When he stopped for the second time, they were

in what Bogner had to believe was one of the seedier sections of Auezov, a run-down residential section on a side street lined with two-story houses most of which were sadly in need of repair and paint. "This is where we get out, gentlemen," Svychi said. "You guys are about to become Kazakh militia."

"What about the train?" Komenich asked.

"That comes later, after you change clothes and meet Mrachak."

Datum: Seven-Two: Headquarters, Odessa Police: 11:17 LT

Two impressive sculptures stood at the main entrance of the old building: one of a lion, the other of a bear. The ornate facade over the portico still betrayed the fact that it was once the Odessa Theater of Dance and Opera. It was said that Galina Ulanova, Rubenstein, even Tchaikovsky had performed there—but all of that was before Yuri Illich's time.

Then, during the reign of Stalin, it suffered an ignominious fate when it was taken over by the Ministry of Public Affairs. Illich had been there then.

Now, the banners were gone, most of the offices were empty, and the building had fallen into disrepair—but the reorganized Odessa Police had moved in anyway.

Yuri Illich took off his hat out of respect for the

once-lovely old building, labored up the marble stairs to the second floor, and headed for the Administrative Offices. He had not called ahead, and he did not even know if Junus Arkadiya was there or would have time to see him.

Illich liked to say the gods were with him when fortunes turned on his behalf—and on this occasion, the gods were with him. Senior Director Junus Arkadiya was not only in his office, he was alone. Illich knocked even though the door was open, and the old man looked up from his work. On a desk cluttered with files and documents, he had been carefully penciling in and shading the facial features over multiple diagrams of a human skull. At the sight of the homicide inspector, the old man smiled and stood up. For Junus Arkadiya it was a gesture both out of character and difficult. He had lost a leg to a land mine, and standing for more than a few minutes was laborious. Walking was impossible.

"It is good to see you, Yuri," Arkadiya said, extending his hand. Illich sidestepped the man's hand and embraced his longtime friend.

"I do not see my mentor often enough," Illich said apologetically.

"We are all too busy these days," Arkadiya replied with a smile. "I hear that even in homicide there is turmoil. The ranks of the police grow thinner—and the legions of hooligans continue to grow."

Illich dropped into a chair and waited for the old man to settle himself again. They exchanged pleasantries but when there was a pause in their conversation, Arkadiya leaned forward. "I would like to think that this is purely a social visit, but I fear that is not the reason you are here."

Illich forced a smile. "You're right. I'm here because one of your pupils has need of your wisdom."

"I am flattered," the old man said.

Illich reached into his coat pocket and produced a piece of paper. "I'm convinced there is something very obvious to a case I am investigating, but each time I review the facts, I draw a blank."

Arkadiya waited.

"Several days ago we investigated the homicide of a young woman whose body was found in an old building on the back lot of the Odessa Studio. Nasty situation; she had been mutilated. Her face was cut away, hands removed—everything that might be valuable in identifying the victim was destroyed."

"Dental work?" Arkadiya inquired.

"Two small fillings; nothing of significance."

"Obviously the woman's assailant did not want you to identify her."

"A logical conclusion, and I would have arrived at the same judgment except for one very significant detail. The woman's purse had been left behind. Some of the contents of the purse had been removed—licenses, identification papers—but not a small amount of money. At the time it appeared that her assailant had overlooked a medical appointment for a woman by the name of Rubana Cheslov—but again, another significant detail and a twist. We have subsequently learned that a Rubana Cheslov reported her purse stolen two days before the victim's body was found. As it turns out, the real Rubana Cheslov is still very much alive."

Arkadiya began sketching again. "I am listening," he assured Illich. "Did you think to bring photographs?"

Illich nodded. This time he reached in his briefcase and handed Arkadiya the lab photographs taken at the autopsy. Arkadiya laid them on his desk and picked up his sketch pad. Despite his age, his pencil glided over the paper with the grace of a ballerina.

"Tell me what you know about the woman," the old man said.

Illich rifled through his papers. "The autopsy indicates that she was young, between twenty-eight and thirty-five, one hundred and seventy-two centimeters in height and approximately sixty kilograms in weight."

Arkadiya listened as he continued to sketch. "The skeletal system would appear to support a muscular system about like so," he estimated. "Now, if we round this frontal bone above the eye socket, and judging from the muscle structure over the mandible and the maxilla, blend it in like so—we have a basic facial structure that could look something like this. . . ."

"Brown hair. She had brown hair," Illich offered, "so it would be dark through there." He watched while Arkadiya deftly shaded the side of the face and around the hairline.

"Was the nasal bone prominent?" the old man asked.

Illich shook his head. "No, not really. Curious. Despite her height, she gives the impression of having been quite delicate."

Arkadiya studied the picture again and changed a few elements of his sketch, drawing in the throat and sketching down to the bust. "What about the eyes?"

Illich shrugged and Arkadiya continued, finally reaching for some colored pencils. When he finished he held the tablet up for Illich's appraisal. "On the attractive side—if that's what she looked like." He tore the sketch off the tablet and handed it to his former pupil.

Illich settled back in the chair and studied the drawing.

"You realize of course that we're dealing with three layers of tissue in studying a drawing of this nature. The subcutaneous layer contains fat cells, and could greatly influence the outer layer of epidermis. She could look a great deal different depending on that fact alone."

"At least this gives me some idea," Illich said.

"You have interviewed this Cheslov woman?"

Illich shook his head. "That's my next stop. This drawing gives me something to go on."

R. Karl Largent

Datum: Seven-Three: The Varna Cafe: 16:51 LT

Rikov Mrachak reminded Bogner of someone who had watched too many thirties-vintage American gangster movies. He was tall, almost as tall as Bogner, had a thin hollowed face, and wore a carefully cultivated mustache. His attire would have done George Raft proud—double-breasted suit with a wide lapel, wide tasteless tie, and even wider cuffed pants. He wore aging patent-leather shoes with cracks in the leather. His Kazakh origins, however, got in the way.

His English was interspersed with his native tongue and occasional profanity; the final result sounded like someone who had learned their English in the streets of Ashkhabad, or worse yet, from Utra Svychi.

Whatever he was, or wanted to be, Mrachak had come prepared. He had been in the room just long enough to learn to pronounce Bogner's name, and spread several maps on the table when Komenich began pressing him about what he knew.

"I know you need help getting a Ukrainian woman off of the train to Alma-Ata. Beyond that I know nothing." Then he paused for a moment before he added, "This Ukrainian woman, she must be very important, huh?"

Bogner nodded, but didn't elaborate. Instead he looked at the section of map showing the tracks running parallel to the Kyrgyzstan border. As he did, Komenich traced the route with his finger.

Red Sand

"Did Sukharev tell you that the person we want to get off that train is in all likelihood being guarded around the clock by Ukrainian militia?"

"It doesn't surprise me," Svychi said. "The unfortunate few who ride the train to Alma-Ata are seldom seen again. It has been called the train to oblivion."

"Tell me about the territory between here and here," Bogner said. He pointed to the area east of Zhambyl and west of Alma-Alta.

"You are talking about three hundred miles of damn near wasteland," Svychi said. "The tracks nestle right up against the mountains most of the way. The elevation is maybe three thousand foot. This time of year you'll run into some snow, but for the most part it will be colder than hell and very windy. When them damn mountain winds blow, the cold cuts through a man to his bones and his fingers turn to ice."

"What about the terrain?"

"Wasteland. Rocks, sand, brush, and bunchgrass," Mrachak replied.

"What about people?"

"You might see one or two peasants—for the most part they are nomads—and you might run across an occasional mining outpost. There are peaks in the mountains to the east and south that run sixteen thousand feet."

"We've been told that east of Alma-Ata the train works a series of bridges and tunnels. Where are they located?"

Mrachak reached into his pocket and took out a gold Cross pen. When he saw Bogner looking at it, he explained that he had obtained it in trade from an American schoolteacher for two tins of Kopet caviar. It was engraved with a picture of the Sears Tower and carried the inscription CHICAGO, 1993 on the barrel. Mrachak used the pen to pinpoint the location of the major bridges and three tunnels.

"Tell me about them," Bogner said.

"This bridge," Mrachak began, "is new. It spans a ravine where the railroad has had several washouts. It is said the rail bed is laid on soapstone and that the ground is difficult to stabilize. As you can see, it is only eighty or so kilometers west of Zhambyl."

"Too close," Komenich decided. "We wouldn't have enough time."

Bogner pushed his finger east along the tracks. "What's this?" he asked.

"The mud-flow control dam. It is less than twenty-five kilometers from Alma-Ata." Mrachak thought for a moment. "If we wish to avoid detection, that would be a poor choice. It is heavily guarded by militia, and the construction crews work around the clock."

Komenich leaned over with his hands on the table. "Where is this so-called seven-mile tunnel we hear about?"

Mrachak hesitated before he pointed to it on the map. "There," he said. "On the border. "You leave Kazakhstan and you end up in China. You would have little difficulty getting on the train in my country. You would have a great deal of difficulty getting off once you cross the border."

Svychi folded his arms. "Whoever this person is, she must be pretty damn valuable if you're going to all this trouble just to get her off the train."

Komenich looked at Bogner before he began. Then he explained just enough for the two Kazakhs to get a feel for the magnitude of the situation.

Svychi began to smile. "If I'd have known all of that, I'd have hit Sukharev up for more money," he admitted. He winked at Mrachak.

Svychi took out a small notebook and began making notes. Then he turned to Bogner. "So far you haven't said anything about the train. What happens to the train? You wouldn't be asking about bridges and tunnels if you didn't have some plan for that damn train."

Bogner frowned. "Our first priority is the woman. Anything else is a bonus. We'll worry about the train later."

"What's the train carrying?" Mrachak asked.

"Six long-range ICBMs, all armed with warheads—maybe bio-chemical," Komenich said. "They were shipped from the Balnecha Arsenal near Kiev less than two weeks ago."

"For the Chinks?" Svychi asked.

Bogner nodded.

"I got a gut feeling tellin' me you intend to make damn sure that train don't deliver them missiles, right?"

"In a perfect world," Bogner said, "we would get the girl off the train and then blow that damn train off the face of the earth. And in the process we'd make certain it would be a long time before they used those tracks to ship the Chinese anything, let alone missiles."

"Now it is getting interesting," Mrachak said with a grin. "Does the American government pay us even more if we help you blow up the train as well?"

Svychi was smiling as well. Now he understood. Sukharev had made the initial contact, but the *amerikanski* was the one with the money. He turned his attention back to the maps. "Then the first thing we must do is decide where we will get the woman off the train. After that, we decide how we're going to rid of the train."

Svychi continued to appraise his newfound source of wealth. Bogner was a lottery. Finally he said, "There is an old Kazakh saying that goes. Making a train disappear costs a lot of money. A whole lot of money." Then he laughed.

Datum: Seven-Four: ISA Headquarters, Washington: 20:30 LT

At eight-thirty in the evening the cafeteria in the basement of the ISA building was all but deserted. The bank of vending machines had been picked over and the table of the fruit vendor was empty. The choices consisted of two kinds of sandwiches, tuna salad or processed cheese, two kinds of Jello salad on slightly wilted lettuce, and stale coffee.

Spitz and Packer opted for the coffee. Miller tried his luck with the tuna salad.

On the other side of the dining area, two custodians were mopping the floor and listening to a sports call-in program from Baltimore. A caller was bemoaning the fate of the Ravens.

"Thanks for bringing it over," Packer said. "I'd sure as hell hate to find out about this through channels." He went over Hurley's note for the third and final time before he pushed it across the table at Miller. "We'll keep this under wraps and check out our end—just in case it goes deeper. Either way, we realize it's not just Jaffe's problem."

"Double agents never are," Spitz said. "Apparently this one is living a little too high off the hog and needs a few extra bucks. Whoever he or she is, they're sticking their neck out selling information to a damn television network."

"What about inter-bureau contacts?" Miller asked.

"For the time being, everything goes through Jaffe," Spitz said. "His biggest concern outside of the fact that he's got a leak in his department is Bogner."

"T.C. is out there on a limb, even without this," Packer said.

Spitz nodded. "I'll close the loop with Jaffe, but somehow you've got to get word to Bogner. He needs to know we've verified that there's a leak."

"He might as well be on the other side of the

moon," Miller admitted. "SOP—no contact until he's recovered the Berzin woman. Even then it'll be difficult."

"What about your man in Odessa?"

"Komenich? He's with Bogner. Toby is calling the shots. They made their last contact last night—before they caught the plane to Auezov."

"What about Borodin?"

"He may have blown his cover. We haven't heard from him and we haven't been able to get through to him."

"Damn," Spitz muttered. He studied what was left of his coffee and scowled.

Packer finished his, grimaced, and shoved his chair away from the table. "Toby talked to me the day before he left. He suspected there was a good possibility someone was working both sides of the fence. He said his ex-wife knew about the Libyan warheads shipment. At that point it was still classified information. She claimed someone was leaking details to one of her foreign analysts at the network even before we had confirmation that the shipments had left Tarhuna. I notified Jaffe as soon as I heard."

"You're simply confirming what Jaffe told me," Spitz said.

"So what's our next move?" Miller asked.

"There's not a helluva lot we can do," Packer said. "If for some reason Bogner does get in touch with us, we warn him to cover his ass."

Red Sand

Datum: Seven-Four: 172 Rudisa Pyeryeulak, Odessa: 09:38 LT

Rubana Cheslov's movements were awkward, a condition she attributed to the fact that she still had not completely healed from the injuries she'd received in the Metro attack. Still, she was gracious as she poured Yuri Illich a cup of coffee and took a seat across from him. The coffee was thin and watery, not like the thick, black, pungent drink the weary inspector was used to.

Her attempts at hospitality included serving some small *kasha prozhnaye*, cereal cakes not unlike the ones Illich's wife often made. He suspected that the extra fuss was designed as much to put her at ease as it was to be an accommodating hostess. Illich was not used to such thoughtfulness. It wasn't often that people treated police officers as guests.

"It was good of you to consent to see me on such short notice," Illich said.

The woman waved her hand as if to dismiss the statement. "You said it was a matter of some urgency," she reminded him. "Is it because you have identified my assailant?"

Illich shook his head. "Unfortunately, no. But your purse and your papers, they have been returned to you?"

The woman nodded. She sat upright, hands folded in her lap, obviously uncomfortable. Illich could not decide whether the nervousness was attributable to the fact that there was a strange man in her apartment or that he was about to interrogate her about the incident on the Metro.

"Tell me what happened the night you were accosted," Illich began.

From the outset it was obvious that Rubana Cheslov was not what Illich would have called a brave woman. She was distressed and easily distracted. In many ways, she reminded him of a cat. He had already recorded the fact that she bore a resemblance to the dead woman, but not as much as he had hoped. She was tall and slender like the faceless figure in the morgue. Her hair was dark, shoulder length, and if he asked her, he was certain she would tell him that she weighed somewhere between 130 and 140 pounds.

"I work in the regional office of the Ministry," she said. There was a tremor in her voice. "We had received new directives from Vice Minister Lavrenti in Kiev regarding reapportionment of resources for—"

Illich interrupted. "And you worked late that evening, is that correct?"

The woman nodded. "I stayed until I finished because I was confident I could still catch the Metro to the Kreshchatil section."

"And you did?"

"It was late. And when it finally arrived it was quite crowded. Several of the passengers talked about attending the circus at Pobedy."

"When and where did the men accost you?"

"It was near the end of my fare. The car was

nearly empty. There were three men. I thought they were laborers."

"They weren't young men?"

Rubana Cheslov shook her head. "No. If they had been young I would have moved forward to another car—at least somewhere that there would have been witnesses. Hooligans are never brave when there are witnesses."

"Can you describe the three?"

The woman thought for a moment. "Rough looking," she finally answered. "They were wearing heavy coats—it was cold and raining."

"Weight? Height? A general description?" Illich asked. "Anything peculiar about any of the three? Scars? Limps? Speech mannerisms? Anything that would make them stand out? Did you notice a cough or something out of the ordinary?"

Rubana Cheslov's face was flushed. She was embarrassed. So far she had not been able to answer even the simplest of Illich's questions. "I am . . . I am afraid I do not remember details well," she said.

"Perhaps that's because you've tried to put the incident out of your mind," Illich suggested. "It's quite common for people who have been through experiences like this to do so. To remember is painful."

"I'm curious, Inspector. You say you're a homicide inspector. If that's the case, why are you here? I was accosted—my purse was stolen—but this isn't a case of homicide."

Illich polished off one of the cereal cakes and

wiped his fingers on his sleeve. "I believe"—he hesitated—"that you were a victim of circumstances, Gaspazha Cheslov. And while I do not wish to frighten you, I believe that you were selected because of your appearance."

Rubana Cheslov mouthed the word "appearance." "I do not understand."

"I can assure you that my investigation is a long way from complete, but I do have a theory. You see, just two days hours after your purse was stolen, we discovered the body of a young woman at the Odessa Film Studio. Her features were mutilated and your purse, containing your medical appointment card, was found at the scene. If it had been a robbery, they would not have left a purse behind. Your purse was planted at the scene to make us believe that it was"—he hesitated again—"that you were the victim."

Rubana Cheslov's eyes clouded. Her hands were shaking. "You are saying that the only reason I was accosted is that I looked like someone . . . and that they wanted my purse and papers to leave with the victim to throw the police off?"

"I believe that to be the case," Illich confirmed. "In a way you can consider yourself fortunate, Gaspazha Cheslov. It was merely your purse they wanted—not your life."

After several moments of awkward silence, Yuri Illich stood up. When he did, the woman accompanied him to the door. He handed her his card. "If you think of anything else that you wish to tell me, you can call me at this number." Illich put on his hat and coat, and the woman, obviously still unnerved by their conversation, closed the door behind him.

Standing in the vestibule of the apartment building, Yuri Illich felt a strange kind of exhilaration. Junus Arkadiya was brilliant. Between his former mentor's sketch and Rubana Cheslov, for the first time, he felt he knew what the dead woman looked like.

Datum: Seven-Five: Falls Church, Virginia: 20:10 LT

Clancy Packer closed the door of his study and dialed the number he had been carrying around with him all day.

Joy Carpenter answered on the second ring.

"Joy, it's Clancy."

"Pack, you sweetheart," she said, but suddenly sobered. He could hear her trying to catch her breath. "This isn't about Toby, is it?"

"As far as I know, T.C. is all right. At least he was last night."

"Damn it, Clancy, don't scare me like that," she snapped.

Clancy Packer was truly sorry. If Toby Bogner was like a son, Joy was like a daughter. He had known both of them since the days when Bogner was in flight school at the Naval Air Station in Pensacola and Packer was recruiting the young pilot for an ISA assignment. Clancy Packer was Kim Bogner's godfather, and that made Joy family.

"This is sensitive stuff, Joy," he said. "I know how journalists protect their sources, but that isn't going to stop me from asking. . . ."

Joy was silent.

"T.C. talked to me before he left. He said you knew about the Libyan warhead shipment before it was confirmed by the Security Council and the State Department."

"You know I'm not going to talk about—"

"All I want is a yes or no, Joy. Was Toby dreaming it, or did you tell him about the Tarhuna warheads before he got it in the next day's briefing?"

"Is Toby in danger?"

"You're the one that suggested a source could be like a two-headed snake; you tell me."

After a long pause, she said, "There's a man by the name of Jeff Rutland in our counteranalysis group. Perhaps you ought to talk to him. Outside of that, Clancy, I don't know anything that can help you."

"He'll never have the vaguest idea how we caught on to him," Clancy promised.

"I'm counting on you," Joy said. Suddenly her voice seemed to lose that old Joy Carpenter confidence.

"That's why we have friends, so that when the going gets rough you'll have people you can count on."

Clancy Packer pressed the disconnect button on

his telephone and hit the automatic dial for Robert Miller all in one motion.

When Miller picked up the receiver, Packer practically hissed his instructions. "Call Jaffe. Tell him we'll meet him at the Carafes Tower at 22:00. And tell him we have a name."

Chapter Eight

The aging Ristovok truck borrowed from a friendly Shymkent meat packer bounced the four men over a maze of washouts, potholes, and gullies as it plowed its way up the long incline toward the arsenal.

Utra Svychi did most of the driving because he knew the road, and until darkness had settled in, Rikov Mrachak had conducted what amounted to a guided tour of the countryside for Bogner and Komenich. Along the way he pointed out topographical features of the land, historical sites, and the location of abandoned missile sites built by the

Russians during the war with Afghanistan.

"They were entrenched in the Hindu Kush and these sites were selected because they were out of the range of anything the Afghans could throw back at us," Mrachak explained. "Even then, there were difficult times."

During the four hours, Bogner had dozed off from time to time, only to be awakened when Svychi was unable to avoid a particularly bad section of the washboard road.

Each of them had changed into the militia uniforms supplied by Svychi: coarse green tunic coats with high collars bearing the green-gold-red insignia of the Kazakh State Yeomanry. In addition, they wore green-colored, ill-fitting trousers and boots. The gloves, greatcoats, and hats, as they were with the militia, were mismatched.

Now, not far from their destination, they rounded a bend in the road and there was a faint glow of light visible on the horizon. Mrachak fumbled in his briefcase until he located an oversized envelope.

"We are less than five kilometers from the arsenal and approaching the central gate," he said. "There will be two sentries. I have the necessary documents. If there are any questions, I will do the talking."

When the arsenal finally came into view, Bogner was taken aback by its size. The high-security fence, spreading away from the central gate, was lighted only at irregular intervals and eventually disappeared into the Kazakh darkness.

"I will inform the guards at the central gate that we have been dispatched by the standby garrison in Shymkent to obtain arms and supplies for new recruits. I will explain our late arrival by simply telling them we got lost. Then I will ask directions to the supply depot. If they respond as they usually do, they will direct us. If one of the guards chooses to take us, we will have a small problem, but one that can easily be solved by Utra."

Utra laughed. "There will be no problems," he assured them. He momentarily displayed a dull black Beretta 92D with a silencer and quickly tucked it back in his coat pocket.

"I take it you two have done this before," Bogner said with a grin.

"The Zeverin Arsenal has proven to be, how shall I say it, an invaluable source of income over the past three years," Mrachak admitted. "I do not think anyone really cares what happens to all of this surplus from the war days. Everyone is trying to forget it."

"Hey, you're talking to the master when you're talking to Rikov Mrachak," Svychi said with a laugh. "A year ago we pulled out of the central gate with a damn flatbed carrying a bulldozer. The shit-eatin' guard was so dumb he couldn't read or write. Rikov here flashed him the papers, he acted like he could read them, gave us the go-ahead, and we were out of there. They probably hung that guy's ass from the highest building in the arsenal when they found out."

Minutes later, Svychi stopped the truck less than twenty feet from the gate and Bogner saw a guard step from the shelter. He was wearing a greatcoat and he pulled his collar up as he approached the truck. Mrachak stepped down out of the cab and met the man halfway. Komenich had rolled the window down to listen.

There were no salutes and a minimum of conversation until the guard took the papers, scanned them, and made some remark about the meat packer's truck they were driving. Mrachak laughed and explained that the garrison was unable to supply them with dependable transportation and he had borrowed it from a militia sympathizer. The guard seemed to understand. Komenich turned to Bogner, his voice low.

"Mrachak knows what he's doing. He's played this game before. Most folks in this part of the world understand broken-down and worn-out equipment; they live with it."

Bogner watched while Mrachak walked to the guard shelter with the man and went through the motions of obtaining directions to the small-arms depot. After several minutes there was more gesturing, more conversation, and finally Mrachak started back for the truck. When he was close enough, Bogner could see that he was smiling.

* * *

Mrachak guided Svychi through a maze of darkened buildings with only an occasional security light for illumination, until they came to a large Quonset-style building in the middle of the compound. Again Mrachak stepped down from the cab of the Ristovok and opened the overhead door. Then he signaled for Svychi to turn the truck around and back into the darkened building. When he did, Mrachak closed the door.

The only light in the building came from two incandescent lamps, one at each end of the low-ceiling structure.

For the most part, the weapons inventory was in chaos. Bogner probed the beam of his flashlight over four-foot-high crates piled high with an assortment of small arms, some containing handguns and others containing rifles. In other crates he located both pressure and scatter grenades, and two kinds of fragmentation land mines.

"Sorta like being in a big boy's toy store," Svychi observed, "except we don't have to pay for it."

"You can thank Gorbachev," Mrachak said. "When the Soviet Union was dissolved there were thousands upon thousands of military personnel with no place to go, no job, and no money. Someone thought it would be a good idea to try to recover as much of this stuff as possible and there was a massive weapons conscription: rubles for weapons. The Zeverin Arsenal was built specifically for the purpose of providing a place to return and store surplus military equipment. As you can see, there is no large armament—that was handled by the individual republics—but small weapons were a different story. We have been told that there is a plan for disposal as soon as the Kazakh Defense Ministry feels regional militia units have had the opportunity to utilize what they find here."

"What Rikov is really saying is, check it out before you haul it out of here," Svychi added. "A lot of it is shit. In most cases, the reason it was turned in is because it don't work. Those guys weren't dummies—they kept the good stuff. Most of 'em knew it would bring a helluva lot more on the black market than it would in the ruble-exchange program."

Even before Svychi was through, Komenich had already begun assessing the inventory. He had slipped a TIE-75 9mm automatic under his tunic and was searching for ammunition clips.

Bogner rummaged through a crate containing an assortment of Czech CZ50s and CZ75s. Most had been partially disassembled or had the action indicators removed. There was a Mauser HSC with a damaged firing pin and a Walther PPK with a scored barrel. Svychi was right; if they had been in good shape, the items would have brought a sizable amount of money on the black market.

"Remember," Mrachak cautioned, "we're going to be covering some pretty tough terrain; take what you need, but if it's going to slow you down, think twice."

At that point, Svychi was still sifting through a

crate containing ammo when he let out a yelp. A large rat scurried out of the box and raced across the floor. Mrachak laughed. While Mrachak was enjoying Svychi's surprise, Bogner was thinking how much he hated rats. Rats fell into the same category as snakes and high places.

"Hey, I think I found what we need," Komenich shouted. "Over here." When Bogner got there, Komenich was shining his flashlight down at a box of Kuskin-77d open-bolt SMGs and fifty-round magazines. "The damn things look brand-new," Komenich exclaimed.

Mrachak reached into the crate and pulled one out. "Exactly what the doctor ordered," he said with a chuckle. Then he looked at Bogner. "This, Captain, is a very fine weapon." One by one, the taller of the two Kazakh mercenaries pulled the 9mm weapons out of the crate, checked the action, and inserted a clip in each before he passed them around. "Anything else is a bonus. But I think we have what we came for," he said.

Just then, Bogner heard a metallic click. When he turned around, a nervous-appearing man in a green greatcoat was pointing one of the Israeli SMGs directly at him.

"You will not move," the man said. His face was hidden in shadows. As he said it, Bogner saw the man's finger curl through the trigger guard. "You," the man said, pointing at Mrachak. "Step forward."

"There is a problem?" Mrachak asked. He held

up his hand. "There should be no problem. I have papers. We are from the citizens militia garrison in Shymkent. We were instructed to come here to obtain small arms for new citizen recruits."

"You have no such authorization!" the man shouted. "We have checked with the garrison commander in Shymkent. No such detail has been dispatched."

"Looks like we didn't fool that guard at the gate after all," Komenich whispered.

"Be quiet," the guard demanded.

Bogner was still trying to size up the situation. As near as he could tell, the guard was alone. But even if he was, he had one big advantage—his Kuskin was loaded and his trigger finger was where it needed to be. Mrachak had taken three steps forward, still trying to show the man his papers. Svychi, who was standing behind the first row of crates, was visible.

Even the lighting was against them. As poorly lighted as the bay was, there was more than enough for the guard to see all four of them and detect any sudden movement. To add to their problems, he looked edgy—and edgy meant quick on the trigger.

"Put your weapons on the floor and raise your hands over your head," the guard ordered.

Bogner and Komenich followed instructions, but Svychi hesitated just long enough to make the guard even more nervous. Suddenly, the guard took a step forward, dropped to one knee, and triggered a burst of bullets that slammed Utra Svychi back against the wall of wooden crates. That gave Bogner just enough time to react. He leaped between a row of crates, crouched, and heard a second burst of bullets spray over his head. Then he saw Komenich hurtle backwards, spin, stumble, and fall to the floor holding his hands over his side.

For Bogner there were several seconds of terror filled with silence before he heard the guard shout at Mrachak again and the sound of slow, uncertain footsteps as the guard began working his way toward him. With each step the man was coming closer, and Bogner tried to push himself back into a narrow space between the crates. By the time he worked his legs around, it was too late. When he looked up, he was staring directly into the barrel of the still-smoking Kuskin. The guard was standing over him, his intent obvious. Bogner knew that any sudden movement would buy the farm. He held out his hands where the guard could see them and clawed his way to his knees. By the time he stood up he was able to assess the damage.

Komenich had managed to sit up, his hands covered with blood. He was trying to stem the flow from two gaping holes spreading a torrent of dark crimson from the ragged perforations in his greatcoat.

Mrachak was still on one knee, dazed. His face was bloodied and he was having trouble seeing. The guard prodded Bogner toward Mrachak with the barrel of the Kuskin, then went back and searched between the crates until he found Svychi. It wasn't until he knelt down to examine the fallen Kazakh that the explosion rocked the building. Crates splintered, debris flew, and shards of shrapnel ripped through the air like a hail of flying glass. Svychi had triggered some kind of incendiary device. Bogner ducked as the place erupted in a ball of flame. He heard one scream—momentary and partially stifled by the roar of an instant inferno. Then he saw the mangled body of the guard rocket backward, sheathed in flames, and he realized he was seeing only half a man—the lower half was gone.

Bogner scrambled to his feet, raced to the truck, threw open the door, and went back for Komenich. By the time he was able to drag him to the cab and pull him to his feet, Mrachak had started to stagger in his direction. Bogner grabbed him, shoved him in beside Komenich, jumped behind the wheel, and turned the key in the ignition.

"If you bastards know how to pray," he muttered, "you better start praying I can get us out of this damn firecracker before that guy's backup gets here and this place blows apart at the seams."

Bogner jerked the aging Ristovok into gear, slammed his foot down on the accelerator, and plowed through the door of the building. Wood splintered and there was a rain of glass as the windshield disintegrated and one of the headlights shattered. He careened several hundred yards between two rows of buildings and headed for the main gate. Behind him there was a chain of violent explosions as one arsenal building after another began detonating in a succession of volcanic eruptions. Zeverin Arsenal had become flaming rubble.

At that point he was no longer driving, he was aiming. The gates were closed and he saw one of the guards step from the building, drop to one knee, shoulder his SMG, and start to aim. Mrachak, still dazed and grimacing, hands covered with blood, had managed to prop his SMG against the truck's dash. He squeezed off three quick bursts and the gate guard pitched backward, arms flailing.

"Hang on," Bogner screamed as the Ristovok rocketed toward the gate. "Head for cover, we're going through." The swerving truck dodged to the right of the gate and slammed into the guard shelter. The tiny structure disintegrated in a shower of fragmented wood, and Bogner threw his arm up to protect his face. The Ristovok slammed to the ground, bottomed out, and Bogner rammed it into third gear.

In the rearview mirror, Bogner could see what had once been the Zeverin Arsenal. A towering wall of white-red flames was spreading, tinderbox buildings were exploding in a chain of devastation—and somewhere in that roaring pyre was the body of Utra Svychi.

He could hear Mrachak crying and Komenich trying to cope with his pain. Five hundred yards from the annihilation, he wheeled the Ristovok onto a narrow side road and tried to catch his breath. Then he looked at Mrachak and Komenich.

Syvchi was dead. Mrachak was shaking. And Komenich had been hit two, maybe three times. At
that moment, any hope of getting Polce Berzin off
of the missile train looked like one helluva long
shot.

Datum: Eight-Two: The Train, Near Zhambyl: 22:22 LT

"You wish to see me?" Dubchek said.

Polce Berzin paused until the guard closed the
door and they were alone. She heard the man assume his position outside the compartment, and
waited for Krislof Dubchek to motion her to a seat.
When he did, it was at best a perfunctory gesture,
halfhearted and curt. Revealing, she thought, his
annoyance at her interruption.

Dubchek's desk was littered with papers and a
cigarette smoldered in the ashtray. His eyes were
bloodshot and he looked tired.

"Are you here because you have complaints, Gaspazha Berzin? Because if you are—"

"On the contrary, General, I have been reflecting
on our conversation. I am curious about what you
meant when you referred to my 'cooperation.' "

Dubchek leaned back in his chair. One by one he
unbuttoned the ornate gold clasps on his tunic, and
picked up a stilettolike letter opener. He did not
smile, but somehow she felt his expression was less
hostile. "First I have questions," he said.

She held up her hand. "No, General. First I have a question for you."

Dubchek waited; he enjoyed the verbal sparring.

"You know who I am, don't you?"

"Perhaps," he said. "But I am more curious about your relationship with Aralov Lavrenti."

"I have already told you, we share mutual interests. He is interested in developing new economic models for our emerging—"

Dubchek was impatient. "Do you deny that you dine with him? That you share private conversations with him?"

"We often dine. The days are long. His schedule requires that he—"

"Not all of your conversations are about these so-called economic models. Is that correct?"

The woman hesitated. "We talk of other things," she finally admitted.

"About the future of our country?"

She nodded.

"And in this 'future of our country,' what is the role of Aleksei Savin?"

Polce looked down at her hands. It had happened. It was as Aralov had told her it would be— the first crack in the veneer, the first flaw in the fabric. "I am afraid I do not understand what the general is getting at."

Dubchek scowled. "On the contrary, *gaspazha*, you know only too well what I mean. You, perhaps more than others, know the Vice Minister's intentions. He is an architect of cunning and deception.

By now he sees that Savin is a political liability, does he not?"

The woman waited the appropriate amount of time before answering. When she did, she made her response as demure as possible. *"Da."*

Dubchek stood up. Instead of striking his usual stance with his hands behind his back, he stood with his arms folded in front of him. He was more relaxed and he appeared to be relieved at her answer.

"Now," he said, "it is time for more honesty."

"What do you mean?"

"When I was informed that the daughter of the Deputy Prime Minister was aboard this train and being held as a political hostage, I was forced to ask myself why? Clearly, *gaspazha,* your presence aboard a train delivering missiles to our allies in the Fifth Academy makes no sense. I am a logical man, and your presence has no logic—unless, of course, your presence has an unstated purpose."

"I was abducted—" she began.

Dubchek moved from one side of the compartment to the other. "When the train stopped east of Kulsary, I instructed Comrade Serova to search your compartment and your luggage. Would you like to know what she found?"

She chose not to answer.

"The bumbling assemblage of rubes and fools my colleague Savin refers to as his militia were merely following instructions. But, and I am sure you know this as well as anyone, those were not Savin's instructions, but those of Aralov Lavrenti. Oh, I am not saying that Savin did not know about it, but the man who engineered your abduction was in reality Aralov Lavrenti. Correct?"

The woman started to protest, and Dubchek held up his hand. "I warned you once before, *gaspazha*, do not play me for a fool."

The woman persisted. "Professor Tairov invited me to Odessa. I was instructed to be prepared to travel. My father wanted to get me out of the country before he gave the Americans his full cooperation."

Dubchek sighed. He returned to his desk and took out a sheet of paper covered with handwriting. "This is Comrade Serova's inventory of your possessions. Note the items she discovered in one of your cases." Dubchek handed the paper to her. He had underlined the references to the French 9mm automatic and two cartridge clips. "Of equal interest are the photographs of Comrade Savin. Is that so there would be no mistaking his identity?"

"Those are not mine," Polce protested. "Olga Serova is lying."

"Is she lying about this?" Dubchek asked. He reached into the drawer of his desk and pulled out a manila envelope containing newspaper clippings. He spread them out on the top of the desk so Polce could see them. "If I am not mistaken, this is a picture of Gaspazha Berzin—taken at the Odessa State Academic Opera and Ballet Theater just last year.

And this is Gaspazha Berzin as she appears in the registry of the Dnepro Academy."

The woman waited.

"It is easy to see, when one studies the evidence, that while the woman who sits in front of me bears a strong resemblance to Polce Berzin, the woman who sits in front of me is obviously *not* Polce Berzin. The question then becomes, who are you?"

For the first time, Dubchek could see cracks in the facade of the woman. There was a perceptible anxiousness in her demeanor, and her eyes betrayed her vexation. Still, she did not answer him.

"Perhaps your true identity is of little importance," he continued. "Perhaps it is your mission, your reason for being here, that should be my main concern. Perhaps knowing that you are affiliated with Vice Minister Lavrenti is of even more significance."

When the woman finally spoke, she had regained her equilibrium. Her voice was steady if not yet strong. "My name is Emita Paukof."

"And your purpose in being here?" Dubchek demanded.

The woman hesitated and Dubchek sagged into the chair behind his desk.

"Let me tell you why you are here then," he said. "This entire charade was arranged by Aralov Lavrenti. Am I correct in my assumption?"

"*Da,*" the woman confirmed.

"For what purpose?"

"I—I have been instructed . . . to see that Aleksei

R. Karl Largent

Savin does . . . does not return after delivering the missiles."

For the first time, she saw Dubchek smile. "To embrace logic is to know the truth. You see, I was right. Within the plot there is a plot. I have observed our illustrious Vice Minister Lavrenti for many years. I know his ways. . . ."

"Savin has become an embarrassment," the woman volunteered, gaining confidence. "He has taken matters into his own hands. The death of the Tairovs is an example."

Dubchek seemed to be pleased with himself. "Let me see if I can deduce the rest of the scenario. While Savin delivers the missiles to our Chinese friends, Lavrenti reveals to our mourning countrymen that he has discovered that Savin engineered the assassination of our beloved President Yefimov, and further reveals that Savin has suffered some ignominious, if providential fate . . . and you are the instrument of that fate."

The Paukof woman remained silent.

"And in the process, two very important objectives have been accomplished in addition to lining the coffers of the Party. One, Lavrenti has successfully disassociated the Party from the unfortunate demise of President Yefimov. And two, in eliminating Yefimov, but revealing the man who killed him, he has practically guaranteed himself—and the Party—a victory in the upcoming elections."

The woman continued to wait while Dubchek reveled in the success of his deduction. Finally, he reached into his desk again and took out the cigarette case. He opened it and offered her a cigarette.

Now that she had dropped her charade of Polce Berzin, Emita Paukof accepted it. "You will, of course, inform Vice Minister Lavrenti that when I discovered your subterfuge, I continued to cooperate. Correct?"

"Of course," Emita Paukof replied.

Dubchek smiled. He made a mental note to applaud Lavrenti. His staging of Savin's demise was worthy of a story by Chekhov.

Datum: A Farm, Near Klin: 23:47 LT

Bogner had driven aimlessly for over an hour until he found a narrow rock road that took him off the main highway. At the end of the road he came to a single farmhouse with one outbuilding, a small barn. He pulled behind it and hid the Ristovok in a grove of scraggly birch trees. They weren't much, but they were the only cover he could find.

During that hour, Mrachak had regained his equilibrium, and he did what little he could under the circumstances to tend to Komenich.

"First thing we do," Bogner said, "is check out that farmhouse."

Mrachak, toting one of the SMGs, was dispatched to the cottage to check it out. Bogner watched him disappear into the darkness, grabbed his flashlight, pushed back Komenich's bulky greatcoat, and used his field knife to cut away the man's blood-soaked shirt.

"Two wars, three border skirmishes—not even a scratch," Komenich said with a grunt. "Then I get in the way of some slob who obviously didn't know what he was doing. To top it off, I don't even get a nurse."

Bogner continued to probe at the Ukrainian's wounds.

"Don't keep me in suspense. How—how does it look?"

"So far all I can find is a couple of small holes," Bogner replied. "You can tell your girlfriend you're going to be a little tender in the love handles for a while. One slug did nothing more than graze the skin, another went clean through. That second one left a hole about the size of a kopeck. You're still bleeding from that one. That's the good news. The bad news is, there is a third bullet hole—and I think the slug is still in there. Can't really tell until I get better light."

"That's me," Komenich said, "Mikos the lucky." He closed his eyes, flinching each time Bogner probed to determine the extent of the damage.

Finally Bogner put his flashlight down, pulled the greatcoat up to cover the wound, and looked up. "I think I hear Mrachak coming back. Lets hope he found something in that cottage we can use for bandages."

When Mrachak returned, he was carrying a lantern and followed by an old man. The man looked frightened. "We're in luck," Mrachak said in English. "An old couple. They live here by themselves. They were asleep. When they opened the door, this damn Uzi scared the shit out of them. Then they saw the militia uniforms. I told them we had a man who had been shot. The old woman asked us to bring him up to the house."

Bogner looked at Komenich. "Looks like it might be fifty or sixty yards up to the house. Think you can make it?"

Komenich reached under the coat, ran his fingers over the bullet holes, and winced. "It's—it's a good thing that guard didn't know what he was doing. Up or over a bit, either way, and you and Rikov would have to get that Berzin woman off that train by yourselves."

"He knew enough to get Svychi," Bogner said.

"Svychi?" Komenich repeated. "Where is he?"

Bogner shook his head.

Komenich's eyes squeezed shut again.

"I saw Utra take two VS-50 blast mines out of one of the crates along with a damn Polish C-12 incendiary," Mrachak said. "He must have detonated it when that goon bent over him to see if he was still alive."

Komenich grimaced and bit his lip. He felt Bogner stiffen.

"He was a tough little bastard," Mrachak said with a sigh. "He claimed he learned it all in your country," he said to Bogner.

"How'd we get out of there?" Komenich asked.

"You missed the fireworks," Mrachak said. "By the time we cleared the gate, the whole damn thing was going up like a cheap rocket. Unless I miss my guess, that weapons depot can't be much more than a pile of ashes by now. We could still see the glow in the sky seven miles from the arsenal."

The old man moved around Mrachak and bent down beside Komenich. When he spoke the words came out in a thick and hesitating Kazakh dialect. Bogner couldn't understand him.

"He says he used to be a veterinarian," Mrachak said. "he thinks he can help."

The old man went to the corner of the barn and moments later with a piece of toweling and two leather thongs. He constructed a pressure bandage, tied it off with the thongs, and stopped the bleeding. When he was finished, Bogner and Mrachak were able to get Komenich to his feet and start him toward the couple's cottage.

It was going on three o'clock in the morning when Mrachak came back up to the cottage. He slumped into a chair across the table from Bogner while the old man and his wife worked over Komenich.

"Damage report," Mrachak said. "Technically, she runs, but that's about all I can say for it. I pried the radiator out away from the fan, figured out a way to rewire the headlights, and taped everything that I could find back in place. We've got no windshield, no second gear, and damn little gas. There's a hole in the oil sump and we might make five, maybe even ten, kilometers before the damn thing blows up on us."

Bogner's shoulders sagged. "How far are we from Zhambyl and that damn train?"

"A helluva lot farther than that truck will get us."

The old man understood more English than he had been letting on. "The Zhambyl station is seventeen kilometers," he said. "I have driven it many times." The old man was still describing the road to Zhambyl when his wife pointed toward the road and began gesturing. She was pointing out a pair of headlights that had pulled off the road and started up the rock road toward the farmhouse.

"Looks like we've got company," Bogner noted. "Just what we don't need."

"It is the local militia," the woman said in broken English. "They are looking for the truck. Zhambyl Radio is saying that a number of militia units have been dispatched from the Centro barracks to search the area for the truck that escaped from the arsenal. They are asking anyone who sees the truck to report it."

"Looks like we didn't get all of 'em after all," Mrachak grumbled.

"Where can we hide Komenich?" Bogner asked.

The old woman was already dragging the large braided rug to one side to reveal a trapdoor in the floor. "When the wind and dust storms come, it is our only refuge," her husband explained.

While the old couple moved Komenich to the

storm cellar, Mrachak and Bogner left through the rear door and headed for the outbuilding. They managed to clear the area just as the militia truck rounded into view.

"What's it look like?" Bogner whispered.

Mrachak was squinting into the darkness. "I think our luck just ran out. So far I count four of them. They're in a Czech-built ML-ta towing a weapons carrier with gun-mount platform. If they are driving an ML-ta, that means they're militia regulars. Worse yet, they've got a fifty-caliber machine gun mounted on a platform over the rear axle and a damned halogen-beam searchlight on that tow platform. It won't take 'em long to find us."

Mrachak inched his way backward, deeper into the shadows. The ML-ta had stopped less than fifty meters from where Mrachak had hidden their own truck.

"If they find that damn truck, all bets are off," Bogner muttered. "They'll be on that radio in nothing flat."

Mrachak and Bogner watched while all four of the militiamen crawled down out of the vehicle. One of the men scrambled up on the trailer platform and activated the halogen. Then he began rotating the beam in a 180-degree sweep from the house to the barn. The first pass was too rapid and one of the men shouted at him; the second was slower—more methodical—more effective.

A second guard, hefting what, from where Mrachak was hiding, appeared to be a Kuskin SMG, headed for the outbuilding while the other two headed for the cottage.

"You're calling the shots, Captain," Mrachak whispered.

"No choice," Bogner hissed. "Take 'em out. That damn weapons carrier is our ticket out of here."

Mrachak was grinning. "I like your style," he said. "Let's go."

Bogner grabbed Mrachak's sleeve. "No matter what happens, Rikov, you make damn certain none of them get back to that radio. I'll take care of the rest."

Bogner shimmied forward in the shadows with the SMG cocked. The beam of the truck-mounted halogen swung momentarily in his direction, than back again, reversing its search pattern until it was again pointing back at the cottage. The light had come within three feet of him.

He saw one of the militiamen probe his flashlight into the old barn and then move cautiously around to the side. When Bogner looked back, Mrachak had managed to position himself within twenty feet of the house. Suddenly one of the militiamen wheeled and spotted him, and Bogner saw Mrachak open fire. The Israeli version of the Uzi blistered the blackness with two rapid-fire bursts of hot orange and both militiamen went down.

The searchlight swung back, picking up Mrachak as he dove into the shadows. Bogner tensed, sighted, and squeezed. There was a series of mocking, miniature explosions . . . a rhythmic firecrackerlike burping sound that only someone firing an Uzi was familiar with. The man on the platform suddenly began performing a grotesque pirouette; his body jerked one way and then another as the 9mm slugs ripped through him and ricocheted off the gun mount.

The beam of the searchlight, swinging free, spun wildly until the beam was pointing up into the darkness.

Bogner dropped to his stomach. Mrachak had taken care of two of them and the ML-ta had been immobilized, but there was still a fourth one out there. Bogner squirmed back into the weeds at the edge of the clearing and waited. He lay there for several moments before he heard Mrachak call out, "Where the hell is he?"

"Behind the barn. I'm going after him. You secure that damn radio."

Mrachak began inching his way through the shadows to the weapons carrier, and Bogner shuddered. This time it wasn't a rice paddy. This time there wasn't a stinking sweat bath and swarms of mosquitoes. This time it was a dusty, bone-chilling stretch of nothingness on the grainy sand-rock soil of a Kazakhstan farm. This time it wasn't the smoldering wreckage of a downed F-4 Phantom betraying his position. This time it was, of all things, a goddamn Russian-built delivery truck that was giving him away. But this time there was one big difference. The odds. This time the odds were on his side. Bogner had Mrachak and whether the militia guard knew it or not, he was all alone.

Bogner bolted for the barn, slammed his body up against the sidewall, checked the bolt on his SMG, and inched his way toward the back of the building. His adversary was an unknown. If he was a militia regular as Mrachak suspected, he was either trying to figure out how to get back to the weapons carrier and radio for help, or he was waiting. Either way, he had the darkness to work with.

Bogner worked his way to a place where he could see the meat truck. It was parked in the sparse grove of birch. In the dim moonlight, the area was a tangle of shadows—a bushwhacker's paradise. He crouched, waited several moments, then started working his way toward the truck again. The realization that he had blundered came too late.

The mine went off less than ten feet from Bogner, showering him with a hail of rocks and dirt. He went down, and more out of instinct than training, rolled over just as the Kazakh militia man opened fire. Now it was Nam all over again. The only difference was there was no infrared, no night vision, no tracers. He swung the Kuskin SMG around, squeezed, and emptied the clip into the darkness. He could hear the bullets shredding metal as they gouged their way into the steel cargo area of the meat truck.

There was an angry shout and sporadic return fire; a spray of bullets ripped into and splayed out chunks of birch and spewed dirt in chaotic patterns. Then, just as quickly, the angry belches of red-orange return fire stopped.

Now came the hard part. Bogner waited for what seemed like an eternity before he drew a deep breath. Finally, he stood up.

The silence was deafening.

Chapter Nine

Datum: Nine-One: Parking Garage, Shermark Hotel: 20:14 LT

Robert Miller was as meticulous about time as he was about everything else. Miller's watch, which was set by Naval Observatory time, now indicated that Jeff Rutland was fourteen minutes and thirty-seven seconds late for their eight P.M. meeting.

"He said he'd be driving a white four-door Mercury and he'd meet us on the second level near the elevators," Miller confirmed. "At eight o'clock. Maybe he got cold feet."

Packer checked his notes and shook his head. "He'll show. If he doesn't, he knows he's got even bigger problems. It doesn't take a genius to figure out you don't have a helluva lot of options when a government agency puts the press on you."

"Time to swing into gear then," Miller said with a sigh. He reached into his briefcase, took out the tiny transmitter, and pinned it under Packer's tie. When he got out of the car, he pocketed the small combination recorder/receiver and walked down the ramp, leaving Packer to wait by himself.

Moments later, a white Mercury eased down the exit ramp from the third level and pulled even with Packer's car. When Rutland rolled down the window, Packer got his first look at the news analyst. Out of habit Packer began mentally ticking off his observations. Rutland appeared to be nervous and annoyed. He was late and obviously eager to avoid both the meeting and the conversation, all factors in Packer's favor.

"Your place or mine," Packer said.

Rutland hesitated.

"Climb in," Packer invited.

Finally Rutland shook his head. "Neither. My way or no way," he said. He turned off the ignition, got out of his car, and motioned to the stairs. "We talk there—or we don't talk."

Packer sighed, stepped out, and walked to the stairs. Along the way Rutland lit a cigarette, took two quick drags, and threw the cigarette away; observations confirmed. At the top of the stairs Packer reached inside his coat and flashed his identification.

"Okay, so you're Clancy Packer. Note this, Clancy

Packer, it's cold and I'm in a hurry. But before we start, I've got my own question. Where the hell do you come off phoning my home, telling my wife you're with the ISA and that you want to talk to me? You scared the hell out of her and the kids."

Clancy Packer smiled and glanced down. From where they were standing he could see the hotel's empty cocktail patio. The tables and chairs had been stored for the winter. "All we want to do is talk to you," he said, "and the sooner you tell us what we need to know, the sooner you can go home to your wife and children where it's nice and warm. Deal?"

Rutland scowled and waited. "The meter's running."

"It seems," Packer began, "that from time to time, you're privy to some very sensitive information. In some cases, that information is so sensitive, it's still classified. We'd like to know how you got it."

"Every newsman has his source."

Packer laughed. "So I've heard. But in this case we're not talking about some senator pimping the press with 'an unidentified source' line of bullshit. We're talking about information that could get someone hurt—and that certain someone is one of my men."

"If you got personnel problems, Packer, that's your predicament. I haven't done anything illegal and you know it. You want to file charges, file 'em. I got the damn Constitution on my side, and you know that too."

Clancy Packer reached inside his overcoat and took a small notebook out of his shirt pocket. "Well, you keep saying I know something, so let's see what I do know."

Rutland leaned back against the cement, shoved his hands in his pockets, and waited.

Packer scanned his notes. "It says here: Jeff Rutland, forty-one years old, married, wife Nancy, two children, Glenna, two, and Murray, five. You've been with NBS five years and the reason you didn't get a raise on your last performance review was that you have a slight drinking problem."

"So?"

Packer sighed. "You know, Mr. Rutland, on the way over here I got to wondering. . . ."

"Wondering what, Packer?"

"Wondering whether your wife, Nancy, knows that your Monday night poker club broke up three years ago, and that you now spend your Monday night with . . ." Clancy glanced down at his notes. "A Miss Carol Taylor, who has an apartment at—"

Rutland held up his hand. "Careful, Packer, you're on thin ice. You try that shit and I'll charge your bureaucratic ass with blackmail."

"In case it didn't occur to you, Mr. Rutland, I have some friends in very high places. Charges like that usually get a little messy. Messy situations usually require lawyers, and lawyers cost money. The question is, are you going to have any money left after your wife's divorce lawyer gets through with you?"

Packer had him at a disadvantage and Rutland

knew it. He lit another cigarette. This time he held onto it. "All right, Packer, you win the first round; ask your damn questions—but be specific."

Packer looked out over the lights of the city. "It seems to us that lately you've been tapping in to someone with a big mouth. And we think that someone is telling you things that get in our way."

"Like I said, Packer, be specific."

"Last year, two Columbian arms dealers slipped out of town after your network did a special on a couple of very nasty arms deals. That special aired less than twenty-four hours before the appropriate government agency filed the documents with the Attorney General."

"Sloppy work on the government's part," Rutland countered.

"We don't think so. We did a little checking, and what we discovered was, you're the one that did the so-called 'investigative' work and fact-finding on that story."

"So I got lucky. Bad timing on your part."

"A week ago, you filed your report on some war-head shipments out of Tarhuna in Libya—only three hours after a top secret meeting on that very subject concluded in the White House. Bottom line, someone tipped you off. My question, Mr. Rutland, is quite obvious. Who tipped you off?"

Rutland laughed. "You know I don't have to answer that, Packer."

"True. As my wife likes to say, so true. By the same token, nowhere is it written that I have to keep this little bit of information about your Monday night poker club from Mrs. Rutland either."

It was Rutland's turn to turn and stare down at the empty courtyard. His hands were shaking. "Suppose, just suppose, we find a way to work out some kind of a deal."

"I have a better idea, Jeffy. Lets just play the cards that are on the table," Packer countered. "You tell me where you get your information and Miss Taylor remains our sordid little secret."

Rutland hesitated. Then he turned back to confront his nemesis. "No deal."

Packer sighed, shrugged, turned, and started back to his car. Behind him, he heard Rutland walk back to his car, get in, and drive away. By the time that happened, Packer was already giving Miller instructions.

"Have Henline pick up his tail when he pulls out of the hotel parking lot. Arrange to keep someone on our boy's ass night and day. Tell whoever's following him we don't want Rutland to take a shit without us knowing time, date, location, and volume."

Datum: Nine-Two: 610 Lenin Podre, Odessa: 08:10 LT

Duna Marava was a vivacious young woman and Yuri Illich had long enjoyed her company. So much so, in fact, that he had been reluctant to release her to the Ministry of Public Affairs when she was offered the promotion. Now the dark-eyed woman was teasing him about that fact.

"Was it because you secretly entertained fantasies about me, Inspector?"

Illich, never adept at small talk, nevertheless was enjoying the exchange. "You would have made a good homicide investigator," he answered. "Unfortunately, I don't see that many trainees with your eye for detail."

Duna Marava blushed. It was one of her charms.

They were still standing in the vending area when Illich bought her a cup of tea and warm milk and invited her to have a seat.

"Your work, it goes well?" Illich inquired.

The young woman wrinkled her nose. "If you are asking me if I find it as exciting as the work I did in your department, the answer is *no*."

"You have the option of transferring back," Illich offered. "Perhaps the work you have been doing will make you a more skilled investigator."

Duna Marava pointed to the stack of file folders she had been carrying when she walked into the vending area. "I'm afraid the Ministry of Public Affairs only prepares one to do what one is doing." She opened one of the files and slid it across the table toward the inspector.

Illich glanced at it. It was a complaint of price gouging by several women who claimed that they were being overcharged by a government supply store.

"The good news," he said with a sigh, "is, if we

can believe what they tell us, it won't be long until the State is no longer operating in the private sector."

Duna laughed. "Not if the Communists come back into power. Then I would be out of a job. Everything will be as it was, and people will know it is pointless to complain."

Illich studied the stack of files. "Surely the Ministry of Public Affairs handles matters more substantive than consumer complaints."

Duna held up her hand and counted on the fingers of one hand. "So far I have delved into such matters as housing shortages, admissions to the university, consumer complaints, and expediting passports."

Illich shook his head. "A waste," he concurred.

"See this one?" Duna asked. She leafed through the folders a second time. "This one cost me an entire weekend. I got a telephone call from a Professor Tairov, asking me to arrange for an emergency passport for the daughter of the Deputy Prime Minister."

Illich stopped sipping his milk tea and looked at the file.

"You'd think someone with Tairov's connections would have called on some of his friends in the Cabinet of Ministers, or the Supreme Council," the woman grumbled, "but no, I had to hand-carry the paperwork through every clearance station and agency in Kiev."

Illich liked Duna, but now he remembered why

he approved the transfer; Duna Marava had a habit of prattling on long after all meaningful discussion had abated.

Still, something was bothering him. He pulled the file toward him and opened it. "What happened? The passport is still in the file."

"I know," Duna said. "I lose two holidays, my work piles up, and this Berzin woman never even bothers to pick up the passport."

"Did you ask Professor Tairov what happened?"

Duna Marava lowered her voice. "You know what happened to him, don't you?" She leaned back in her chair and smiled coyly. "Of course you know what happened," she said. "How unfortunate. Don't you agree?" She suddenly felt foolish, selfish, and too talkative. She had dominated the conversation, and thus far she had not even asked him how his work was going.

"The passport would have done her no good," Illich commented. "Passports require a current photograph."

Duna rifled through the file until she produced a photograph. "I was going to have this one reduced," she said. She showed the photograph to Yuri Illich, and was starting to put it back in the file when he reached for it. "Let me see that, please," he said.

When she pushed the photograph back at him, he took Junus Arkadiya's sketch out of his pocket and compared the two. "What do you think?" he said. "Do they look alike?"

"There are some similarities," the woman admitted.

Illich was disappointed. "Not that much, huh?"

"The one in the sketch is older. Perhaps it is nothing more than the difference in age between the two women."

Illich closed Duna's file, put the Arkadiya sketch back in his pocket, and picked up his hat. Then he caught himself doing not one, but two things that were completely out of character for him. First, he winked and patted the young woman's hand. It was purely a paternal gesture. Second, he invited her to stop by the homicide division if she was considering transferring again. It was true that Duna Marava talked too much, but Illich was convinced that another trainee of the caliber of Fedorovich could do nothing but hasten his own retirement.

By the time he walked to the bank of vending machines, it occurred to him that there was one question he had not asked. "This Berzin woman," he said, "where did she work?"

Duna Marava shrugged and dug back into her files. She traced her finger down through the reams of information. "Ah," she said, "she was a high-level analyst with the Dnepro Institute."

"Dnepro Institute?" Illich asked. "Do I recall reading that it reports to Vice Minister Lavrenti?"

Datum: Nine-Three: Near Klin: 02:17 LT

Bogner and Mrachak spent most of the early morning hours revising their plans. Now, with the

Czech-built ML-ta weapons carrier at their disposal, they no longer had to depend on the borrowed butcher truck; they had a way out. Their only remaining task was to dispose of the bodies of the militiamen and the old truck the trio had used to escape the Zeverin Arsenal the previous evening.

In the process of stripping the bodies, Mrachak had discovered militia papers in the pockets of one of them. The papers ordered the men to assemble with a detail of Kazakh militia men boarding the train at Zhambyl to relieve troops escorting the missile shipment to Alma-Ata.

He handed the papers to Bogner. "Well, my *amerikanski* friend, it looks like our luck just took a turn for the worse," he said. "All four of these men were assigned to the same garrison. These papers are official orders, instructing them to join with a formation *subotu* at *syem chasov*."

"Saturday at 07:00 hours," Bogner repeated. "Too risky. If it was several garrisons, we might try it. We'd have a chance of getting lost in the masses. We'll have to find a way to get on that train somewhere further east."

Mrachak nodded in Komenich's direction. "I'm afraid our friend is an even bigger problem. If he is strong enough, we take him. If he is not, then we will have to leave him behind."

Bogner walked over to the old woman. At Mrachak's request, she had been repairing the bullet holes in the tunics of the militiamen. "How is he?"

The old woman shook her head. "He has lost

much blood," she said. "He is very weak."

When the woman's husband joined them, he was frowning. "She is right, it would be dangerous to move him. I was unable to remove the bullet that is lodged near his kidney. I have neither the proper instruments nor the necessary antiseptics . . . and there is the increasing danger of infection."

Bogner took Mrachak aside and kept his voice low. "How much danger is there in leaving Mikos here?"

"The danger is to the old people," Mrachak said. "If the militia discovers that they have given him sanctuary, they will be arrested for harboring an enemy of the State. At this point we are all considered enemies of the State."

Bogner frowned. "Let me put it another way. What's the chances of them finding him if they aren't looking for him?"

"They will continue to look until they do," Mrachak said. "They have nothing better to do."

"Not if my plan works."

Mrachak waited.

"Remember that narrow bridge we crossed last night, the one over the ravine? Suppose they found that old butcher truck we borrowed at the bottom of that ravine with the bodies of three men dressed in the militia uniforms Utra had us wearing. What then?"

Mrachak's frown began to dissipate. "It would take them a while to identify the bodies," he admitted.

Red Sand

."It would take 'em a helluva lot longer if the bodies were badly burned," Bogner said.

Mrachak was beginning to see the possibilities.

"My first thought was we would have to take the bodies of those four Kazakh militiamen out somewhere and bury them in shallow graves until we had time to get away from here. But this idea could work even better. We're wearing their uniforms— so why not put ours on them? Even if the bodies aren't burned beyond recognition, it'll take some of your forensic experts several days to put the pieces together and figure out what happened."

"What is it Svychi would have said?" Mrachak asked with a smile. "Works for me." The Kazakh paused for a moment and the smile faded. "I will miss him," he admitted.

Mrachak, with Bogner following in the weapons carrier, succeeded in getting the old butcher truck across the bridge, turned around, and headed away from the arsenal before the engine seized. It was still smoking when Bogner and Mrachak carried the bodies of the four men from the cargo area around to the cab. Then Bogner removed four incendiary devices and two road flares from the weapons cache at the base of the machine-gun mount. He opened the caps on the incendiaries, an impact type designed to be fired by a handheld rocket launcher, set them for forty-five seconds, and attached them to the frame of the truck near the gas tank.

Mrachak wedged the flare between the firewall and the floorboard, peeled back the cap, waited until it ignited, and shoved the gear shift into neutral.

Moments later, after the crashing, clattering sounds of an aging Ristovok truck plunging two hundred feet into a dry river bed under a bridge, there was a momentary silence. Later Bogner would think of that brief silence as a wake for both man and machine.

Then came the explosion. The inferno that followed bathed the craggy walls of the ravine in an eerie red-orange light as it consumed its victims.

When Bogner looked at Mrachak, he realized that the Kazakh had bowed his head in prayer.

Finally, Mrachak spoke. It came in the form of a rhetorical question. "This Berzin woman, she is worth all of this?"

Bogner shook his head and shrugged. He did not have an answer.

Datum: Nine-Four: The Train, 06:31 LT

Emita Paukof, no longer burdened with maintaining the identity of Polce Berzin, had spiraled into a deep sleep for the first time in four days. That sleep was now being interrupted as she felt the slow-moving train lurch to a stop. She opened her eyes and looked around the darkened compartment for several moments.

Then, still mired in that first drowsy awareness, she rolled over and pulled back the heavy drape over her sleeping compartment window. The sky along the horizon revealed the first feeble light of morning and a barren, rock-strewn landscape void of trees and civilization. She saw no change; her view was the same as it had been for the last eighteen hours, a featureless and dreary expanse of impoverished countryside that had been laid waste by eroding winds and severe winters.

Knowing that a return to the deep sleep she had been enjoying would be unlikely, she turned on the small night-light over her bed and lit a cigarette. It was another of the pleasures that she no longer had to deny herself because of the cessation of the Berzin charade. As she lit the cigarette, her mind drifted back again to her last meeting with the Vice Minister and the explicitness of his instructions. As always, Aralov Lavrenti had left nothing to chance, carefully explaining his reasons why and meticulously going over every detail.

She recalled how they had met that night. He was a man of large disciplines and small customs. They met in a small cafe across the street from the former Intourist Cultural Center the night of Yefimov's assassination.

"You have heard?" he asked as he sat down.

"Just as you planned," she said. "There is a feeling of elation?"

"It has only just begun," he admitted. "There is still much to do. As you well know, the death of our beloved President is only the first step."

"And this is where I come in. Correct?"

Lavrenti lowered his voice. "Your task may be even more difficult than that of your comrade earlier today. Seven years ago when I selected you from the ranks of the GRU, you exhibited great resourcefulness. It is that resourcefulness that I am counting on now."

Emita Paukof had ordered a licorice drink prior to his arrival, and she reached for it to take a sip. Lavrenti looked around to be certain their conversation was not being overheard and waited for her to finish.

"Listen carefully," he cautioned. "Tomorrow morning, I will inform my staff that I have scheduled a meeting with the Berzin woman at the Dnepro Institute. At the same time, you will call in and inform your superior that you are being called away on a family matter. You will be distressed, and although out of character, you will leave no contact information."

Emita Paukof listened as Lavrenti continued.

"Through my many conversations with Deputy Prime Minister Berzin prior to leaving for America, I know full well his intentions. He intends to reveal to the Americans that the missiles and warheads intended for disassembly by the French are being diverted to the Fifth Academy in direct violation of our nuclear agreements. Because he fears for his daughter's safety when that revelation is made, he has made arrangements for an associate, a Dmitri Tairov, in Odessa, to arrange passage out of the country for his daughter."

Red Sand

Emita Paukof nodded her understanding.

Aralov Lavrenti slid his hand across the table. When he lifted it there was a key and an airline ticket. "When you leave here, you must go directly to the Berzin woman's apartment and wait for Tairov's call. When he calls, tell him that you will arrive in Odessa as soon as possible. Do not tell him which flight you will be arriving on—we do not want him to know that you already have a ticket."

"What about the Berzin woman?" Emita asked.

"That has already been taken care of. My associates have been quite clever. It will take the Odessa authorities quite some time to unravel our machinations. In Odessa, you will visit the Tairovs and as they attempt to get you out of the country, you will be abducted."

"Abducted?"

Lavrenti held up his hand. "Abducted," he repeated, "and put aboard the train carrying the missiles. It is important for my colleagues to believe that Polce Berzin is aboard that train. I want them to think that I have fulfilled my part of the arrangement in preventing Polce Berzin from leaving the country."

"But I am there for a reason, correct?"

Lavrenti seldom smiled, but this time he did. "In the struggle for power it is often necessary for wise men to consort with fools, Comrade Paukof. Until such a time as I reveal that my colleague, Aleksei Savin, is responsible for the assassination of our beloved President Yefimov, and he falls out of favor with Party hard-liners, I cannot count on their vote in the upcoming elections. When it becomes apparent to the people that he is unworthy of their support, I will reluctantly step forward and become the standard-bearer for the Party."

"How do you want this to appear?"

"It must be made to appear that Comrade Savin took his own life after he learned of the groundswell against him. Comrade Savin is a man of considerable infirmities; it will not be difficult.

"The missile shipment must be accomplished. There will be other shipments, and the sale of such missiles will continue to fortify the Party in the days to come. That is, until such time as we have need of them for our own purposes."

"You do not wish to give me instructions as to how—"

"What I have given you are your constraints," Lavrenti said. "When you return to Kiev, you will reassume your real identity—and, of course, you will be appropriately rewarded."

"Would it be indelicate of me to ask how?"

"How do you *want* to be rewarded?" Lavrenti countered.

Emita Paukof recalled how she had smiled and informed the man who had selected her from the ranks of the GRU that her reward was something she wished to think about.

Now, as she lay in the darkness, reflecting back on that conversation, she was forced to merge those thoughts with the voices and sounds in the corridor outside her compartment. It was only reasonable to wonder what the addition of Dubchek to the equation meant. She was still thinking about that when the knock on the door of her compartment broke the contemplative mood. She sat up and extinguished her cigarette.

"*Da*," she said. The door opened and Olga Serova entered.

Emita had seen less of her designated companion since she had reached her "understanding" with Dubchek. Now Olga, dressed in a heavy flannel nightgown, inquired if she had heard about the delay.

"I know we have stopped," Emita snapped, "but I do not know why."

"We have arrived at the Gretchkah station," Olga informed her. "In the past we have only stopped here if we have business at the Zeverin Arsenal."

"Arsenal?" Emita repeated. "Why would we stop at a Kazakhstan arsenal?"

Olga Serova bent over Emita's bunk and peered out the window. "I do not know," she admitted. "I only know that when we stopped, three men boarded the train."

The man, an officer in the Kazakh militia, saluted Dubchek when he entered the general's compartment. Dubchek, still seated on the edge of his bunk, ignored the salute and endeavored to get his thoughts organized. The vodka had induced a deep sleep.

"The general will excuse this inconvenience?" the man said. "I wish to inform you that early yesterday evening three, possibly four, men destroyed the Zeverin Arsenal in Klin."

Dubchek tried to clear his head. He could hear the commotion in the corridor outside his compartment and he stood up. "I—I am curious, Captain, as to why you think I would be—"

"We are searching the train, General," the man said. "Our commander has dispatched search units throughout the area. The damage to the arsenal was extensive."

"And why do you think that this would be of interest to me?" Dubchek pressed.

"There have been raids on the arsenal in the past, some of which were perpetrated by dissidents which resulted in disruptive actions that—"

Dubchek stood up. He was wearing only long underwear. "I would remind the captain that this train is carrying property of the Ukrainian government and is authorized to proceed unimpeded through Kazakh territory—an authority granted by the Kazakhstan government. There have been no stops since we left Zhambyl, and in order to maintain our schedule, our engineers are under orders not to stop until we reach Alma-Ata. If you persist in your search and it results in further delays, I will have no recourse but to report your actions to your superiors."

The Kazakh officer stiffened. "You are denying us access and authority to search?"

"That is exactly what I am doing, Captain. Now, order your men off of the train."

The officer turned to leave the compartment. This time there was no salute. He stopped just long enough to inform Dubchek that he would inform his own superiors of Dubchek's reluctance to comply with the search order. Then he left.

From the window of his compartment Dubchek watched until the Kazakh officer and his men stepped from the train. Then he went to the door and spoke to the guard.

"You will remind the engineers that once they are under way again, they are under orders to stop for nothing until they reach Alma-Ata. It is imperative that the true nature of our cargo not become general knowledge."

Chapter Ten

Datum: Ten-One: Near Klin: 07:17 LT

Bogner climbed back up the stairs from the farm-house storm cellar and shook his head. "We'll have to go on without him," he said. "He's too weak to travel, and even if it was safe for him, he'd slow us down."

Mrachak looked up from his maps. He knew what was going through Bogner's mind. Bogner was questioning whether or not two men could accomplish a task that had originally been designed for four. More to the point, he was questioning if they could accomplish what they needed to do without the Ukrainian. Perhaps even deeper than that, Bogner could be questioning whether or not

Mrachak was willing to stick it out to the end. Mrachak had portrayed himself as a mercenary, a paid gun, saying it mattered little to him whether the Chinese had the warheads or they were still in the hands of the Russians. Warheads were warheads. Money was money. There was no family to protect, no country to save. His needs motivated him—not his political philosophies.

"Do we go on?" Mrachak asked.

"You tell me," Bogner said.

Mrachak allowed a subtle smile to play with the corners of his mouth and alter ever so slightly the lines of his craggy face. "You still have to get the girl off the train, do you not?"

Bogner nodded.

"And there is still the matter of the missiles?"

Bogner nodded again. "Things haven't changed in that respect."

"Then it is time to revise our plan," Mrachak decided. "You pay Mrachak Svychi's share and he does the work of two men."

Bogner agreed. "You got yourself a deal."

"All we have to do," Mrachak said, "is devise a way to accomplish our plan with two men. On one side we have this man you refer to as Savin and his KON militia, and on the other side we have Mrachak and one *amerikanski*. In the streets where I grew up, I would assess those odds at being about even."

"Then you're still in?"

"Of course I am in," Mrachak laughed. "I know where we are going and you have lots of money.

Mrachak asks himself, who better to align himself with than a man that has much money?" He shoved the map across the table at Bogner and pointed to an area he had circled. "While you have been worrying, Mrachak has been planning."

Bogner moved the candle closer to the charts and watched Mrachak's finger trace a trail to a village midway between Zhambyl and Alma-Ata.

"Mrachak has gone over the papers he found in the pockets of the militia officer. We know that group was part of a militia detachment relieving the detachment already aboard the train. The detachment is small, consisting of only twelve men. It is not the size of the detachment that bothers Mrachak, it is the familiarity. If they know one another, we will be recognized as outsiders. Our presence will be questioned."

"All right . . . what do we do?"

"Mrachak has developed a better plan. West of Alma-Ata is a small village. It is called Abay. It is high in the mountains. There Mrachak has a cousin, too old and too infirm to help us, but we can launch our plan from there."

"So, if those militia papers indicate that Zhambyl is the last stop before Alma-Ata, how do we get aboard the train?"

"You have not attempted to board a moving train, *amerikanski*? I have done so many times when I was a youth," Mrachak said. "It was considered a test of *machiavo*, our manhood."

Bogner sat down. "Okay, I'm still with you. We're

on the train and we get the girl—how do we get her off? If I understand what you're telling me, we're in the middle of some pretty rugged terrain."

Mrachak laid the pencil down. "First we get the girl, then we worry what we do with her. If she is pretty, perhaps Mrachak will take her for a wife."

"How far to this village where you have an old and infirm 'cousin'?" Bogner asked with a grin. He suspected there was more to it than Mrachak was letting on.

"We have time," Mrachak assured him, "but prepare yourself for a long and uncomfortable journey."

Bogner glanced back at the door to the open storm cellar. "What about Mikos?"

The old man stepped forward. He had been listening. "You have friends. We will take care of him, and when he is able we will see that he is able to return to his home."

Datum: Ten-Two: Near Klin: 09:02 LT

Major Ustan Varmii walked slowly back to the drop-off and stared down into the dry creek bed where the remains of the truck still smoldered. The winds had picked up, and now he was forced to contend with a light snow. Below him, he could see two of his men poking through the twisted wreckage while a third had walked upstream looking for any indication that someone might have survived.

When he received no signal, Varmii returned to

the two peasants who had reported discovering the still-burning debris some two hours earlier and continued his interrogation.

"Tell me again what happened," he demanded.

The peasants, both old farmers, huddled next to their truck to stay out of the wind. Thus far Varmii had been successful in getting only one of the two men to talk. The other was either mute or too frightened to say anything. Varmii figured that it was perhaps his uniform—the newly formed Kazakh militia had not yet earned the people's trust—and given the history of both the former Red Army and the KGB in the region, he understood why.

When the man spoke it was in a regional dialect, reflecting both the Kyrgyz and Kazakh languages. Varmii had difficulty understanding him. He tried repeating what the man told him to see if he had heard it correctly.

"You came over that hill there." He pointed to the east. "And you saw the fire burning down in the ravine. You stopped your truck and tried to get down to see if you could help anyone that might be trapped."

The man's head bobbed with each word, urging the major to continue.

"But it was too hot, the flames were still burning. Could you see bodies in the wreckage?"

Before the peasant could answer, one of Varmii's men returned from the scene of the wreck. His face was flushed, he was carrying a plastic bag, and he was out of breath from the steep climb. He confirmed what the peasant had been telling him.

"They are all dead, Major. It is impossible to tell how many were in the truck, the bodies are badly burned."

"But it is the truck."

"I believe so, sir," the man said. "It is not one of our vehicles. The guard at the Zeverin Arsenal said the men were wearing militia uniforms and I found this. . . ." The young soldier opened the plastic bag and showed Varmii the severed hand and wrist of one of the victims. It protruded from the remnants of a sleeve of a green greatcoat.

Varmii, by profession an instructor at a nearby agricultural college, and a reserve officer in the militia, had been called to duty because of the raid on the arsenal. When he saw the arm and hand, he turned away to regain his composure.

Finally he asked, "Could you tell? Was there more than one body? Did anyone survive? Could anyone have escaped?"

The soldier shook his head. "There is more than one body in the wreckage," he confirmed, "and I do not see how anyone could have survived."

Varmii walked back to the staff car, opened the door, and instructed the driver to get on the radio. While he waited he braced himself against the raw, gusty wind and noted that the snow was beginning to accumulate. Despite his heavy coat, and a hat that covered his ears, a chill had encompassed most of his body. At that moment, Major Ustan Varmii would have been hard pressed to tell whether the chill was the result of the rapidly dropping temperature or the sight of the severed hand and wrist carried by the young soldier.

When he was informed that the regiment dispatcher was on the line, he said, "Inform General Armanov that we have located the truck that escaped from the arsenal. And also tell him that we will need an autopsy expert. Indications are there are no survivors."

Datum: Ten-Three: Alma-Ata: 10:30 LT

Aleksei Savin's appearance belied his dossier. He was an exceedingly frail man, yet he was a man that others feared. Standing no more than five feet, eight inches tall, he weighed a mere one hundred and thirty pounds and used a portable oxygen tank to support his breathing.

It was not the physical man that others feared; it was his reputation, the legend, and the record. At sixty-eight years of age, he had survived the purges of Khrushchev and Brezhnev. Because of his failing health, he had resigned his position as Deputy Director of the Ministry of State Security. Despite this he was, as Nikollai Ezhov, then head of the GRU, once described him, "the embodiment and the essence" of the KGB.

Now he was the hope of the Party, not only in his native Ukraine, but in other former Soviet states that, like the Ukraine, fervently hoped for the Party's return to power. He had come to Alma-Ata, not as a man from another country, but as the man Kazakh Party loyalists believed would lead them back to the glory days of the Union.

Seated in his hotel suite, breakfasting on a thin soup and eggs, *bul'yon* and *yaytsa*, he studied a topographical map of the area between Alma-Ata and the Chinese border and waited for the arrival of General Armanov, the Commanding General of the Kazakh Regulars.

Armanov, himself an avowed Bolshevik, had scheduled the meeting to review plans for boarding the train at Alma-Ata and delivering the missiles to Mao Quan.

When Armanov finally arrived, he was fifteen minutes late and looked harried. He embraced the former KGB director and as he had been advised, avoided inquiring about Savin's health. Aleksei Savin, despite his portable breathing apparatus, regarded his failing health as a matter of private concern only.

"It is good to have you here," Armanov said. "The Party rejoices in your continued efforts to—"

Savin waved his hand in annoyance. His disregard for small talk and social amenities was equally well documented. "You are late," he reminded the general.

Armanov, who normally smoked, refrained from reaching for a cigarette. "I will be able to keep my appointments when we once again assume power and rid our country of hooliganism," he said with a sigh. "Unfortunately, it has been a long night."

Even though Savin did not ask why, Armanov launched into a lengthy explanation. "The Zeverin Arsenal, near Klin, was raided last night. Regrettably, they succeeded not only in laying waste to much of the facility, they managed to escape. But only for a brief period of time. My men were able to track them down and the hijackers were disposed of not far from the arsenal."

Savin appeared only slightly interested. Despite Armanov's record and stature, he regarded the man as nothing more than a conduit, a political necessity for pulling the Union together again.

"Upon learning of the raid on the arsenal," Armanov continued, "I instructed one of my officers to board the train at Gretchkah station to inform your General Dubchek of the situation."

"There were to be no further stops after the train left Zhambyl," Savin reminded him. "We have assured Colonel Mao Quan of security integrity. Alma-Ata was to be the only other stop."

To Savin's surprise, Armanov refused to back down. "I thought it best to inform General Dubchek of the raid on the arsenal. Perhaps General Savin is not aware that twice in recent months, nonconformists and enemies of the State have initiated actions designed to be both disruptive and an embarrassment to my country."

"It is part of the general decadence that afflicts our people," Savin wheezed. "We can take comfort in the fact that it will cease when Party control is reestablished."

Armanov was still standing, waiting for the aging Party leader to offer him a chair, when two of Savin's aides entered the room. One carried a samovar. The second carried a tray containing an assortment of condiments and dry toasts. When the aides finished serving, Savin excused them.

"But we are here to discuss other matters, are we not?" Armanov said. "Among them the protocol for the completion of the first shipment."

Savin moved his wheelchair across the heavily carpeted hotel room and took up a position next to the windows. He was silhouetted against the listless gray day beyond. "I am curious, General Aramanov, what preparations you have made."

The Kazakh officer took a sip of his tea. "A detachment of Kazakh militia regulars will have boarded the train prior to your entourage appearing at the terminal. The train will be delayed just long enough to add one sleeping car. The switching will take place and you and your staff will be escorted aboard the train at approximately 09:30 hours."

"The sleeping car has been refurbished?" Savin inquired.

"As you requested. Half of the sleeping compartments have been removed and replaced with a conference table where the signing will take place. There is even a small roomette where Mao Quan can refresh himself before the signing ceremony."

Although he gave no visible indication, Savin

seemed pleased. "You have arranged for photographers?" he asked.

Aramanov had been warned about Savin's obsessive preoccupation with detail. Now he was seeing it firsthand. Even though he knew Savin had read his report, the man wanted a complete briefing.

"The photographers will board after your entourage at the People's Revolutionary Station in Alma-Ata. They will take a few photographs and leave the train. From Alma-Ata, the train will proceed through the high elevations up to the Jinghe Tunnel."

"I am curious about the tunnel," Savin admitted. "I am told it is only partially complete."

"But passable," Armanov assured him. "The tunnel is a joint project between the People's Republic of China and the Kazakhstan government to facilitate trade. It is approximately seven and one half kilometers in length and in the middle of the tunnel the train crosses over from my country into China."

"But not complete," Sevrin repeated. "I have heard there are still many men working in the tunnel."

"It is true, General. At present, only one track is finished. Our Chinese friends have experienced construction delays."

"Perhaps the Chinese are not as industrious as our countrymen, General Aramanov," Savin offered.

"It was necessary for them to first complete the construction of their hydroelectric dam at the exit of the Jinghe Tunnel. When the train emerges from the tunnel, it does so at a point halfway up the wall of the canyon between the top and base of the dam. And it is there that Mao Quan wishes more pictures taken—specifically, of you, General Savin, the great Ukrainian Party leader, and next President of the Ukraine, congratulating Mao Quan on his forward-thinking socialist achievements."

Savin studied the topographical model and pointed to a switchyard downstream from the hydroelectric station. "The missiles will be off-loaded here?"

"They will," Armanov confirmed, "and the train will be turned around at that point for the return trip."

Savin reflected for a moment. "There is a sense of history in all of this," he observed.

Again, without saying so, Aramanov knew Savin was pleased, not only with the details but with Armanov's thoroughness.

"Tomorrow morning, Comrade General," Savin said, "when we board the train, we are, in effect, setting our countries on a new course of destiny."

Aramanov stood up, walked over to the samovar, and poured himself another cup of tea. "May I pour one for you, Comrade Savin, to celebrate the commencement of the new beginning?"

Savin moved his wheelchair across the room and held out his cup. As he did, Aramanov commented on the weather. "I hope you are fortified with warm clothing. Between Alma-Ata and the Jinghe Tunnel the weather can be expected to be quite foul."

Datum: Ten-Four: Regional Militia Offices: 14:11 LT

The reams of bureaucratic paperwork associated with the incident at the Zeverin Arsenal kept Major Ustan Varmii from meeting his afternoon classes at the agricultural college, and he was now regretting his decision to file his patrol reports before the autopsy documents were complete. Still, he stayed with his chore, realizing that if he completed his work, he would miss only one day of class.

He was about to finish one report and begin another when his phone rang. When Varmii answered, he was informed that a woman wished to see him.

"I am very busy," he informed the young soldier tending the phones in the garrison lobby. "See if she can wait."

"She says it is important and that she doesn't have much time."

"Very well," Varmii said with a sigh, "send her in."

Moments later, when the woman appeared at the door of his small office, Ustan Varmii was surprised. She was elderly and apprehensive. The militia major escorted her into the room, offered her a seat, and took her coat.

"You wish to see me?" he asked.

Red Sand

The woman nodded.

"Then let's start with your name," Varmii said. He took out a tablet and made note of the time.

Finally, the woman made an attempt to speak. Her voice was small and hesitating. Like so many in the area along the border between the two countries, she spoke in a mixed Kazakh and Kyrgyz dialect.

"I—I—do not have much time," she said. "My—my husband is buying *lyekarstva* and *mas'*—the man is *kravatyechyeniye*."

"Who is bleeding?" Varmii demanded. He was catching only occasional words.

The woman hesitated. "The—the young man," she finally said. "The—young man—who—who was shot."

Varmii got up and walked around his desk. "What young man are you referring to?"

The old woman looked around the room as though she suddenly realized she had been catapulted into another world. Her eyes were tired and at the same time nervous. "He—he is—is one of them," she said. "They—they are the ones—the ones who escaped from the arsenal."

"Who escaped from the arsenal?" Varmii asked. He was careful not to raise his voice a second time.

The fear-filled eyes began to well with tears and her hands trembled. "There were three of—of them," she managed. "They shot the men in the militia truck who came after them—then—they drove their own truck into the ravine—it burned. . . ."

Ustan Vermii was beginning to put the woman's tortured bits of conversation and information together.

"We—we are old," the woman sobbed. "If the authorities learn what we have done—they will take away our pension—they will—"

Varmii put his hand on the woman's arm. "Are they still there?" he asked.

"The one who is bleeding is," the woman said. "He is very weak. . . ."

"Where are the others?"

"They left. They are using the militia—the militia truck. It—it—it has something—something to do with a train."

Varmii repeated what he thought she had told him. "You are telling me that the men who robbed the arsenal came to your home in the middle of the night."

The woman's nod was barely perceptible.

"And you are telling me that they killed the four militiamen who followed them . . . and then drove their own truck off the bridge?" When the woman again confirmed what he was saying, he asked, "Do you know where they were going?"

"*Nyet,*"

"And the one who is bleeding, can you take me to him?"

"My husband will be angry," she said.

"You have done the right thing in reporting this incident to the authorities," Varmii assured her.

"You will not hurt us?" the woman asked. "You will not put us in prison?"

Varmii ignored the question and reached for his telephone. "Yastof," he barked. "Arrange for a carryall. I wish to leave in twenty minutes." As an afterthought he added, "I will not need a driver."

Datum: Ten-Five: Village Grove, Maryland: 22:14 LT

Jeff Rutland waited well over an hour until he was certain his wife and children were asleep. Then he got out of bed, went to the kitchen, closed the door, and picked up the telephone. He dialed the number from memory.

"I heard you were trying to reach me," the voice on the other end of the line said. "What's the problem?"

"The *problem* is, we have a problem—a very big problem," Rutland snapped. "Last night I got a call from Clancy Packer down at the ISA. They're on to us."

"What do you mean, 'on to us'? How the hell could they be on to us?"

Rutland glanced around the darkened kitchen to make certain Nancy hadn't followed him. "I mean exactly what I said. Somehow Packer knows I'm getting information from someone before the damned information has been cleared for the public."

"Impossible."

"Impossible or not, he knows, and he knows about Carol," Rutland blurted out. "He knows all about the poker club breaking up and where I've been going on Monday nights."

"Looks to me like you're the one who has the problem."

"Wait a damn minute," Rutland barked. "You're the one that set me up with Carol Taylor, dammit. You're the one that's been feeding me the damned information. We've been paying you good money—"

"All networks have their sources—and their dirty little secrets. Besides, there's no way to trace that money, and you know it."

Rutland lowered his voice again. "You fed me that damn information on the warhead shipment out of Libya before the damned stuff was declassified."

"So, what are they telling you?"

"They're saying I either divulge where I'm getting my information or Packer and his people tell Nancy all about my affair with Carol."

"You play with fire, you get burned."

"Get this straight. I'm not getting my ass hauled through a messy divorce case and lose everything I've worked for just to protect a source that's been feeding me classified information."

"You knew what the score was when you sat down at the table."

"I sure as hell wasn't looking for classified information."

Red Sand

There was a silence on the other end of the line for several moments. "All right, relax. I've got a plan. First thing you do, go in and wake up your wife, tell her the network called and they've got a late-breaking story with some international implications. Tell her they want you to come in to work on the background info. It's happened before; she'll buy it. Then meet me at the Carver Club on Milhausen Road. I'll be there in an hour."

Mel Henline had long since decided he would take any assignment Packer offered, anything to get out of Washington. He had given up hope that they would reopen the Omaha office, but he had heard rumors that Bill Goeglin was getting ready to retire in Dallas—and Dallas, despite the heat, he decided, would be a whole lot better than spending another six months in Washington.

Now, as he periodically glanced up at the darkened, sprawling single-story ranch house belonging to Jeff Rutland and sipped coffee, he twisted the dial on his radio, hoping to find one of the all-night talk shows that he knew would keep him awake.

A wet snow with huge flakes, the kind a person could almost count as they fell, had been falling for over an hour, leaving a streamlined residue of moisture as they slid down the windshield and, for brief moments, impaired his view of the house.

He closed his eyes for a second, yawned, stretched, and when he opened them, saw a light go on in the Rutland garage. When the garage door opened a few minutes later and a white four-door Mercury backed out, Henline hit the button on his car phone.

Peters was working the night shift. "What's up?"

"A car just backed out of Rutland's garage. With this damn snow I can't even tell if it's Rutland or his wife. Either way, though, I'm following. It's chancy. Hell, for all I know he may be doing nothing more than heading for the nearest drugstore."

"Want me to stay on the line?" Peters asked.

"Naw, I'll let you know what's happening, if anything does."

Datum: Ten-Five: Cabinet Building, Gidropark, Kiev: 10:30 LT

Aralov Lavrenti rolled the business card over in his hand and studied it:

> *Chief Inspector Yuri Illich*
> *Homicide Investigation*
> *Odessa Police*

"Well, Inspector, if nothing else, you are a long way from home. What brings you to Kiev?"

Illich had not bothered to take off his wet coat. Nor had he seen a place to hang it if he had. Instead, he took the seat across the desk from Lavrenti, and hoped that the coat would not drip on the Vice Minister's ornate Persian rug.

"It was good of you to find time to see me," Illich

said. After he said it, he realized his voice didn't have quite the ring of professionalism he had hoped it would. He had sounded subservient. That was something he had not intended.

"I am always eager to assist the police when I can," Lavrenti said. "Now, what is it that brings you all this way?"

Illich picked up his briefcase and fumbled through it until he found the folder he was looking for. He took it out and laid it on the Vice Minister's desk. "It's a homicide case, sir," he said. He opened the folder and laid three pictures on the man's desk. The first was a picture of Polce Berzin, the second a picture of Rubana Cheslov, and the third was Junus Arkadiya's sketch. "Would you happen to know any of these women, Vice Minister?"

Lavrenti picked up each of the pictures and studied them. "They all look very much alike, Inspector. Are they the same woman?"

"Two of them may well be," Illich admitted. "But look again, sir. Is it possible that you know any of them?"

Lavrenti picked up the photograph of Polce Berzin a second time. "This one looks a great deal like a young analyst from the Dnepro Institute," he said.

"And how would you know her, sir?"

"Inspector, I'm surprised you would ask. In my capacity as Vice Minister, I often work with personnel from the Dnepro. Dnepro Institute is responsible for many of the economic models we use to judge the health of our economy."

"Do you know her name?" Illich persisted.

"If it is who I think it is, Inspector, this woman is the daughter of Deputy Prime Minister Berzin, a very talented young economist."

"When is the last time you saw her?"

Lavrenti leaned back in his chair, tented his fingers, and closed his eyes. "Let's see," he said. He thought for a moment and reached for his desk calendar. "I do recall that the last time I was supposed to have a meeting with her, she was unable to attend, something about a family matter she had to take care of. If I recall correctly, she informed her supervisor that she was going out of town."

Illich continued to scribble notes in his day book. "Did she inform her supervisor where she was going?"

"Why don't you ask her? Or her supervisor at the Institute. Would you like to use my telephone?"

"I have tried," Illich said. "She has not returned to work. In fact, no one has seen her since the day before your scheduled meeting."

"Has anyone had contact with her?" Lavrenti asked.

"Only her supervisor, who spoke to her on the telephone the morning she informed him that she would be gone for a few days."

"I am trying to put two and two together, Inspector. You are homicide. She has not reported to work. Do you suspect foul play?"

Illich wanted to be careful. He had not shown

Lavrenti the picture of the Vice Minister and Polce Berzin together—and he wasn't sure why.

Datum: Ten-Six: Carver Club, Milhausen Road: 23:46 LT

The Carver Club in its prime had been a Washington hot spot—but that was in the days of Prohibition. It had enjoyed a revival during World War II when senators and high-ranking military men needed a place to entertain and not be bothered with the nettlesome concerns about ration stamps and political alliances. There had been an *understanding* in those days as well; no one talked about who they had seen or what they had done at the Carver Club. It was the place to go if you were a Washington insider.

But that too faded. Now it was nothing more than one in a series of forgotten roadside watering holes, closed and shuttered and waiting to be torn down.

In order to get to the Carver Club, Jeff Rutland had to negotiate an abrupt, unmarked turnoff and a narrow, one-lane, creaking wooden bridge over a creek without a name, and avoid apartment-size potholes in a parking lot that he was convinced hadn't been repaired in the last thirty years.

That parking lot was where he waited.

Fifteen minutes later, he was still waiting. A car had passed the turnoff just a few minutes after he had pulled in, and another, going in the opposite direction, had passed a few moments later.

Twice he thought he saw movement inside the old club, and decided his mind was playing tricks on him; the Carver Club had been closed for over a year now.

The snow had stopped and a light drizzle, which alternated between an irritating mist and occasional periods of rain and snow mixed, brought with it a fog that hugged the ground and further impaired his vision. Rutland checked his watch, leaned his head back, and closed his eyes.

It was the sound of tapping on his car window that awakened him. When he rolled the window down he was staring into the barrel of a .45. "Jeff, old buddy," the voice said, "like you said, you've got a problem, and judging by our phone conversation, it sounds like you're not handling it very well."

"Are you out of your—"

The man cut him off before he finished. "Get out of the car," he ordered, "and bring your keys."

Rutland got out of the car and the man ordered him to open his trunk and crawl in. When Rutland hesitated, he felt the barrel pressing against the base of his skull. "I said get in the trunk."

"What the hell are you—"

Before Jeff Rutland had a chance to finish his protest, the man brought the barrel crashing down hard across the back of his skull and Rutland felt himself pitching forward into the darkness. It was then that Jeff Rutland realized that his hands and arms wouldn't move and his world was all confusion and chaos. A raging pain began twisting and turning up through his neck, corkscrewing its way into his brain. There were explosions, quick and large, savage and terrifying, as he tried to hold on to reality.

Then, for a moment, there was nothing. Helpless, he watched the man walk slowly away until he disappeared in the fog. Then he reappeared, carrying a large container. He opened it and began pouring the contents on Rutland. The aroma was pungent; there was a sensation of icy cold.

Rutland tried to speak, to protest, but the words were mushy, disconnected, and meaningless. He identified the smell—gasoline—and he could feel the cold wash as it cascaded over him. He shivered, or was it a convulsion? The fear had constricted his breathing. He was gasping, pleading, praying, babbling, all in one tangle of terrifying confusion.

The man lit a match, set the matchbook on fire, threw it in, and slammed the trunk lid of the car shut.

There were moments when Jeff Rutland's screams reached a near-crescendo. There was even a brief moment when his executioner could hear him pleading. There was even less time to hear him screeching a rage of profanity.

In the end there was only the sound of the hissing, angry, consuming flames.

The man who had solved Jeff Rutland's problems walked back to his car, got in, and drove away.

Moments later, as he pulled out of the driveway, he heard the explosion—and for one brief moment, the old Carver Club was a hot spot all over again.

PART THREE

Chapter Eleven

Datum: Eleven-One: Near Abay: 17:07 LT

Bogner adjusted his binoculars and scanned the now not-so-distant range of snowcapped, icebound ridges. Many of the peaks were shrouded in clouds and the valleys, for the most part, concealed in cloaks of hoarfrost and ice fog.

"Behold our magnificent passage to nowhere," Mrachak said. "It is a good place to separate two countries, no?"

"Where's the Jinghe Tunnel?"

Mrachak made a sweeping motion back to his right. "The railroad follows the valley of the Kushi up to the pass at Tien Shan. Tien Shan Pass is the lowest point in the chain of ridges between Prevlasak and Bakta. The tunnel is located there."

"Length?"

Mrachak was still pointing. "A little over seven kilometers. The tunnel begins near where my cousin lives, not far from the village of Abay, and emerges near the great hydroelectric dam near Yining."

"This cousin of yours . . . ?"

Mrachak laughed. "We call ourselves cousins but he is not truly a cousin. A man would have to be very unfortunate to share the same genetics as someone like Serafim. No, Serafim and I served together for many months in the war against Afghanistan. We decided then that we were family. Otherwise we could not have stood each other."

"So how does this so-called cousin of yours fit into the picture?"

"What you are really asking is, can he be trusted."

"Something like that," Bogner admitted.

"Serafim is what you Americans would call a laborer. He has worked on the tunnel since the war. He knows a great deal about the tunnel and he will be able to tell us how work progresses."

"Progresses? You mean the tunnel is not finished?"

Mrachak laughed again. "Perhaps in the next millennium. Progress is slow. Someday the Jinghe Tunnel will accommodate two rail beds, one for traffic heading east, the other for trains heading west. There will also be a highway for motor vehicles. At present only one of the rail beds is complete. Now, when a train crosses the border and enters into China, the train must descend all the way down the mountain before it can be turned around at the Kashi rail yards."

"Earlier you talked about a hydroelectric dam?"

Mrachak bent down and began drawing a diagram in the red-brown dirt. "Here is Abay, here is the tunnel, and here is the hydroelectric dam. When an eastbound train emerges from the tunnel it does so at the rim of the dam. The rail bed descending into Kashi has actually been dynamited out of the wall of the canyon. If it was not against my nature to give the Chinese credit for anything, I would admit that it is quite an engineering feat." At that point, Mrachak stood up.

Bogner studied the crude sketch, shivered, and pulled his collar tight around his throat. The snowfall had begun to accumulate. In the short time they had been there, it had already concealed their footprints and covered the path from where the ML-ta was parked.

The cold, now that they were near Abay, was intense and penetrating. At over six thousand feet, the altitude made breathing difficult. Joy would have used the word "exhausting" to describe the conditions. Bogner refused to use the term because it implied an inability to go on. Less than five hours from Abay an inability to go on was not an option.

For two days the two men had kept to the back roads, sleeping under the ML-ta at night, and sustaining themselves on the food rations the militia squad had requisitioned for their journey to Alma-Ata to join Aleksei Savin. Bogner was willing to concede that if "exhausted" wasn't acceptable, maybe "drained" or "dog tired" was.

"Have you seen enough, *americanski*?" Mrachak asked. "If you have, we will continue on to my cousin's house."

"How certain are you that we can trust this cousin of yours?"

Mrachak turned and started down the hill toward the ML-ta. He was smiling. "When I write my journal someday, I will write that you people are even more suspicious than my own countrymen—and we, *americanski*, are the father of the KGB."

Datum: Eleven-Two: The Rail Yards at Alma-Ata: 09:41 LT

From the window of the refurbished sleeping car, Krislof Dubchek watched as the black Moskvitch limousine inched its way through the heavy snowfall of the previous night.

He checked his watch; on schedule—Aleksei Savin was always on schedule.

The car stopped less than thirty yards from the rail platform, and Dubchek quickly checked to make certain the militia squad was in place.

The front doors of the Moskvitch opened and two uniformed aides popped out. One scurried to open the door for the general; the other deftly maneuvered the wheelchair into place. One aide assisted

Savin and the other positioned the oxygen tank in a rack on the back of the chair. It was a obviously a maneuver the two men had performed repeatedly.

Savin, wrapped in a greatcoat and wearing a fur hat, was quickly ushered up the ramp to the small elevator that had been installed at the rear of the car, lifted to floor level, and pushed inside.

"Comrade General," Dubchek greeted him as Savin was wheeled down the corridor into the compartment where the conference table had been situated. The ailing general disregarded Dubchek's perfunctory salute and dismissed his aides. Then he wheeled himself to the window and looked out.

"How many men in the militia garrison boarding the train?" Savin demanded. His voice was little more than a tortured wheeze.

"Twelve," Dubchek replied, "all regulars. I spoke to General Aramanov. He assures me that they are among his finest."

Savin sneered. "General Aramanov is not only a fool, he is also a poor judge of his men's readiness. It was a squad of Aramanov's so-called Kazakh finest that botched the capture of the hooligans that raided the Zeverin Arsenal."

"They have not been captured?"

Savin, ignoring the question, wheeled himself back toward the conference table in the middle of the room. "These twelve bring the total complement of militia aboard the train to how many?"

"Twenty. I have retained eight from the original

garrison that left Odessa with the shipment. There are also four technicians aboard."

Savin nodded and moved his wheelchair closer to the table. "The warheads have been installed?" As usual, there was no small talk. Savin seldom wasted time on trivials.

Dubchek, prepared for the inevitable, laid a file on the table. "The installation is complete. I have inspected them myself."

Savin opened the file, leafed through it, and closed it again. "What about our schedule?"

Dubchek glanced at his watch. "As soon as the militia garrison boards and the second engine is in place, we will proceed. From the north station at Alma-Ata, where we are situated now, it is approximately one hundred and seventy kilometers to the Jinghe Tunnel on the border." Dubchek paused momentarily, weighing his words. "The general is aware, of course, that our progress will be quite slow because of the decided increase in elevation to the Tien Shan Pass. It is an increase of almost four thousand feet."

As usual, Aleksei Savin gave the impression that he was only half listening. But Krislof Dubchek knew better; the crippled former KGB chief possessed a mind renowned for its alacrity and its retention of detail. Dubchek knew that, if pressed, Savin could have easily repeated Dubchek's report word for word.

Still, as Dubchek recited the details of their schedule, Savin appeared to be distracted. Finally he pressed the bell calling for his aide. When the young corporal appeared at the door to the conference room, Savin ordered glasses and a bottle of Kuban. When the aide left, Dubchek finished his report.

Savin was still staring out the window at the snow. Then he turned to his longtime comrade. "Excellent, General. As usual, you have been very thorough, but I find it curious that you have not mentioned our guest. You did not forget, did you?"

Few but Savin would have detected the transient display of annoyance that anointed Dubchek's usually implacable expression. "A mere oversight," he apologized. "The girl is little more than an inconvenience."

Savin leaned back in his chair. "Inconvenience? A curious choice of words, General. Should I assume from your observation then that you have talked to her?"

"I have," Dubchek admitted, "on several occasions."

"I am told that the daughter of our esteemed Ukrainian Deputy Prime Minister is an attractive young woman. Would you agree with that assessment?"

Dubchek hesitated. Savin's question had caught him off guard. It was out of character. Was it possible that he suspected something? He discarded the possibility almost as quickly as the thought had occurred to him. No one could possibly know of their conversations. No one had left the train. They had maintained radio silence—there was no way Savin could know. "I will defer to the general's opinion in such matters," he said.

"And when will I meet her?" Savin continued.

"At the general's leisure."

"Good. Then you will ask her to join us at dinner tonight."

"The general realizes, of course, that the Berzin woman is being detained against her wishes. Her demeanor can hardly be expected to lend itself to dinner conversation."

"Perhaps I will explain to her that her abduction was arranged by Comrade Lavrenti and that she is being detained for no other reason that to dissuade her father from revealing the full nature of our arrangement with Mao Quan."

Dubchek was silent.

"Then it is settled," Savin decided. He dismissed Dubchek with a wave of his hand. "Inform Miss Berzin that we will dine at 20:00 hours. I will instruct the cook to prepare *salyanka baranina* with *garokh* and *kartofyel*. You do like lamb, do you not, General Dubchek?"

"I find the choice of dishes curious in view of the fact that you seldom eat meat, General Savin."

Savin enjoyed a rare laugh. "Do you not see the delicious irony of all of this, my old comrade? We are leading the unfortunate lamb to slaughter—the lamb of our esteemed Deputy Prime Minister."

As Krislof Dubchek stepped from the compartment of Aleksei Savin's private car into the corridor and passed the two young aides, the disturbing notion that Savin knew of his arrangement with Emita Paukof occurred to him again.

Moments later he felt the train lurch and begin to move. He felt a sense of relief. It was snowing again and the winds had increased. The grainy red sand soil of the Kazakh steppes would soon be obliterated by the storm.

Datum: Eleven-Three: Paskov Bal'nista, Klin: 16:31 LT

Ustan Varmii had waited until his classes were finished for the day before visiting the Paskov Bal'nista. The Bal'nista was a sprawling five-story regional medical center constructed during the halcyon days of the Soviet Union to serve the city of Klin and the sparsely populated steppes surrounding it.

Varmii, dressed in his militia uniform, parked his two-door Zhiguli in the parking lot across the street from the hospital. He walked through the now deserted Worker's Park featuring a statue of poet Mikhail Sholokhov, and used the pedestrian bridge to cross over to the entrance.

In days past he would have had to present his Party card to the security guard in the lobby. But those days were gone. Now security was too lax. Now the basement and underground corridors that connected the wings of the sprawling complex were home to some of the city's more unsavory types.

Varmii had heard reports of drug deals, racketeering, and even rape in the hospital's bowels.

He caught the lift to the third floor and worked his way past the *myetsyestra* station without either of the women looking up from their charts. When he came to Room 3-7a-b, he took off his hat and greatcoat and opened the door quietly. Mikos Komenich was awake.

Varmii approached the bed and stood looking at the man reputed to be one of those responsible for the destruction of the Zeverin Arsenal.

Komenich glanced at him briefly, then looked away. To Varmii the man appeared different; he supposed it was because one of the volunteers had shaved and bathed him. He examined the progress chart for several moments before moving around to the side of the bed.

"Do you know where you are?" Varmii asked.

Komenich looked at him but did not answer.

"You are in the third-floor security ward at the Paskov Bal'nista in Klin. When you were brought here, you were quite weak and sometimes unconscious. Therefore I expect you to have little if any recollection of what has transpired in the last two days."

"Security ward?" Komenich asked. His voice was weak.

"Indeed, a security ward. Technically you are my prisoner. More to the point, you are an enemy of the people. From what the old woman who reported you told me, you and your colleagues raided the Zeverin Arsenal four days ago. And although I have not witnessed the extent of the damage myself, I am told you left little more than a pile of ruble."

To Komenich's surprise, the expression on the face of the man standing beside his bed betrayed a half smile. "I don't know what you are talking about," Komenich said.

"Of course you don't," Varmii said. The smile intensified. "So let's start at the beginning. I have been through your meager possessions and there is little to go on. So we will start with your name."

Bogner and Mrachak had been thorough. They had seen to it that nothing was left behind—nothing that would tie Komenich to the attempt to rescue Polce Berzin or the plan to stop the delivery of the missiles. "At the moment I can't think of one," Komenich said.

"Then 3-7a-b will have to do," Varmii said with a shrug. "Names aren't absolutely essential. Our firing squads have dispatched more than one man to his eternal reward without establishing an identity. But that does bring us to my second question. Do you know where your associates are?"

Komenich shrugged. "I don't know what you're talking about."

"Such loyalty is fascinating in view of the fact that they left you to die, which you would probably have done in a very short period of time if the old woman had not reported your whereabouts."

"I still don't know what you're talking about," Komenich repeated.

Varmii pulled a chair up next to the bed, opened his briefcase, extracted a sheaf of papers, and glanced over them. "Since your memory seems to be a bit cloudy as it relates to these events, 3-7a-b, perhaps my version, which admittedly is little more than an educated guess about what happened, will remove some of the cobwebs. Would you like to hear it?"

Komenich turned away.

"In my version, you and two, possibly three, of your comrades infiltrated the Zeverin Arsenal four nights ago. In the process, you stole and destroyed property belonging to the provincial government of the Republic of Kazakhstan. Still later, you and those same colleagues killed four Kazakh militiamen who had been dispatched to investigate the incident. Somewhere along the way, you were wounded. Your wounds were sufficient to incapacitate you and you were left in the care of an elderly couple. An elderly couple, I might add, who were sufficiently loyal to the present Kazakh regime to report your crimes to the local militia garrison."

Komenich turned back to his interrogator. "I don't have the slightest idea what you're talking about."

"That is most unfortunate." Varmii sighed. "Unfortunate because you are in a position to save yourself, 3-7a-b. All you have to do is cooperate . . . more specifically, tell me where your colleagues are and why you chose to raid the arsenal. You see, I am in a position to recommend leniency at your trial."

Komenich turned away from the Kazakh officer.

"Very well. I suggest then that you get some rest, citizen, and I would caution you to enjoy what little time you have. I assure you, your accommodations when you leave here will be far less conducive to recovery."

Varmii moved away from the bed, reached in his pocket, turned off the tiny voice recorder, picked up his greatcoat, and walked out in the corridor. The nurse was waiting.

"Keep him sedated, heavily sedated, and make certain no one else talks to him."

Datum: Eleven-Four: The Train, East of Alma-Ata: 14:14 LT

"You sent for me?" Emita Paukof asked.

Dubchek motioned the woman into his sleeping compartment and instructed her to close the door. When she was seated, he walked to the door and locked it. "The time draws near," he said, taking his seat behind the desk.

"He is here?"

"*Da*, he boarded the train along with his entourage and a garrison of Kazakh militia regulars before the train left Alma-Ata this morning."

"More militia? Will that not make our task more difficult?"

"On the contrary, the journey from here to Tien

Shan Pass will be long and monotonous, made even more so if the storm continues. Under such conditions the militia will tend to become lax in their duties and our task will be even less daunting."

"You have a plan?"

Dubchek leaned back in his chair and closed his eyes as if he was savoring the moment. When he spoke, he kept his voice low. "You cannot know this, *gaspazha*, but our general's vices are playing right into our hand. General Savin has requested your presence at dinner this evening."

"Vices?" the woman repeated.

"Indeed, despite his advanced years and quite obvious failing health, the general still enjoys the company of an attractive woman."

Emita Paukof lit a cigarette, paused, and exhaled a cloud of slate-gray smoke. "I am told he is quite old, confined to a wheelchair, and is sustained by a breathing apparatus." She smiled.

"True. It is also true that a man of his age enjoys revisiting the pleasures of his youth. I suspect he views you as a possible conduit to those reflections."

"I trust you have a plan?" the woman asked.

Dubchek closed his eyes. "I am told there is evidence that the majority of our fellow countrymen are repulsed by the assassination of our beloved President Yefimov. Comrade Lavrenti has shown great insight in his assessment that the Ukrainian populace would view Savin's act as one of cowardice and avarice."

"And what is General Savin's reaction to this groundswell of outrage?"

A smile played with the corners of Dubchek's stern mouth. "He refuses to acknowledge it. He believes that the alliance with Mao Quan and the Fifth Academy will overshadow the public perception of odium that surrounds Yefimov's death."

"You still have not revealed your plan," Emita reminded him.

Dubchek held up his hand in a halting gesture. "We must be patient, *gaspazha*. At first you must appear distant and distrusting. Remember, you are outraged at your abduction. Despite your demeanor, I feel certain the general will steer our dinner conversation to the subject of ideologies. When he does, you will listen. From time to time you will counter the general's views, expressing the more democratic views you learned from your father."

"Josef Berzin, of course."

Dubchek nodded. "Excellent. You will be just pliant enough in your views that our general will begin to believe that his passionate and persuasive skills are starting to win you over."

Paukof smiled. "I believe I know what to do."

"Ultimately, it must appear that he took his own life. When the time comes I will assist you. The task will be easy. The general suffers from bouts of extreme discomfort because of the atrophy in his legs. On such occasions he has been known to over-indulge in the comfort of Kuban. When the pain becomes unbearable, he has even been known to resort to heavy doses of morphine. The dosage is usually administered by one of his two longtime aides, but there is evidence that he has also relied upon others when the aides were not available."

"There is a way to insure this added discomfort?"

Dubchek opened his desk drawer and removed a small envelope. He opened it and displayed four small tablets. "This should induce the desired discomfort," he said.

Emita Paukof reached across the desk and examined the contents of the envelope.

"Strychnine in small doses is often used as a stimulant," Dubchek explained. "The cumulative dosage contained in these tablets, administered over a two-day period, will be sufficient to cause our general significant discomfort. A tablet at dinner tonight and two more tomorrow will be more than adequate. And you, Gaspazha Paukof, his increasingly charming dinner partner, will doubtless be called upon to administer the morphine. The combination of excessive amounts of Kuban, strychnine, and morphine will be more than his sixty-eight year-old and already weakened heart can stand."

Emita Paukof extinguished her cigarette, leaned back in her chair, and smiled. "You are clever, General," she whispered. "I see you come by your reputation deservedly."

Dubchek leaned forward with his arms on the desk. "And you, my nefarious colleague, are reminded that you have yet another role in this intrigue. When you return to Kiev, you will inform

Comrade Lavrenti of my cooperation in this matter."

Emita Paukof leaned forward and picked up the tablets. "It will appear then that the good general simply died of an overdose of morphine . . . and only you and Lavrenti will know the truth."

Dubchek pushed himself away from the desk and stood up. "Dinner at eight," he reminded her.

As Emita Paukof stepped from Dubchek's compartment, she was again smiling. For the first time since the train had left the Odessa station, she felt a sense of purpose and exhilaration.

Datum: Eleven-Five: Washington: 16:13 LT

Joy Carpenter cradled her whiskey sour between her hands and wished she had ordered the bourbon straight up. The tears had ceased but there was still that gnawing, empty feeling in her stomach. "I feel so damned sorry for Nancy. What the hell will she do now?"

Clancy Packer had known Joy for a long time, long enough to remember when Joy was pregnant with Kim and Toby was fresh out of flight school at Pensacola with a new commission. He had been honored when the young couple asked him to be Kim's godfather, and he had cried when Joy announced that she and Toby were getting a divorce. He had watched as her career at NBS blossomed, and he had worried every time Toby was sent off on one of his myriad of ISA assignments. Now he wanted to console Joy, he wanted to tell her that Nancy Rutland would be all right, but he didn't know the woman any more than he knew the man whose funeral they had just attended. In the end, he said nothing. He sat there, wishing he knew how to comfort the woman that he loved as much as a father could love a daughter.

"How long did you know Jeff Rutland?" he finally asked.

"Long enough—ten years maybe. I remember when he came to work. He was a digger. He could find information in an empty bottle. Everyone in the news department respected him. He propped us all up."

"Did you know him socially?"

"The usual news department parties, that sort of thing . . ." Joy's voice trailed off and the tears welled in her eyes again. "Jesus, Clancy, that's a helluva way to die. What kind of sick bastard would it take to do that to another human being?"

Clancy Packer bolted his drink and motioned for a refill. He wished now he had asked Sara to attend the funeral with him. Sara would know how to console Joy; she would know what words to say. He reached across the table and held Joy's hand. She was trembling.

"Why the hell haven't the police come up with something?" Joy blurted out. "No one commits an atrocity like this without leaving some kind of clues."

Clancy kept his voice low. He realized that now

was probably not a good time to ask questions, but he reasoned that there would probably not be a good time and he blundered ahead. "What did you know about Rutland's private life? Who did he run around with? Who did he talk about?"

Joy shook her head. "The usual. He belonged to the Press Club and the Athletic Club. He played golf, and he used to laugh about how he never won at his Monday night poker club."

Clancy considered telling her that the reason Jeff Rutland never won was because he didn't play—at least not poker. That would involve telling her about the woman named Carol, and now didn't seem like the time.

"He was in the Naval Reserve, you know," Joy volunteered. It was an afterthought, the kind people have when they are reflecting back on a man's life and small bits of seemingly irrelevant information come to mind. "Three years ago, he attended a seminar with a bunch of his cronies; he talked about it for weeks."

Clancy Packer removed a small piece of paper from his pocket, unfolded it, and glanced at the list of names. "Did you ever hear Rutland mention any of these people?" He began reciting the names, pausing after each. "George Armitage . . . Joseph Hoffman . . . Mark Stern . . . Betty Annaman . . ." Almost as an afterthought he added the name of Carol Taylor. When he did, Joy's eyes betrayed her.

"You know about Carol?"

"Only that when Rutland's Monday night poker club broke up, he began seeing her."

"Do you know this Carol Taylor?"

Joy leaned back in her chair and stared at her drink. "In a group our size, you hear things. There was talk. Where there's talk, there's usually smoke. Where there's smoke there's usually . . ."

Clancy unfolded another piece of paper and read it aloud.

> *Carol Taylor*
> *24345 Baden*
> *Hamal Hills*

"Have you talked to her?" Joy pressed.

"Not yet, but I plan to."

"Do you suppose Nancy knows?"

Clancy Packer shrugged and slipped the pieces of paper back in his pocket. "It's not my job to tell her. Although I suppose that if she did know, it might make the job of mourning a little easier."

"Not if she loved him."

Packer glanced at his watch, finished his drink, and appraised the woman that he knew in so many different ways. "Sorry to put you through all of this."

When Joy pursed her lips, Clancy knew what was coming.

He shook his head. "You know I can't tell you where Toby is. I can't even tell you that he's all right. But I can tell you that as of five days ago, he was alive and well."

Joy Carpenter knew that Clancy had told her as much as he was allowed to tell her. She reached for her purse, pushed her chair away from the table, stood up, and walked around the table to where he was sitting. Then she bent over and kissed the ISA chief on the cheek. "Make sure nothing happens to him, Clancy. I don't want to be another Nancy Rutland."

Datum: Eleven-Six: Abay: 19:43 LT

The snow had stopped, the winds had increased, and the temperature had plummeted by the time Bogner and Mrachak reached the outskirts of Abay. Mrachak had hidden the ML-ta in an abandoned toolshed near a played-out rock quarry at the edge of the village and covered it with the tattered remnants of old tarpaulins and blankets. As a final precaution, he had stacked an assortment of empty crates, barrels, and containers in front of the vehicle to further conceal it. By the time he had finished, even the tracks of the ML-ta had been obliterated by the shifting winds.

Bogner shivered in the cold. "How far?"

"Less than a mile." The Kazakh smiled. "And welcome to the beginning of the long winter, Kazakhstan style." Mrachak looked off into the blackness and braced himself against the wind. "Now you know why I question the sanity of my old friend. At least during the war there were times when we were warm. What you see now, *americanski,* is what Abay is like most of the time. Serafim used to laugh and say that if the people of Abay were fortunate, summer would occur on a holiday and the entire village could enjoy it."

Wind-whipped grains of sand stung Bogner's face and he closed his eyes. He had already decided there was little to see except the lights of a small covey of buildings huddled together several hundred yards down the hill.

"It is a small village, less than two hundred people," Mrachak volunteered. "There is a government-owned emergency provisions station for the train, a mill, and what you people would call a general store. You would not know it from looking at it now, but Abay was a thriving village back in the days when our portion of the tunnel was being built. Now the Chinese provide most of the labor. While it is true that a few Russian technicians are still here to operate the heavy equipment, for the most part the only people that remain are the ones the government deemed too old to resettle."

"What about your so-called cousin?"

"Serafim?" Mrachak laughed. "Serafim stays because he has no place else to go. Occasionally he finds work in the government store and he has his pension from the military. Together it is enough to sustain him. You will understand better when you meet him. In the meantime, we still have a long way to go."

Chapter Twelve

Datum: Twelve-One: The Train: 20:00 LT

Emita Paukof was surprised by the elegance of the dinner. The *salyanka baranina* was exquisite. Despite her evenings with Lavrenti, Emita could not recall having dined on lamb before. Nor could she remember drinking Kuban from ornately carved and monogrammed lead crystal glasses. The dinner concluded with *zapyekanka*, a baked pudding, liberally sprinkled with *sakhar* and *yagada*, sugar and berries.

Finally, Savin called for the cognac. Savin's aides poured it for both Emita and Dubchek while Savin continued to pour himself drinks from the silver flask of Kuban.

Throughout dinner both Savin and Dubchek discussed ideologies, and on several occasions, Savin would pause long enough to ask Emita what she believed. As the evening progressed, Savin's questions became more penetrating and trenchant, yet the woman Lavrenti had entrusted with seeing that Savin did not return to Odessa managed to hold her own. At times she even appeared to be charming her host.

Two hours after they had begun, Savin ordered the dishes cleared. An aide moved the general's wheelchair into the sitting compartment and Dubchek and the woman followed.

"Tell me, Gaspazha Berzin," Savin began, "are you comfortable in the accommodations we have given you?"

"Considering the fact that I am being detained against my will, they are acceptable." Emita Paukof looked across the sitting area at Dubchek to make certain she was playing her role to his satisfaction. His expression had not changed.

"Most certainly you must admit being beguiled by the view from your compartment window," Savin continued. "The mountains, vast stretches of fir forests, the rivers—"

"One is hardly beguiled by dirty snow and the boundless monotony of sand and rock. Even the mountains lack color and charm."

Even though he did not smile, Savin was obviously enjoying their exchange. "You have only your father to blame for your disillusionment. He consorts with our philosophical enemies. There is no place in the new Union for a man with such views," Savin said.

"Gaspazha Berzin and I have discussed her father on several occasions," Dubchek interjected. "She does not share all of her father's beliefs."

"That is good to know," Savin said. "I would hope such beauty is not encumbered by views detrimental to the new order."

Emita studied the frail man sitting across from her. He was dressed in full uniform. His epaulets displayed the two stars of his rank. His loose-fitting tunic was adorned with four rows of service ribbons. From the waist down, he was covered by a blanket. The face was thin and his parchment like skin was heavily veined. His eyes were phlegmatic, almost ghoulish at times. But it was the hissing, cumbersome presence of the breathing apparatus that she noticed most. It occurred to her that if Lavrenti had not been intent on making it look like suicide, it would be just as easy to dispose of the man by shutting off his supply of oxygen.

"Has Comrade Dubchek apprised you of our itinerary for the next two days?" Savin asked.

"He has not," Emita replied. She tried to make it sound both as if she had no prior knowledge and as if she did not care. "My only concern, General, is when I will be allowed to return home."

For the first time she saw Savin's expression change. For a fleeting moment she thought she detected a smile.

Savin looked away and out the window. Beyond it was a wall of blackness, a sparsely populated land made all the more stark by the early vestiges of winter. "In less than thirty-six hours we will arrive at the Tien Shan Pass. It is said that on a clear day, one can see for almost forty kilometers in every direction. An inspiring sight."

Emita Paukof managed a pout. "You will forgive me, General Savin, if I do not share your enthusiasm. I would find the sights of Kiev and Odessa far more to my liking."

Dubchek glanced at his watch and stood up. "I am afraid that all good things must come to an end. The hour is late, and I have work to do. Before I retire for the night, I must make my rounds. I must check with the militia garrison officer, and make sure the missiles are secure. Even now I can feel the engines slow to accommodate the grade. Would you like me to escort you to your compartment, Gaspazha Berzin?"

"I too will retire," Emita said, taking Dubchek's cue. She stood up. Savin said nothing to detain her. "It was a delightful dinner," she continued, "and the conversation was, if not altogether agreeable, certainly most stimulating."

Savin inclined his head forward to acknowledge their departure. Quite suddenly he appeared agitated and as they left the compartment, she saw him reaching for the small button to call for his aide.

Outside in the corridor, they passed the younger

of Savin's two aides. The corporal was holding a hypodermic needle and a small vile of morphine. He nodded, entered Savin's compartment, and closed the door behind him.

Datum: Twelve-Two: Abay: 21:21 LT

Serafim Volokitin was a tall, emaciated man with a sparse head of hair, absurdly large hands, and a warm but nearly toothless smile. He embraced Mrachak, laughed, cried, embraced him again, and only then acknowledged Bogner.

"You see why I call him old and infirm?" Mrachak said. "He is too ugly to have a wife, too stubborn to move away from this place, and too lazy to hold a job—but he is my friend."

"*Nyet*," Serafim corrected him, "we are cousins. We agreed to that in the war; we are family." Serafim scurried about the small cabin, brewed *kofi* in a pan over the wood-burning stove, and apologized because he could not offer them *kan'yak* or *votka*. When he finally sat down with his back to the fireplace, he said, "And what, my cousin, brings you to this abysmal place?"

"To see you, of course," Mrachak answered with a smile.

Serafim beamed. "It is good to see you. Often I think about you and wonder what you are doing."

Mrachak looked around the cabin, first at the fire and then at his old comrade's meager belongings. "Are you well?" he asked.

For the first time, Serafim's expression sobered. "I make do," he said. "I do not need much. My pension and a couple of days' work on the railroad or in the tunnel are all I need."

"How does the tunnel progress?" Mrachak asked.

Serafim Volokitin shook his head. "It does not go well. Progress is slow, even though I am told a great train is coming." He looked up at the calendar and back at his guests. "If the rock slides do not continue, it is expected in less than two days."

"Rock slides?" Bogner repeated.

Serafim nodded, and Mrachak realized he had not introduced the two men. When he finished, Serafim repeated the word *americanski* with a kind of awe.

"He refers to the rock slides resulting from the tremors in the mountains," Mrachak said. "There are frequent earthquakes in these mountains. Most of them are inconsequential, but they do just enough damage to the rails to cause delays. In truth, the delays are little more than minor inconveniences.. The rail officials have come to expect them."

Serafim refilled their cups, put another log in the fire, and patted his "cousin" on the shoulder as he sat down. He was still smiling. "Now that you have warmed Serafim's heart," he said, "you must tell me why you are really here."

Bogner looked at Mrachak before he began. "We are here," he said carefully, "because we have an assignment to get someone off the train."

Red Sand

Serafim's eyes darted from Bogner to Mrachak. "I do not understand. Why do you not just instruct this person to—"

"It's a bit more complicated than that," Mrachak interjected. "Perhaps it would be better if I told you what has happened. . . ."

For the most part, Bogner no longer felt quite so chilled. He stood close to the fireplace and polished off a second cup of thick, black coffee while Mrachak regaled his friend with a lengthy description of events leading up to their arrival in Abay. He told him about the raid on the arsenal, the death of Utra Svychi, the encounter with the militia garrison, and their three-hundred-kilometer journey to Abay, accomplished mostly on the back roads east of Alma-Ata. Finally, he explained the presence of Bogner and how the American had been sent to rescue the daughter of Josef Berzin. He finished with a flourish, lifting his cup to his old comrade. "We have two tasks left: get the woman off the train and slow the missile shipment. We believe you can help us."

"How?" Serafim asked. "As you can see, I am no longer agile. When the snows and cold come, I am barely able to get around. The rail officials at the provisions store tolerate me only because I have a pension and they are duty bound to do so."

While Mrachak and Serafim talked, Bogner began looking around the tiny cabin. The floor was constructed of rough-hewn planks, the furniture handmade. The sink, little more than a galvanized tub with a hole in the bottom, was serviced by a hand pump, and the walls were covered with pictures torn from magazines. Included among them was a poster from the Moscow Circus and a diagram of a section of the railroad at the Tien Shan Pass. Bogner pointed to it.

Serafim explained that the thirty-kilometer section of track Bogner was looking at was the stretch of track between Abay and the Jinghe Tunnel. "Where the train passes through, the walls of the gorge are very narrow, and when the ground rumbles there are often rock slides. It is my job is to make sure the tracks are clear of boulders and debris. When I am told a train is coming, I walk along the track and check it. It is a simple task."

Bogner looked at Mrachak. He was smiling.

"What happens if you can't move the boulders by yourself?" Mrachak asked.

"Either they will send men out from the provisions store to help me or, as usually is the case, the men from the train will assist me."

"That means," Bogner asked, "that if the track isn't clear in that narrow gorge, then the train has to come to a complete stop until you can get help?"

Serafim nodded.

"Have you been told when the next train is coming?" Bogner pressed.

Serafim looked at his calendar and pointed to a crude X penciled through the date. "The next train comes the day after tomorrow—in the morning. I am told it is a supply train from Odessa in the Ukraine."

Red Sand

**Datum: Twelve-Three: Hamal Hills Suburb,
Washington: 20:17 LT**

Carol Taylor had been crying. Her eyes were
swollen and her face was puffy. Despite that, she
seemed pleased that Clancy Packer had called her
and that she had agreed to see him. Now, as she sat
across the room from him, she seemed almost eager to talk.

"I must apologize," Packer said, "and I have to
admit that now that I'm here, I'm not certain I know
how to begin."

"You want me to tell you about my relationship
with Jeff Rutland. Is that correct, Mr. Packer?"

"This is a rather awkward situation, Miss Taylor.
I—I suppose I should ask you to start at the beginning."

Carol Taylor was not at all what Packer had expected. She was a short, somewhat frail-looking
woman with dark hair and plain features, not the
kind he would have suspected of being involved
with Rutland. She was dressed in a wool skirt and
a plain white sweater. She wore no makeup and no
jewelry.

"Have the police talked to you?" he finally asked.

"Are you the police?"

"After a fashion," Packer admitted. "I'm with the
ISA, the Internal Security Agency, and the only reason I wish to talk to you is that we believe Jeff Rutland was involved in activities that come under the
purview of the ISA."

"Was he in trouble?"

"Frankly, yes. He was under investigation by the ISA at the time of his death."

The woman shifted in her chair. "Does his wife know about me?"

Packer shook his head. "We don't know, Miss Taylor. Frankly, that's not our concern."

"You're beating around the bush, Mr. Packer. If you have something to say, I wish you'd come out with it."

"All right, let me lay my cards on the table. At the time of his death, Jeff Rutland was illegally obtaining classified information from someone. The ISA was putting pressure on Rutland to reveal his source. We think he was about to reveal the identity of that source when he was killed. Our question then is, did Jeff ever discuss his work or any of his cohorts with you?"

"Indiscreet pillow talk, is that what you're talking about?"

Packer nodded. "I know this is painful, but I'd like you to think back about some of your conversations."

The Taylor woman closed her eyes and choked back a sob. "I was very lonely when Jeff came along. I was, as all the magazine articles like to say, on the rebound. He was married, not all that appealing in a lot of ways, didn't have a lot of money, but he was here—knocking on my door—and I let him in. Silly, huh?"

"Did he ever talk about his friends, his business

acquaintances, the people he ran around with?"

"No, but a few of his friends did know he was seeing me. Sometimes they would call here."

"What about names? Do any names come to mind?"

"No . . . wait, there was a man named Muldoon, or Mikan, or something like that, he called here several times. One night he called and Jeff had to leave—he said it was important—it had something to do with his job."

Packer jotted down the names Muldoon and Mikan. "Any others come to mind?"

Carol Taylor shook her head.

Packer put his notebook back in his pocket and wondered what questions he hadn't asked.

"Thank you," Carol Taylor said. "Thank you for giving me a chance to talk about Jeff. That's not something the *other woman* gets a chance to do, you know." She paused before continuing. "I went to the funeral. I sat in the back of the church. I had to be careful. I even had to be careful how much I cried. . . ."

Packer stood up. He felt awkward.

Carol Taylor showed him to the door and closed it behind him. Even with the door closed, he could hear her crying.

From her second-floor window, Carol Taylor watched as Clancy Packer crawled into his car and pulled away from the curb. Then she picked up the telephone and dialed the number from memory. "A man from the ISA was here, asking questions."

"What did you tell them?"

"I didn't tell them everything I know, if that's what you mean."

Datum: Twelve-Four: The Train: 19:58 LT

Emita Paukof was eating with Aleksei Savin for the third time that day. She had breakfasted with the general, lunched with him, and now they were having dinner. The last meal of the day featured *katlyeti pakiyefski*, an excellent chicken Kiev—one of Emita's favorites. At the conclusion of the meal, Savin again called for aides, and this time they served berries and cream along with the *kofi*.

Savin had been drinking heavily most of the day. Dubchek had advised her of that fact before she went to the general's compartment.

"Now is the appropriate time?" she had asked.

Dubchek had smiled. "Now is the time. With four doses of strychnine in him, he will call for the morphine."

"And when he does?"

"Administer it," Dubchek had said. "Then send for me."

"You will not be dining with us this evening?"

"It is more likely to happen if you and the general dine alone." Dubchek had said. Then he had handed her the syringe and the vial of morphine. "Simply open his tunic and inject him with the entire contents of the vial—in the heart. The combination of the strychnine and the heavy dose of morphine, injected in the right place, will be more than his heart can take. He will appear to have simply gone to sleep. Call for his aides. When they are unable to revive him, call for me."

Now, as the aides cleared the table and Emita Paukof reflected on her conversation with Dubchek, Savin leaned forward. "So, Gaspazha Berzin, what shall we talk about tonight? Have we exhausted our somewhat superficial debate concerning the supremacy of socialism over all other forms of government?"

Emita smiled, but did not respond. Instead she studied the aging general to see if the three previous doses of strychnine were having any effect on the man. Dubchek had indicated that the former chief of the KGB would first exhibit an unquenchable thirst, which he would try to satiate with vodka, before the telltale lethargy set in. Finally, Dubchek had assured her, Savin would begin to experience unbearable pain. When that happened, she could expect him to call for the morphine.

"We will talk about whatever the general wishes to discuss," Emita said, reaching across the table and refilling his glass of Kuban.

Savin squinted. "Something is different," he observed. You have been very accommodating, Gaspazha Berzin. Why is that?"

"Do you want me to be honest?" Emita asked.

Savin leaned back in his chair. "By all means. But let me assure you, I am always on my guard. I know how difficult it is for a woman to be honest." Savin laughed to demonstrate his delight at his observation.

Emita Paukof moved forward. She was still smiling. "The general is wise, but he should know, not all women are like that. The general is powerful—and power can be very appealing."

Savin closed his eyes for a moment and his head lolled briefly to one side. "Move around to this side of the table," he said, the words slightly slurred. "Savin is no longer capable of being with a woman, but your perfume fascinates me."

Emita stood up and walked slowly around the table. She cupped the loaded syringe in her hand, stood next to the old man, and leaned against the table. Savin's hand, with its prominent purple veins and nearly transparent skin, reached out for her. He began by caressing her hand and then slowly working his way up her arm.

Aleksei Savin closed his eyes again as his fingers began trailing down from her shoulder toward her breast, only to have Emita stop him and gently push his hand away.

"Why do you stop me? Would you deny that Gaspazha Berzin, like Savin, is hungry for the pleasures of the flesh?"

"I would not deny it," Emita whispered, "but first we must do something about the general's pain. The general cannot enjoy the pleasures of the flesh when he is in such great pain." Emita Paukof leaned forward and unbuttoned the top buttons of his tunic. Then she slipped her hand inside until it was touching the flesh of his chest. His skin was cold, but she resisted the impulse to recoil.

Savin closed his eyes again in expectation and Emita Paukof plunged the needle of the syringe into his chest just above the heart. When Savin raised his hands in protest, she jerked the oxygen tube away, clamped her hand over his nose and mouth, and emptied the contents of the syringe.

It took the sixty-eight-year-old former head of the KGB several minutes to die. Finally his hands went limp and his head lolled to one side. Emita Paukof removed the needle, replaced the breathing apparatus, rebuttoned the general's tunic, walked back around the table, picked up her purse, replaced the syringe, and took out a small mirror. Then she held the small mirror under Savin's nose to make certain there was no trace of breathing.

Satisfied that he was dead, she straightened her hair, walked slowly around the table making certain nothing was out of place, took a drink of cognac, braced herself, walked calmly to the door, and stepped into the hall. The aides were waiting.

"General Savin appears to be in a great deal of discomfort," she said. "Perhaps you should check on him."

Savin's aides had worked feverishly over the aging general for more than thirty minutes, looking for a heartbeat and checking for evidence of breathing before finally giving up. All the while, Dubchek paced back and forth and the woman the aides knew as Polce Berzin stood by, waiting. Emita Paukof was proud of her performance.

When it was apparent that nothing else could be done for Savin, Dubchek instructed them to check the general's oxygen supply to see if it had malfunctioned. After examining the tubes and the valve settings and determining that there was still oxygen in the cylinders, both aides confirmed that the old man's breathing apparatus appeared to have been working properly at the time of his death.

Finally, Dubchek turned to Emita. "Once again," he demanded, "tell us what happened."

Emita's voice was barely a whisper when she answered. "I do not know. There was no protest of pain. He simply closed his eyes. I called out to him several times but he did not respond."

Dubchek was standing with his hands behind his back, glowering at Savin's aides. "I want this compartment sealed off until I can complete a full investigation. Inform the train authorities—but no one is to enter this compartment except me."

Savin's aides acknowledged the order.

"In the meantime, I will escort Gaspazha Berzin back to her quarters and you will place General Savin's body on his bed."

When Krislof Dubchek closed and locked the door of her compartment, Emita Paukof sagged down on the edge of her bed and breathed a sigh of relief. "I am still shaking," she said, "but at last it is done."

Red Sand

"On the contrary, *gaspazha*, the task is only half complete," Dubchek said. "There is a great deal more to be accomplished. The Serova woman indicated that you had a 9mm French automatic in your possession. Where is it?"

Emita looked at the man. "In my luggage, why?"

"We must be cautious. You were the only one with Savin when he died. There is bound to be an investigation. I do not want the investigators to find a weapon in your possession. It would be inconsistent with the story we will be telling the authorities. Most assuredly, the daughter of Josef Berzin would not have been carrying a weapon such as you have in your possession when she was abducted."

Emita Paukof frowned, stood up, and walked over to her luggage. She opened it, moved several garments to one side, and handed Dubchek the automatic with both clips. Dubchek inserted one of the clips and pointed the gun at her. "Now Gaspazha Paukof, I must exercise the second part of my plan. Because of General Savin's prominence, we can be quite certain the authorities will find it necessary to conduct an autopsy. And unfortunately, that autopsy will reveal the heavy doses of strychnine you have administered, as well as the excessive amounts of morphine in his system. That, my dear *gaspazha*, will lead them to suspect foul play . . . and we cannot afford to arouse their suspicions."

Emita Paukof stiffened. "What are you saying?"

"I am saying, Gaspazha Paukof, that you have played out your role in our little melodrama. You are no longer of use to me." Krislof Dubchek's eyes narrowed and he took a step forward with the muzzle of the automatic pointed directly at the woman. "Now, *gaspazha*, I must ask you turn around."

The woman hesitated.

"Come, come, Gaspazha Paukof, do not make the inevitable more difficult than is necessary. You see, my dear, you have committed a crime against the Ukrainian people and one of its leaders. For that you must pay the price."

For Emita Paukof, the struggle was brief. Krislof Dubchek grabbed her by the arm, turned her around, clamped one hand over her mouth, and raised the 9mm to her head with the other. In one continuous motion, he shoved the muzzle against her temple and pulled the trigger.

There was a momentary, muffled explosion and Emita Paukof's suddenly violated body rocketed to one side as Dubchek released her and she slumped to the floor of her tiny compartment.

Dubchek waited several moments, studying the way the woman had fallen before bending over, placing the gun in her hand, and lacing her finger through the trigger guard.

When he was satisfied with the way the scene had been set, he left the compartment and closed and locked the door behind him.

Datum: Twelve-Five: The Train: 21:31 LT

By the time Krislof Dubchek returned to Savin's compartment, the general's aides had summoned the train's conductor. The conductor, a small, officious man in an ill-fitting uniform, was both visibly upset and unnerved. He was demanding access to Savin's compartment.

"We have been instructed to allow no one in the general's compartment," the older of the two aides informed him.

"By whose authority?" the conductor demanded.

"By my authority," Dubchek said, entering the compartment and taking charge. "Under the circumstances it will be necessary to stop the train at Abay to transfer the general's body from the train. I will contact my superiors and make arrangements to have the general's body flown back to Kiev."

The conductor cleared his throat. He knew that Dubchek was important because of his uniform, but he had been given explicit orders. The train, once it left Alma-Ata, was to make no further stops until it arrived in the rail yards at the east end of the Jinghe Tunnel. When he repeated those instructions to Dubchek, the man once known as the "Butcher of Ekonda," the conductor's voice was almost apologetic.

Dubchek dismissed the man with a wave of his hand. "With the death of General Savin, I am now the ranking officer on this train and I will assume full responsibility. With all due respect, comrade, when you were given your orders, no one could have anticipated such a misfortune as that which has befallen General Savin."

The little man looked at Dubchek, then into the

compartment at the body of the general. Savin's aides had placed the body on the bed and covered it with a sheet. The tall, stern man was right, of course. It would be necessary to do something with the general's body.

"If we must stop at Abay, then I will have to inform the engineer," the man explained. "He was given the same instructions—and he knows nothing of what has happened here."

"Do what is necessary," Dubchek ordered, "then inform me what time we can expect to arrive in Abay."

Chapter Thirteen

Datum: Thirteen-One: Abay: 07:19 LT

The day dawned with a heavy overcast, promising more snow and a biting wind that swirled the ever-present sand down the slope of the mountains. Serafim Volokitin and Rikov Mrachak, bracing themselves against the gnawing cold, worked their way from Volokitin's cabin down to the government-owned emergency provisions station.

At the entrance to the squat and sprawling one-story building, Serafim was greeted by a workman constructing an oblong-shaped box. The man was using odds and ends of the lumber from supply skids. Inside, Viktor Konyef, the sober-faced director of the provisions station, and the man who usually hired Serafim to clear the boulders and debris from the tracks, was sorting supplies. He looked up when he saw the two men approaching. The fact that Serafim was accompanied by someone whose face he did not recognize did not seem to faze him. Konyef, only recently transferred from the railroad provisions store at Biysk, still had not met everyone in the tiny mountain village at the mouth of the Jinghe Tunnel.

"Word travels fast," Konyef commented without looking up.

"According to my calendar the train from Odessa will pass through sometime today," Serafim reminded him.

Konyef looked up from his work. "Unfortunately, it will do more than pass through. We have been informed that the train will stop in Abay." He sighed.

Serafim looked at Mrachak. "I was told the train would pass through without stopping," Serafim said. "I was prepared to spend the entire day in the ravine in the event of a rock slide."

Konyef glanced at Mrachak. There was a trace of a smile on his craggy face. "And you brought someone to keep you company, huh? If I were going to have to spend the entire day out in this weather, citizen, I would have found someone who could also keep me warm."

"This is Mrachak, my cousin from Zaysan. He has offered to help me."

"This time you are in luck," Konyef said, stopping

to light a cigarette. "Your vigil will be brief. We have been informed of a death aboard the train. We are told one of the officials died of an apparent heart attack. We have been instructed to build a coffin and make arrangements to have the body returned to Alma-Ata. From there it will be flown back to Kiev."

"The one who died, he must be a very important man," Serafim said.

Konyef shrugged. "If you listen to my superiors, everyone is a very important official."

Serafim stomped his feet to ward off the cold. "I will need a truck to drive up to the ravine," he said. "It has been several days since I have checked the tracks. I will take my cousin, Mrachak, with me. When I have finished I will report back to you."

Viktor Konyef pointed to the rear of the building. "Take one of the trucks in the shed out back."

Serafim and Mrachak circled back to Serafim's cabin and picked up Bogner before heading for the stretch of track that snaked through the ravine. Serafim parked the wheezing Penza truck on a bluff overlooking the ravine and began pointing. "That is the west end of the ravine. As you can see, the grade is quite steep. I am told that when the track was constructed, the engineers, in order to avoid passing over the summit, decided to dynamite their way through the Tien Shan Pass. This also enabled them to avoid an equally steep decline on the other side of the pass as the train approaches the tunnel."

Bogner inched his way down and looked over the edge into the ravine. "How far down?"

"At this point, fifty, maybe sixty feet," Serafim estimated. "If you wish to board the train here, it would be possible to tie a rope and descend to a small ledge that would accommodate you until the train passes. You could then leap from the ledge to the train."

Bogner winced. "How fast is the train going when it comes through the ravine?"

Serafim thought for a moment. "I do not know the speed but it is slow, very slow. Progress through the pass is agonizing. I have stood on this ledge and watched many times. The engineers fear boulders on the tracks, the tremors are frequent, and there is always the wind."

"Suppose we did try it here," Bogner said. "Is there a place where we can safely get the woman off the train before it passes through the tunnel?"

"There is only one place where that would be possible," Serafim answered. "There is a three-kilometer stretch at the end of the pass, just before the tunnel. But it will be a steep climb out."

Bogner turned to Mrachak. "What do you think?"

The Kazakh studied the sheers walls of the ravine. "I do not *think* when it comes to situations like this, *amerikanski*. I consider the alternatives. If there is a safer one, I take it."

"All right, what's our chances of getting aboard the train when it stops in Abay?" Bogner asked.

"I have seen the trains from the west stop in Abay

on many occasions," Serafim replied. "If the train is carrying militia, as it often does, the militia will be deployed. They will stand guard while the supplies are taken off the train."

"Key question. How many militia?"

"Usually no more than six or eight men."

Bogner frowned. "Suppose we found a place to hide near the tracks. Possible?"

Serafim thought for a minute. "Possible," he admitted. "There is a small freight yard, like a staging area, near where the train will stop."

"Then, when the train stops and they are taking the body off the train, we board, locate the Berzin woman, and hustle her off before the—"

Mrachak nodded. "I like that better than trying to get on the train here."

"It will not be easy even at Abay," Serafim countered. "If she is on the train, she will be under guard and it could be difficult to find her."

"I don't think so," Bogner said, looking at Mrachak. "Remember what Mikos told us? When the train left Odessa, there was one sleeping car. At the KON meeting he learned that another sleeping car would be added later, probably at Alma-Ata. That second sleeping car is strictly for Savin. My guess then is that she is being detained in the other sleeping car."

"What about the train itself?" Mrachak reminded him. "How are you going to stop it?"

Bogner scowled. "You know the territory, Serafim. You've been in that tunnel. Got any ideas?"

The man Mrachak called "cousin" thought for a minute. "The Jinghe Tunnel is slightly over seven kilometers in length. One set of tracks is complete. The parallel tracks are less than half complete. If there was a way to use some of the heavy tunnel construction equipment to block the tracks . . ."

"And then seal the tunnel off," Mrachak continued for him.

Bogner held up his hand. "I think you're on to something, Serafim. Instead of worrying about the train, we blow up the tunnel while the train is in it."

"There is a way," Serafim said. "At the midpoint of the tunnel, there is stockpile of supplies and equipment. If the rails were to be disrupted there . . .

"I have only been there once, to assist in the delivering of supplies," he reflected. "There is a small construction depot and a staging area. That is where the supplies are kept and the great hydraulically operated tunnel-boring machine is positioned. It is being used to bore the adjacent tunnel."

"How many men at this mid-tunnel depot?" Bogner asked.

"Only a few Kazakh technicians. But there are many Chinese working on the section of track to the east of the supply and staging area."

"All right, think back," Bogner said. "What's this damn tunnel-boring machine look like? Is there some way we can use it to block the tracks?"

Serafim had to think for a moment. "It is not on

rails, so it can be maneuvered. The drilling bits are attached to a heavy steel plate that is part of the excavating apparatus. That same plate also acts as a shield to protect the operator. The grout is carried back to railcars on a conveyor belt that is both powered and moved by a locomotive. But the locomotive has not been in place for several days now. The Chinese have not explained why."

"Will this so-called tunnel-boring machine operate independent of the locomotive?"

Serafim nodded.

"Then it could work," Bogner said, watching Serafim finish his sketch. "All we have to do is get that big bastard on the same tracks the train is using . . . load it up with some explosives . . . and boom . . . big boom. Good-bye train and good-bye tunnel.

"But how do we get Polce Berzin off the train and get to the service depot before the train gets there?" he asked.

"This is where Mrachak earns his money, *amerikanski*," Mrachak said. "While you get the woman off the train, I will find a way to get to the depot."

"The service depot is approximately three and a half kilometers away," Serafim said, "and the train from Odessa is due to arrive at the Abay station in less than two hours. We do not have much time."

"Get me back to the depot in Abay, Serafim," Bogner said. "Rikov, you start for the service area in the tunnel. I don't care how you do it, but find a way to block that damn tunnel—then get the hell out of there."

Mrachak looked at his longtime friend. He was smiling. "You see, my dear Serafim, life in Abay need not be boring. All you need is an occasional *amerikanski* to stop by and stir things up."

Datum: Thirteen-Two: Paskov Bal'nista, Klin: 14:14 LT

Mikos Komenich was feeling stronger. For the second day in a row he had been permitted to get out of bed and sit in a chair where he could look out the window. Now he watched the one who called himself Major Varmii get out of his car and cross the street to the *bal'nista*. The militia officer was on his way to conduct another of his interrogation sessions.

Komenich waited for the sound of the elevator and the inevitable shuffle of footsteps in the corridor. There would be a brief pause while the man spoke to the nurse and then the polite knock on the door before he entered.

Komenich braced himself for the inescapable.

"You are feeling better today?" Varmii asked. He took off his coat and hat and laid them on Komenich's bed. Then he pulled up a chair and sat down. There was a chart at the foot of Komenich's bed, and the militiaman studied it. When he was finished, he laid the chart aside. "Are you aware that you will be released tomorrow?"

Komenich shrugged. "One prison or another. Does it make a difference?"

Red Sand

Varmii sighed, stood up, walked to the window, looked out at the barren gray day for several moments, then closed the blinds. When he took his seat again, he moved his chair closer. From their earlier conversations, Komenich had learned that the militia major was an instructor at the university. Now, as usual, Varmii began speaking in his low monotone, and Komenich wondered how his students managed to stay awake during his lectures.

"Does the name Utra Svychi mean anything to you?" Varmii asked.

Komenich tried to conceal his surprise. "Should it?"

"We have identified the body of one of the men who broke into the Zeverin Arsenal. His name was Utra Svychi. We have traced this man called Svychi to Zhambyl."

Komenich shrugged. "That's all very interesting, but I'm afraid I can't help you."

"Our investigation further shows that Svychi and a man by the name of Rikov Mrachak obtained militia uniforms for themselves and two other men, and that they borrowed a truck."

Komenich looked at his hands. "I still don't see what all of this has to do with me, Colonel."

"Let me refresh your memory, comrade. Let me tell you what I believe happened. After the raid on the Zeverin Arsenal, you left your fallen comrade behind and the three of you who managed to escape sought refuge in the farmhouse where we found you. When the militia squad from Klin came to investigate the farmhouse, you and your colleagues subdued them—more accurately, killed them. Then, knowing that you were unable to continue and thinking you were safe with the elderly couple, your colleagues left you there and continued their mission. They used the miltia vehicle to effect their escape."

"That's quite a story, Major. You should write a book."

Varmii leaned forward. "I do not know who you are, comrade, but I can assure you, before I am through, I will learn your identity and I will discover why you raided the arsenal."

"Don't bet on it," Komenich replied.

Varmii shrugged, but his smile was surprisingly warm as he stood up. "Tomorrow, at fourteen hundred hours, you will be released into my custody. I want to again remind you that you can save yourself a great deal of discomfiture, comrade. All you have to do is reveal your colleagues' whereabouts."

Komenich closed his eyes and leaned his head back. He counted the militia officer's footsteps as he crossed the room, opened the door, and left. He waited several minutes before opening the blinds. When he did, he realized that it had started to snow again.

Datum: Thirteen-Three: The Train: 11:31 LT

"And you have touched nothing?" Dubchek demanded.

Red Sand

Olga Serova backed away. "Everything is . . . as I found . . . it, General." Her words came in frightened fragments as she tried to regain her composure.

Krislof Dubchek leaned against the small writing desk in the corner of Emita Paukof's compartment. The conductor, already unnerved by the death of General Savin, was doing his best to calm Olga Serova. "If you would, please, Citizen Serova, tell us exactly what happened," the conductor said.

Her voice was halting, betraying her anguish. "I— I noticed—noticed that the Berzin woman—did not—did not come to the troop car for *zaftrak*. Only twice since we left Odessa has she not taken breakfast. Those times were yesterday when she dined with General Savin, and once before when she was taken ill. It was her custom to eat shortly after the militiamen finished their morning meal."

"Go on," the conductor encouraged.

"Thinking—that she might again be ill or had overslept, I brought—brought some *kofi* with *slifki* and *pyechyen'ye* to her compartment. When she did not—not respond to my efforts to awake her, I—I used the key to let myself in. I found her as you— as you see her . . ." Her voice trailed off and she began to sob again.

The conductor moved cautiously around the body of Emita Paukof, and studied the way she had fallen. "From her position, the location of the wound in her head, and the way she is holding the gun, it would appear that she took her own life," he said. Then he looked at Dubchek for some sort of confirmation of his theory.

Dubchek appraised the situation with an air of detachment.

"Do you know the woman's identity?" the conductor finally asked. "Because this is a military train there is no passenger manifest."

Dubchek avoided looking at the body. "Berzin. Her name is Berzin, Polce Berzin. She is the daughter of the Deputy Prime Minister, Josef Berzin."

The aging conductor, already unsettled by the death of Savin, further paled at the news that the dead woman was the daughter of one of the most powerful men in the Ukraine. "I—I—I did not know," he stammered.

Dubchek glared at the conductor, then turned toward Olga Serova. "And as for you, Gaspazha Serova, you have obviously been negligent in your responsibility. You were instructed to keep an eye on the Berzin woman, were you not?"

The frail woman backed away from Dubchek without responding.

"I would agree with you," Dubchek finally said, looking at the conductor. "It is quite obvious what has happened here." He bent down and touched Emita Paukof's face. Her skin was cold to the touch. The blood had pooled, giving a sickly blue hue to what remained of the left side of her face. There was a puddle of dried blood under her head. "This woman died by her own hand," he concluded. "That seems quite obvious." Then, standing up again, he instructed the conductor to assist Olga Serova in moving the woman's body over to the bed. "After you have finished here, Gaspazha Serova, you will bring the woman's personal effects to my compartment."

Olga Serova nodded her understanding.

Finally, when he looked at his watch, it was evident that Krislof Dubchek had already put the death of the woman known as Polce Berzin behind him. Now he was occupied with other concerns. "How soon will we be arriving in Abay?"

The conductor glanced out the window. The intensity of the winter storm had increased and the train had slowed. "Assuming that the storm does not cause further delay, General, we should arrive in Abay at approximately fifteen hundred hours."

Datum: Thirteen-Three: Cabinet Building, Gidropark: 12:41 LT

Aaralov Lavrenti's administrative assistant was a politically passionate young woman who had come to him by way of the City Collegium of Advocates in Moscow. Originally from the Ukraine, she had jumped at Lavrenti's offer and the opportunity to return to her homeland following the breakup of the Union.

Because she seemed to work both night and day, it was not surprising that Achina Levin was the one who logged in the communique from Abay. She carried it immediately to Lavrenti and stood by while he read it.

Abay, Kazakhstan-04-7731-77-priority 1 urgent-urgent

    At approximately twenty-one hundred hours 21/10/ General Aleksei Savin, former KGB director and founder of the pro-Party KON, was found dead in his compartment aboard . . .

Lavrenti read the communique in its entirety, then read it again. "Get Grechko on the telephone," he instructed.

Achina Levin dialed Grechko's office and handed Lavrenti the phone.

"Leonid," Lavrenti roared, "you can relax. A great burden has been lifted from the shoulders of the Party."

"You have confirmation?" Grechko asked.

Aralov Lavrenti read his comrade the entire text of the dispatch.

" . . . the cause of death of General Savin, who has been in ill health for several years, has not been determined. . . . "

"And your little songbird, Aralov, what about her?"

"General Dubchek's instructions were very specific. He was to assist Gaspazha Paukof in her clandestine endeavor, and as soon as the task was completed, he was directed to see that she suffered sufficient remorse to take her own life."

"Most ingenious, comrade. When the story of what happened aboard that train is revealed to the people, they will believe that the daughter of Josef Berzin, in a fit of familial and political passion, retaliated by taking the life of the man reputed to have engineered the assassination of our beloved President Yefimov."

"Comrade Dubchek has done well. He has followed his instructions to the letter. We knew that the wire services would pick up the story of Savin's death as soon as Dubchek issued the communique. This was planned from the outset. When the train arrives in Abay, he will contact me through confidential railroad channels. Then I will learn more of the details."

The two men congratulated themselves again and Lavrenti handed the receiver back to his assistant. Only then did Lavrenti notice that the woman was holding a business card in her hands.

"Someone is waiting to see me?" Lavrenti asked.

Achina Levin nodded and glanced at the card. "He has been waiting for quite some time now. His name is Yuri Illich. He is a homicide investigator with the Odessa Police."

The smile faded from Aralov Lavrenti's face. He took the card and laid it, face up, on his desk. "Very well." He sighed. "Tell the inspector that I will see him now."

Datum: Thirteen-Five: ISA Offices, Washington: 09:04 LT

Millie Ploughman drained the last few drops of coffee from her cup, and leaned back in her chair. "We just hit the wall," she said. "Rutland's personal phone records and the records from the phone company don't tell us a thing that we didn't already know."

"Did you check out the leads from Carol Taylor?" Packer asked.

"No Muldoon and no Mikan. There are four people in Rutland's book whose names begin with M, a Frank Milstrom, who does his taxes, a fellow by the name of Tad Morgan, who used to work for CBS, now with CNN. Morgan claims he hasn't seen or talked to Rutland in the last five years. The Markland that's in his book is a Baptist minister, and the McNeil is a stockbroker. Markland and McNeil are both clean."

Miller slumped down in his chair. "Damn, it's like looking for a needle—"

"Don't say it, Robert, I hate cliches." Millie growled.

Miller grinned. "Millie's right, Pack, we've played out the string. We've checked out all the names Joy Carpenter could come up with, and everything Carol Taylor could think of."

Clancy Packer stood up and began pacing back and forth. "Dammit, Jeff Rutland was getting his information from someone. The question is who?"

Miller frowned. As was his habit, he had begun doodling on a piece of paper. "Usually in a case like this, the person selling the information gets a little careless, starts spending some of that money. But so far, no leads."

"Let's approach it from a different angle," Millie said. "Who has access to the kind of information Rutland was buying?"

"Damn near every agency in Washington," Miller answered. "We might as well start looking through the phone book."

Millie shook her head. "All right, lets come at it from the other side of the barn. Who was monitoring that chemical weapons plant in Libya?"

"Oscar Jaffe's boys were doing the dirty work. They had an eye in the sky."

"Then let's start with the CIA," Millie suggested. "The question is, will Jaffe cooperate?"

"He has so far, but it's a long shot. They've been squeaky clean since the Aldrich Ames debacle." Miller laughed. "Oscar is already paranoid."

Packer had been listening to the exchange. "Millie may have something, Robert. Why not talk to Oscar again? See if you can find out who was following the progress of that chemical weapons plant in Tarhuna. If he's willing to give us names, then we can find out who they talked to. Who knows, maybe we'll come up with something."

**Log: Thirteen-Six: Arlington Hotel, Washington:
11:17 LT**

In the thirteen years that Clancy Packer had
known Oscar Jaffe, they had never met anyplace
other than the small room heavy with the smell of
kitchen grease and dirty linen adjacent to the
kitchen of the Arlington Hotel. Packer could almost
predict the brown mug, the inevitable cigarette,
and the Jaffe frown.

Packer entered through the alley door, made his
way through the kitchen, past the walk-in coolers,
down the hall to a door marked PRIVATE, knocked
once, and opened the door. Jaffe looked up without
smiling. As usual, his tie was loose and his feet were
propped up on table. "What the hell is this all about,
Clancy?"

It took Clancy Packer the better part of fifteen
minutes to bring Jaffe up to speed. He recounted
Joy's conversation with Bogner about the bio warheads shipment from Tarhuna, the meeting with
Rutland in the parking garage, putting a tail on
Rutland, and the violent death of the NBS analyst
in the parking lot of the Carver Club.

"That's all very interesting, Pack, but I still don't
see how this involves the agency," Jaffe drawled.

"Rutland was having an affair. The woman's
name was Carol Taylor. I talked to her. She didn't
seem to know much about Rutland's professional
life and she didn't give us much help. But she did

say there was one man who called several times and left messages for Rutland."

"Did she have a name?"

Clancy shook his head. No names, but she thought the man's name began with an M."

"First name or last name?"

Packer shrugged.

"Have you subpoenaed her phone records?"

"Yes, and there's nothing that would tie her or anyone else to Rutland."

Jaffe took a sip of coffee. "You still haven't told me why you think I can help."

"Your people were monitoring the Tarhuna situation. They were the ones that discovered the shipment of those bio warheads. We think it's likely that someone inadvertently or on purpose relayed that information to Rutland's contact."

"And you think it could be one of my people?" Jaffe scowled.

"We think it's a possibility."

Jaffe finished his coffee, snuffed out his cigarette, and stood up. As he was putting on his coat he said, "I don't have to check my files, Pack. I know who was following the Tarhuna situation. They're some of my best people."

"It's worth a little of your time, Oscar. Poke around and let me know if you find anything."

Oscar Jaffe grunted. For Packer that was good enough.

Chapter Fourteen

The door was open, but out of deference for the man's position, Yuri Illich knocked anyway. Junus Arkadiya looked up, obviously irritated by the interruption. Then, as soon as he saw the senior homicide inspector, the craggy frown dissolved into a vague half smile. "Come in, come in," Arkadiya said. He motioned for Illich to have a seat.

With his coat draped over his arm and his hat still in his hand, Illich dropped down in the chair across the desk from his former mentor. "According to the Prefect, you are only working part-time,"

314

the inspector said. "I am fortunate to find you here, no?"

The old man scanned the clutter of papers, files, and reports. "As you can see, my friend, part-time is insufficient. At this rate I will never catch up."

"For that very reason I am reluctant to take up your time," Illich said, "but I have need of your counsel."

Arkadiya feigned disappointment, cleared away a stack of reports, and leaned forward with hands on the desk. "When you get to be my age," the old man mused, "a social visit by a former pupil is often a high point in the day. It is testimony to the fact that I am well remembered."

Illich knew that the old man would gladly indulge in a few reminiscences but only if they were brief. He reached in his pocket and pulled out the sketch Arkadiya had prepared for him on his last visit. Though wrinkled and worse for the wear it had received, it was still intact. "Do you recall this?" Illich asked.

Junus Arkadiya studied the drawing for several moments before looking up. "Indeed. Is this not the likely countenance of the young woman whose body was found at the Odessa Film Studios some time ago?"

Illich indicated that it was. "You have a good memory."

"You are still on the case?"

Illich sighed and slumped back in his chair. "I

am," he admitted. "But when I was here before, I was a man without a theory."

"And now you have one?"

Illich nodded. "I have a theory, but as yet I have not found a way to prove it."

Arkadiya smiled. "And you are here to test that theory. Am I right?"

"I admit that it is rather convoluted, but like a haunting, it does not go away."

Arkadiya rummaged around until he found his pipe under a stack of papers, filled it with tobacco, tamped it, and lit it. He savored several puffs before motioning for Illich to continue.

Illich's voice seemed hesitant as he began. "You will recall that the woman's body was found in the basement of a seldom-used outbuilding on the back lot of the studio. The body was mutilated, facial features destroyed, and hands amputated."

"Dental records?" the old man asked.

"Forensics made a valiant effort, but we do not even know if the woman was Ukrainian. In the end they could not help us."

"And your theory?"

"Suppose I told you that I believe the victim was disfigured not so much to hide the identity but because she would have been readily identifiable."

Arkadiya looked puzzled. "Are they not one and the same? Or are you reluctant to say what you really think?"

Illich cleared his throat. His former mentor had cut to the heart of the matter.

"It is too complicated. But I am certain of one thing. This was not a crime of passion. This crime was carefully planned. When you step back and look at everything, you see what amounts to a meticulously constructed puzzle, a body, a purse that leads us to another woman—a woman by the name of Rubana Cheslov, who admits that she was attacked, but who also admits that her attackers seemed more interested in her purse than her person—and finally to a woman who informed me that she was pressured to obtain a passport for one Polce Berzin."

"The daughter of Josef Berzin?"

Illich nodded. "And when I tried to follow up on Polce Berzin, I was informed by her place of work that she has not been seen since two days before the body was found in the Odessa Studio back lot."

Arkadiya frowned. "So far all I hear is uncertainty."

Illich opened his briefcase and took out the pictures. One was the picture of Polce Berzin, the other of Rubana Cheslov? "Compare the photographs with your drawing."

Junus Arkayida laid the drawing beside the photographs. "There are similarities," he admitted.

Illich smiled. "I believe . . ." He hesitated. "That the body may very well be that of Polce Berzin."

"And?"

"I am convinced that she was murdered by the KON."

"That would be difficult to prove."

Illich paused. "And I am convinced that Aralov Lavrenti is somehow involved."

The old man sagged back in his chair. His expression betrayed his concern. "Have you told anyone else of this conviction?"

Illich shook his head. "As I said before, it is only a theory; I have no proof, only circumstantial evidence."

"You would be wise not to articulate this theory to anyone unless you trust them implicitly."

Illich gathered up his photographs and papers and shoveled them back in his suitcase. He searched Arkadiya's face for direction. "I am looking to my former mentor for guidance," he admitted.

"Say nothing until you are certain. Even then, it will be difficult. Men like Aralov Lavrenti are above the law."

Illich nodded. Arkadiya was correct. A further attempt to interrogate Lavrenti now would be foolhardy. A third visit to the office of the Vice Minister would do nothing more than tip Illich's hand—and that would afford the Vice Minister even more of an opportunity to cover his tracks.

Illich stood up.

"What do you intend to do?" Arkadiya asked.

Illich sighed. "I have no choice," he said. "Unless I can come up with something more concrete, I am afraid that there is nothing I can do."

Red Sand

Datum: Fourteen-Two: The Jinghe Tunnel: 12:47 LT

Even though compressed air was being fed into the unfinished cavity around the work area, the air circulating through most of the tunnel was dank with a prevailing foul odor. For that reason, Rikov Mrachak found it easier to breathe now that he was in sight of the slumbering TBU.

From a vantage point behind a stack of supply crates he watched three men in coveralls emerge from a small construction shack where lighting was supplied by two generators. The men were ignoring the TBU and working on the GR-4 diesel-powered locomotive that pulled the muck cars to the east end of the tunnel. He pulled out Serafim's crude sketch of the massive percussive drilling unit and compared the sketch to the actual TBU. The sketch was accurate. The electro-hydraulic drills and the hulking hammers which pushed forward and struck the drill rod shanks were located forward. The controls were located in a safety cage at the rear of the platform, which was elevated midway to the ceiling of the tunnel, where it supported a conveyor belt which carried the stone back to the muck cars. From where he hid, the controls appeared to be a confusing array of gauges, levers, panels and switches. Despite the maze of controls, Serafim had assured him that the massive tunnel-drilling machine could be operated easily by one man. Now, after seeing the beast, Mrachak wasn't so certain.

Then, while Mrachak watched, the three technicians turned their attention to the TBU and began swarming over the unit, checking and tweaking, performing what appeared to be some kind of inspection procedure. Two of the men worked at the giant control panel, while the third danced the beam of his lantern into the recesses of the undercarriage. In the distance, further to the east, there were the sounds of heavy construction, earth movers, bulldozers, and an assortment of heavy equipment cleaning away the debris and rubble where the huge cement panels were being lifted into place on the second section of the tunnel.

Mrachak moved closer. Now he could hear the three men. The technicians were Chinese and they kept up a steady line of chatter as they worked on the control panel. Finally one of the men crawled down and worked his way forward through the maze of drills to a large hydraulic boom capable of positioning the drill plate. He used a wrench to adjust the gears on the lift, instructed one of his coworkers to cycle the drill plate, and stood back to assess the boom's performance. The machine cycled twice, then stopped again. At that point the one who appeared to be the lead technician was standing no more than thirty yards from Mrachak with his back to him. Mrachak waited until a second attempt was made to cycle the massive unit, and then inched his way closer. He knew he would not be able to understand the spoken exchange, but he hoped to be able to get a better look at the controls.

He had moved to within twenty feet of the TBU when he saw the three technicians look up. The lights of an approaching vehicle were suddenly bathing the walls of the tunnel with a white-yellow glow far brighter than the faint illumination provided by the string of shielded incandescent lamps over the work site.

Mrachak ducked back into the shadows and waited for the vehicle to come to a stop. The unit was a light-duty combination half-track and truck, built low to the ground, operating on batteries and using oversized balloon tires. It carried three men, all of whom were armed. Unlike their Chinese counterparts, these three appeared to be Kazakhs and Mrachak could understand them. There was a brief exchange, accompanied by gestures and instructions, before one of the Chinese technicians crawled into the safety cage and began checking the wiring on the control panel. A second Chinese technician dropped to the floor of the cave, worked his way forward to the bulky drill shield, and began inspecting the quartet of electro-hydraulic hammers. The third, meanwhile, began a systematic inspection of the connections in the recesses in the undercarriage. The superstructure of the giant TBU was a maze of heavy steel beams and oversized hydrokinetics. Mrachak shook his head; at best the massive piece of equipment was a maintenance man's nightmare. Mrachak, who had worked in tunnels before, knew that such machinery existed, but he had never actually seen it. The question was, could he move it without the aid of the locomotive?

He moved closer to get a better look. In his conversations with Bogner and Serafim, they had discussed possible ways of stopping the missile train. Serafim, who knew the configuration of the tunnel, had first suggested diverting the train in mid-tunnel by rerouting it into the section of track that led into the partially completed adjacent second tunnel.

Finally, though, they had agreed on blocking the track and using explosives at the point of impact. In order to do that, Mrachak would have to commandeer the TBU and maneuver it back onto the main track to straddle the rails. He would have to load the drills with explosives, short out the lighting, and clear the tunnel. When the train collided with the TBU, any concerns about the train crossing over into China would be a thing of the past.

Mrachak kept low and moved still closer. He was close enough now to be able to pick up fragments of conversation from the three Kazakhs. The three Chinese technicians had finished their inspection and were listening. He was no more twenty feet from the six men when his luck ran out. In the darkness he stumbled, and it was just enough noise to alert the work crew. Even though Mrachak was able to duck back into the shadows and stand motionless, it was too late. When the beam of one of the Kazakh flashlights, accompanied by what Mrachak recognized as the muzzle of the Chinese equivalent of an M-16, ferreted out his hiding place, Mrachak was trapped.

"Come out into the light," the Kazakh ordered. Mrachak was prodded to his feet and instructed to hold up his hands. His captors were led by a paunchy-looking little man in a Kazakh militia uniform. There were no chevrons to indicate rank. He was flanked by his two Kazakh comrades, neither of whom appeared to be armed. Without the M-16 knockoff, the trio didn't exactly look formidable. The three Chinese technicians had all stayed back, near the TBU.

The rotund one kept the beam of his flashlight shining in Mrachak's eyes. "Who are you and how did you get in here?" he demanded.

"I could ask the same question," Mrachak bluffed. "Who are you?"

"I am security," the man snapped, "and I will ask the questions."

"Well, then, you should know that the provisions people sent me here to inform you that the train from the Ukraine is running ahead of schedule. The provisions officer must be assured that the track is clear—no construction equipment is to be allowed on the tracks." In the dim light of the tunnel Mrachak couldn't tell if the fleshy little security man was buying his story.

The Kazakh scowled. "How did you get here? I heard no tram."

"You heard no tram because it broke down a mile

or so back down the tunnel. I managed to get it off the tracks, but I had to walk the rest of the way."

The Kazakh was still scowling. "Why have I not seen you before?" he demanded.

"I'm new. I'm assisting Serafim Volokitin. He is my cousin."

The Kazakh scoffed. "Volokitin is a nothing. Why did he not come himself?"

"He's cleaning the debris from the tracks that run through the ravine. The provisions officer has instructed him to remain there until the train clears."

The Kazakh turned and looked at his two comrades. "Do either of you recognize him?" he demanded.

Both men shook their head.

"You will come with me," the security man ordered. "I'll call the provisions officer."

Mrachak breathed a sigh of relief. He had taken the precaution of cutting the temporary phone lines at two different points as he worked his way into the tunnel. Those downed phone lines, plus the fact that so far only one of the men appeared to be armed, gave him hope. He still had a chance.

Datum: Fourteen-Three: Paskov Bal'nista: Klin: 14:14 LT

Mikos Komenich moved from his bed in the darkened room, dressed, and took a seat near the window. There was nothing to do now but wait for the inevitable. He had heard there was a large government prison at Taldykurgan where political prisoners were incarcerated, and he assumed he would be sent there. The hospital personnel spoke of it often, indicating they frequently provided medical services for inmates transferred from the prison facility.

When he heard the elevator doors open across the corridor from his room, he knew the time had come. The Kazakh major was slightly late. He'd promised to return at two o'clock.

Varmii was smiling as he entered the room. "Ah, the patient is up and dressed. Excellent."

Komenich frowned and pointed to the nightstand beside his bed. "I have been released. The doctor signed the papers less than an hour ago."

For a change, the militia major was not wearing his uniform. Instead he was attired in a drab gray suit with a stiffly starched shirt and a plain blue tie. Varmii walked to the nightstand, picked up the papers, signed them, and turned toward Komenich. "Now, 3-7a-b, you will come with me."

Komenich, still weak, stood up and preceded Varmii out of the room. Two nurses, standing in the corridor outside of his room, watched as Varmii escorted him into the elevator and closed the door.

At the doors to the main entrance, a dark blue Chaika limousine waited. It was snowing: a wet, heavy, clinging snow that, despite its beauty, added nothing but chill. A young woman, bundled in a heavy black coat with the collar buttoned tight around her throat and wearing a knit cap pulled low over her ears, was sitting behind the wheel. The bundling was so complete, Komenich was unable to determine whether or not she was pretty.

Varmii, to Komenich's surprise, crawled in and sat down beside him. He waited until the woman pulled into the flow of traffic before he opened his briefcase and spoke.

"What does the name Borodin mean to you?" Varmii asked.

"Never heard of him."

Varmii sighed. "I compliment you, Mikos Komenich. You do indeed live up to your reputation."

Komenich stared out the window as the Chaika pulled onto an esplanade lined with barren trees and dirty snow. "Do you expect me to capitulate just because you have learned my name?"

Varmii had an easy laugh, the kind people trust. "I know a great deal more about you than just your name," he said. "You come from Odessa, you are a member of the KON, and you were sent here with an American by the name of Bogner. Would you like to hear more?"

Komenich was stunned. How could he know? There was no way he could—unless Bogner had been discovered. He turned away from the window and looked at the man who had been interrogating him for the past five days. "I know nothing of this matter. Nor do I have any idea who this Komenich is of whom you speak."

"You met Bogner in Odessa shortly after the train

carrying the missiles left the rail yards," Varmii continued.

"Look," Komenich said with a scowl, "I do not know how or where you got your information, but if you expect me to say anything, you are as the Americans say, barking up the wrong tree."

Varmii leaned forward, picked up the intercom, and spoke to the driver. "Bakan, Leah," he said. "You know the place."

Now that Varmii knew his identity, Komenich wondered why the militia major was being so casual.

"Now, Citizen Komenich, I will ask you again, does the name Borodin mean anything to you?"

Komenich refused to answer. Sure, he knew who Borodin was. Borodin was the Americans' Kazakh contact. But Borodin had disappeared, gone underground, and no one had heard from him in over two years. The assumption in most quarters was that he was either dead or had been discovered.

"Very well," Varmii said with a sigh, "let me tell you what I know about Borodin. He is a conduit to certain people for the American government. He is, in fact, to this part of the world what I am told you are to the people of your country."

Komenich looked away. "You must have me confused with someone else," he insisted.

Varmii leaned his head back and closed his eyes. "Listen carefully. Bakan is a small village approximately sixty kilometers from here. When we arrive in Bakan, you will change clothes and identity. You will become Colonel Boris Turchin of the Kazakhstan People's Militia." Varmii reached in his attaché case a second time. "Here are your papers and, if you will excuse the irony of it, your green Party card. You will speak only if absolutely necessary. The less you say, the less likely you are to be discovered."

Varmii handed Komenich the set of militia travel orders and the necessary identification papers. Komenich took the papers, glanced over them, and looked up. If Varmii was trying to trap him, he was going about it in a strange way.

"From Bakan, you will travel to Zhambyl by bus. In Zhambyl, you will ask directions to the train station. Your contact in the bus station will be a young woman by the name of Sasha. You will know her by her impairment; she is confined to a wheelchair. When you see her, you will ask, *"Kakaya slyed uyushaya astanofka?"* That is your password and she will tell you where you go next. There are two train stations in Zhambyl and she will know which one is the safest."

"I—I don't understand," Komenich said. "How will you account for the fact that—"

"For the fact you have disappeared?"

Komenich nodded.

"There will be no questions. If you will reflect back upon your three-day stay in the *bal'nista*, you will remember that you talked to no one except the staff and me during that time. If questions arise, there is an unfortunate cadaver in the morgue of

328

the *bal'nista*, about your age, height, and weight. He has a bullet hole in his side, just above the kidney; he is identified only as 3-7a-b. It will be enough to satisfy the curiosity of anyone who does ask questions."

Komenich looked at the papers. It appeared as though Varmii had thought of everything, even bus tickets. "Who are you?" Komenich asked.

"Fortunately for you, my friend, the old woman came to the one officer in Klin that could help you."

"That still doesn't explain—" Komenich said.

"For the record, Borodin is alive and well." Varmii smiled. "If you are wondering why it took me so long to reveal who I am, I had to be certain you were not a plant by my government. I think you will agree, treachery works both sides of the street."

Datum: Fourteen-Four: The Train Station in Abay: 14:11 LT

Bogner watched as Serafim Volokitin threaded his way through the maze of empty supply crates in the yard across from the provisions depot. It was snowing again and Mrachak's "cousin" was having difficulty breathing by the time he worked his way up the small incline to the area where Bogner was hiding.

"What the hell's going on down there?" Bogner asked. "None of those cars were there this morning. The place is crawling with people."

Serafim hunkered down between the crates and

brushed the snow off his coat, struggling to catch his breath. "I am told they are journalists and television people. They are here covering the death of a Ukrainian official aboard the train."

"Ukrainain official? Who?"

"A General Savin. Inside they are saying they received a a communique from the train which indicated that the general was murdered late last night by a Yefimov sympathizer. They are listening now to the radio. It is already being reported on the news programs."

"Savin?" Bogner repeated. "Do you know who Savin is?"

Serafim shook his head.

"Aleksei Savin is the former head of the KGB. When I left Washington, our people had it pretty well figured out that he was the one who engineered Yefimov's assassination. Supposedly he was going to be the Party's choice in the upcoming Ukrainian elections."

"The body is to be flown back to Kiev," Serafim said. I am told they are arranging a funeral cortege."

"That means the train will be here longer than we thought. What's this do to their schedule?"

Serafim shrugged. "I am told that the delay here in Abay will be extended while the general's body is taken off the train and the necessary official reports are filed. The provisions officer indicated that the communiques from the train have not revealed any of the details surrounding the general's death other than that he was murdered."

"If the train is delayed here longer than we anticipated, and they send someone ahead to check the track . . ."

"If I see that one of the security people is sent ahead, I will follow him. There will be no problem," Serafim said. "First we must worry about the woman. No?"

Bogner nodded. "You're right. First the Deputy Prime Minister's daughter, then the missiles."

Serafim smiled and began drawing another of his diagrams in the snow. "It is standard procedure to add an additional locomotive to an eastbound train at Alma-Ata. This is done to accommodate the increase in grade as the train approaches the steep grade at Tien Shan Pass. Since that is the case, we will assume that the train consists of two locomotives, three flatbeds, which are no doubt carrying the missiles, a troop car, and two sleeping cars. The troop car will be carrying any laborers and militia troops. I overheard the provisions officer informing the journalists that General Savin's sleeping car was added to the train at Alma-Ata."

Bogner studied Serafim's drawing in the snow. "This is where it starts to get sticky. But maybe it will turn out that Savin's death is a blessing in disguise—especially if it gives us more time. If Berzin's daughter is still on that train, she's probably being detained in the first sleeping car. If that's the case, I slip aboard while they're taking Savin's body off the train, find the girl, and get her off while they're making out their reports and informing the journalists about what happened. Make sense?"

Serafim nodded and pointed to the tracks. "When the train pulls into the terminal it will stop about there. The train will be between us and the provisions station. We will not be able to see what is going on. It will be risky."

Bogner shook his head. "Chances are, they'll use some of the militia to move the body to the provisions station. If they do leave any of the troops on the train, it's a good bet they'll be distracted by what's going on. I'll slip aboard the first sleeping car from this side, find the woman, get her off, bring her back up here, and we'll wait until things settle down before we take her back to your place."

"You are going aboard the train alone?" Serafim sounded dubious.

"In this case, one is better than two," Bogner assured him. "Now, how long before the train gets here?"

"We will not have long to wait. I have learned the sounds. The ground complains and the tracks sing. The train is not far away."

Datum: Fourteen-Five: Jinghe Tunnel: 14:13 LT

The youngest of the three Kazakh security men was little more than a youth. Unlike his rotund superior, he did not wear a uniform nor did he sport a mustache. When it was his turn to guard Mrachak, Mrachak regarded him with more suspicion than his counterparts. The senior security guard told the youngest where to sit and how to hold what Mrachak had now decided was a French variation on an old Model J semiautomatic.

To Mrachak's surprise, the three Chinese technicians had departed toward the east end of the tunnel. At the same time, none of the three-man Kazakh security team had made any further effort to check on his story. The squad leader had tried several times early on, but as time passed, the trio had seemed to relax. They had begun laughing and joking with Mrachak, apparently buying his story that he'd come to advise of a change in the train's schedule.

Now the squad leader seemed content to register an occasional complaint about the phone lines always being down and the lack of information from his superiors. When his comrades no longer seemed interested in his caviling, he addressed his litany of complaints to Mrachak.

"The phones have never worked as they should," he lamented. "One time it is the equipment, another the lines are down, or the phones are left unattended. Each time there is a tremor, our communications fail."

Serafim had informed Mrachak of the frequent tremors, but he'd insisted that they were generally minor in nature and of little consequence.

The young man was still glaring at him and juggling the semiautomatic as he lit another cigarette. He failed to notice that the senior guard was approaching again. The soft little man was smiling.

"So you say Serafim Volokitin is related to you?" the man said, "I know Volokitin. You have more hair and are better looking." He laughed. "I have always said that it is good Volokitin does not have children—they would be homely, like him."

The young Kazakh saw little humor in what the old man was saying, and continued to frown. He was taking his job seriously.

"We served in the war against Afghanistan together," Mrachak volunteered. "He saved my life when I stepped on one of their land mines." As he said it, Rikov Mrachak reached down and pulled up his pants leg to show his captors a scar. It had nothing to do with an land mine but it served his purpose.

His timing was perfect. The younger of the two was lighting still another in his endless chain of cigarettes when the older one bent over to examine the wound. Mrachak jerked his knee up into the man's face. He felt the man's fleshy features turn pulpy under the force of the blow and the man reeled backward. The startled youth tried to bring the semiautomatic up, but it was too late. Mrachak leaped, threw a handful of dirt at the youth, and threw his shoulder into the young man's chest. He brought his forearm up and slammed it into his surprised face, dove for the semiautomatic, missed, and felt the youth land on top of him as he rolled over.

Mrachak kicked, swung his elbow, and made contact. The security guard let out a yelp like a startled puppy and curled up in the fetal position. Mrachak scrambled to his feet again, grabbed the weapon, and assessed the damage. The kid's nose was splattered against the left side of his face and gushing blood like an oil well. He was whimpering and he had lost all interest in playing hero. He was clutching his face in a futile effort to stem the flow.

The pudgy one had suffered much the same fate. Somehow he had managed to get to his knees, but his progress had stopped there. His face was a bloody mask of loosely connected parts and he was gulping in air through his tortured mouth. Mrachak figured it would be a long time before his nose functioned the way it was supposed to.

"Okay, you two," Mrachak growled, "on your feet. Let's go find your playmate. Where is he?"

The older one either refused to answer or couldn't get the words past his loose teeth. The youth, Mrachak decided, wasn't able to respond or didn't know. He was still on his hands and knees coughing up a syrup of thick red-black mucus and blood. He was groping for his pack of cigarettes.

"One more time," Mrachak said threateningly, "where is your comrade?"

The soft little man in the uniform managed to gargle out a reply and point in the direction of the TBU. "He's—he's fueling—fueling the—the diesels on the—" His voice was choked off in a fit of coughing.

Mrachak located a spool of primer cord, cut it, and tied the two men's hands behind their backs. Then he forced them into a kneeling position, and tied their legs to one of the spare drills. As a final precaution, he rummaged through a crate of debris and trash until he found an oily rag, ripped it in half, and stuffed the halves in each of their mouths.

"You might as well relax," Mrachak said with a grin, "because if everything goes according to plan, you two are going to be here for a while."

Mrachak checked the clip in the semiautomatic and began working his way toward the TBU. He dodged from one shadow to the next until he was less than twenty feet from the machine's superstructure. The third of the three Kazakhs, taller and heavier than his counterparts, had just finished checking the reserves in the diesel fuel drums and was preparing to top off the tanks.

Mrachak crouched and waited until the man uncoiled the fuel hose and started his climb to the platform level. Then Mrachak lunged and slammed into the Kazakh just as he reached the third rung of the ladder. The force of the blow knocked the fuel hose out of the guard's hand and sent both men sprawling. Diesel fuel spewed out, saturating the ground around the TBU.

Unlike the other two, this one was quicker, stronger, and decidedly more agile. He shoved Mrachak off him, scrambled to his feet, sprang forward, and caught Mrachak in the chest with his shoulder just as Mrachak was starting to get up. Still dazed, Mrachak rolled sideways and felt the Kazakh land on top of him. Somewhere the man had picked up a rock, and he used it to land a blow to Mrachak's head before he brought his knee up into Mrachak's crotch.

Rikov Mrachak felt a stabbing pain in his groin and the sickening bitter-acid taste of bile flooded his mouth. His world started spinning and he swung blindly at his assailant with the semiautomatic still clutched in his hand. The barrel of the gun caught the man across the face and catapulted him backwards. Sprawling in the fuel-soaked dirt, he unleashed a string of profanity, rolled over clutching his face, and tried to claw his way back into reality.

Bleeding and dazed, Mrachak couldn't capitalize on his advantage. He managed to get up and take two steps forward before his rubbery legs deserted him. He stumbled, pitched forward, and landed in a heap, still trying to swim through a sea of somersaulting images and the choking stream of bile pumping up from his stomach.

The Kazakh, still disoriented, finally got to his feet, staggered to a nearby workbench, and picked up the first thing he could find, a blowtorch. He opened the valve, waited for ignition and the blue-orange flame, locked the fuel jet in the full open position, and started back toward Mrachak.

Rikov Mrachak, still unable to get to his feet, did

the only thing he could; he rolled over, scissored his legs, kicked, and tried to take the guard's legs out from under him. The first effort missed, but he flipped over on his back and kicked again. The second effort knocked the blowtorch out of the man's hand, caught him on the side of the leg, buckled his knees, and pitched him sideways.

Mrachak seized the opportunity. He managed to get to his feet and jump back just as the blowtorch landed in the fuel-soaked dirt and ignited. The flash fire lasted no more than minutes—but that was all it took.

Mrachak covered his eyes, recoiled from the cloud of black, acrid smoke, and backed away as the fire played itself out.

Chapter Fifteen

Datum: Fifteen-One: The Provisions Depot, Abay: 14:37 LT

It was snowing again as Bogner, crouching in the spares yard, watched the Odessa missile train roll into the tiny depot at Abay. The two ancient, lumbering locomotives, both dark gray in color, bore the crudely painted symbol of the trans-Ukrainian and Kazakhstan railroad displayed above the center buck-eye coupler.

By the time Bogner could get a good look at the train, it had slowed to a virtual crawl. The missile train's arrival was accompanied by a symphony of unpleasant screeching sounds and the complaint of disc brakes as the train's engineer brought the ice-covered cars to a stop. Bogner watched the giant wheels peel off the thin sheen of ice that had accumulated on the tracks and gouge their way down to bare steel on the rails.

The train finally rolled to a halt with the three oversized flatcars directly in front of him. Each of the missile cars was shrouded with heavy military-type tarpaulins carefully secured to the transport bulkheads. Both sleeping cars and the troop car transporting the militia garrison had been stopped adjacent to the long loading platform in front of the depot and provisions building.

For Bogner one thing was certain: The engineer hadn't done him any favors. Before he could get on the train he would have to negotiate an open area of nearly thirty yards between the spares yard and the first sleeping car. He was depending on the confusion, the snow, and the uniform he stripped from the dead Kazakh militia man in Klin to give him the cover he needed.

Earlier Bogner had watched a small cluster of people, mostly men, congregate on the depot platform. The depot's tiny parking lot was crowded with cars. He assumed they were the journalists Serafim had told him about. They were dressed in heavy coats, repeatedly stomped their feet to ward off the cold, and like Bogner appeared to be unaccustomed to the thin air in the high altitude of the Tien Shan Pass. Serafim circulated among them, periodically glancing in Bogner's direction to make certain they still had contact.

Red Sand

The plan to get the daughter of Josef Berzin off the train was simple. Bogner intended to board the train at the point where he could get the easiest access and conduct a compartment-to-compartment search until he located the woman. Timing was critical. He knew he had to allow her sufficient time to put on enough clothes to keep warm after he hustled her off the train. Serafim had reminded him that, with all of the activity, there was a strong possibility they would have to hide in the spares yard until darkness.

Getting the woman off the train was only half of the problem. Then there was the matter of making sure the train didn't cross over the border into China. Once the train pulled out of the Abay station and entered the tunnel, that was up to Mrachak. Both Bogner and Mrachak had listened and watched as Serafim carefully sketched the layout of the mid-tunnel construction area and described the operation of the giant tunnel-boring machine positioned in the unfinished adjacent tunnel. Serafim had even prepared a list of the kinds of materials and equipment Mrachak would have to work with when he finally got there. As far as Serafim was concerned, he had told his former comrade everything he knew. "Now you know as much about the Jinghe Tunnel as I do," he had said, handing Mrachak the sketch.

Krislof Dubchek, in full-dress uniform with both battle ribbons and braid, was accompanied by one of his militia officers as he stepped off the train. He saluted the provisions depot officer, stepped down into the snow, and moved to one side to make way for the six uniformed militiamen that followed him. The provisions officer, likewise dressed in the uniform of the Kazakhs, returned Dubchek's salute, did an about-face, and led the entourage up the hill to the provisions building. In Abay, and under the circumstances, it was the best they could do in terms of the military protocol due a fallen leader.

Serafim and the covey of correspondents waited in silence while the pallbearers entered the drab supply structure. They emerged moments later with the crude pine coffin the provisions officer and his staff had constructed from wood taken from supply crates. They marched back down to the train, and disappeared into the second sleeping car.

Dubchek and his aide waited in the snow, staring past the journalists and curiosity-seekers assembled on the station platform, choosing instead to look at the barren landscape beyond Abay. Twenty minutes later, the pallbearers emerged from the train carrying the closed coffin containing the body of Aleksei Savin. The lid to the makeshift casket was closed and the Ukrainian flag had been draped over it. Dubchek and his aide fell into formation at the front of the cortege, and trudged up the path to the provisions building, where Savin's casket was placed on a freight cart. The six militia pallbearers remained with the casket as Dubchek requested a moment of silence and turned to the journalists.

His voice was somber. "I feel certain," he began, "that the news of the passing of General Aleksei Savin comes as a shock to all of you. Because of his untimely death and the conditions under which it occurred, I have conducted a thorough investigation into the circumstances surrounding his passing and can assure you that the leader of the Ukrainian people died with great dignity."

Dubchek reached into the pocket of his greatcoat, took out a piece of paper, unfolded it, and began reading from a prepared statement.

"General Aleksei Vsevolod Savin, age sixty-eight, hero of the war against capitalist oppression, defender of the Union, and beloved champion of the worker, was found dead in his sleeping compartment at approximately twenty hundred hours on the night of . . ."

Bogner could hear Dubchek's voice as he moved closer to the train. He stood up, buttoned the collar of his militia greatcoat, squared his fur balmoral, and boarded at the rear of the first sleeping car. As he stepped forward over the coupler and opened the door to the car, two young militiamen started toward him. They were wearing the green and white insignia of the Free Ukrainian Yeomanry and one of them was carrying a bottle of Starka. The two men edged past him in the narrow corridor, decidedly more interested in seizing a rare opportunity to have a drink than exploring the identity of the stranger in the gray-green Kazakh greatcoat.

Bogner waited until they moved on into the troop

car. Then he knocked on the door to the first compartment. There was no response. He tried the door, discovered it was locked, and moved on. He was about to try the second when he heard a voice behind him.

The man was shorter than Bogner and wearing a uniform with an insignia on his epaulets Bogner didn't recognize. He was sporting a half-intoxicated smile. "Looking for the *gaspazha*, comrade?" he slurred.

Bogner nodded, and the man slumped against the door of the compartment.

"Haven't you noticed?" the man slurred. "The old man has been keepin' the bit of kitty to himself. Usually there's a guard at the door."

Bogner tried the door; it was locked. "Which one does he keep the girl in?"

The man shook his head. "We don't know," he admitted. "There are two of them, you know. One is young, the other is old . . . but after being on this train for so long, even she would look good to us."

The man paused for a moment and closed his eyes—as if the gesture would help him collect his disjointed thoughts. "We—we have—have been ordered to keep away from the general's sleeping car. But we see the *gaspazha*. . . ." The little man's lazy voice trailed off as he entertained his fleeting fantasy. He squinted at Bogner and shrugged, his expression twisted, almost lopsided. "If you are successful, comrade, be sure—be sure to come back and tell Matvei what it was like. . . ."

Bogner gave the man a playful nudge and winked. "I will do even better than that, comrade. I will share every detail with you."

The man thanked him, wavered for a moment, and turned to follow the other two into the troop car. When the door closed behind him, Bogner took a quick glance through the corridor window to make certain Dubchek was still engaged with the journalists. He tried the third door, and it opened.

The startled woman started to get up, but Bogner grabbed her, spun her around, and clamped his hand over her mouth.

"Keep your voice down and you won't get hurt," he whispered. "I am looking for Polce Berzin. Where is she?"

Olga Serova struggled and finally nodded compliance. When she did, Bogner took his hand away and turned her around. The woman was too frightened to speak.

"I'm looking for Polce Berzin," Bogner repeated. "Where is she?"

"Who—who are you?" Serova managed. She was shaking and her eyes were riveted on Bogner. "You are not one of them—you—you do not have that cruel look in your eyes."

"Look, I don't have much time. Where will I find Polce Berzin?" Bogner stepped back into the corridor to check on the progress of Dubchek's impromptu press conference. "Where is she?"

Olga Serova looked at him, still frightened. "You do not know?" she said, backing away.

Bogner grabbed the woman by the arm, twisted, and pinned it behind her back. "Look, there isn't time to explain. You tell me where the Berzin woman is and I let go of your arm. Keep mumbling and I break it in little pieces. Understand?"

Tears welled in her eyes. "The—the woman you seek—is dead," she cried. "The general, he is angry because I did not stop her."

Bogner was stunned. He released the woman's arm and spun her around again until she was facing him. "Dead?" he repeated. "How? When?"

Serova's words came out in fragile, terrified fragments. "She—she committed—suicide," she said. "First she killed General Savin—then she returned to her compartment and took her own life."

"When?" Bogner was looking out of the window again. Dubchek had concluded his session with the journalists and was talking to the provisions officer.

Olga Serova's voice was gaining strength. "Each morning Gaspazha Berzin would come to the small area set aside in the troop car for us to take our meals. This morning she did not come and I went to her compartment to find out if she was ill. It was there I learned that she did not come for her *zaftrak* because she was already dead."

"How do you know she killed Savin?" Bogner asked. In the back of his mind he was already wondering who would have the unpleasant task of informing the Deputy Prime Minister that his daughter had taken her own life. Josef Berzin had lost a daughter. There would be little consolation in knowing his daughter had made the ultimate sacrifice to insure that Savin did not return the Party to power.

Serova had regained a measure of composure. She held her finger to her mouth, cautioning Bogner to lower his voice, and told him to follow her. She made certain the way was clear before stepping into the corridor and leading Bogner to Polce Berzin's compartment. She opened the door and stepped aside so Bogner could enter.

The body of the young woman Olga Serova knew as Polce Berzin was stretched out on the bed, covered with a sheet.

Bogner moved quickly to the bed, lifted the sheet, and felt his stomach do a fast retreat. The entry wound was a tidy round hole with traces of powder burn, a fiendishly deceptive indication of how much devastation had been caused by the bullet. It was the exit wound that had twisted and distorted the woman's face into an ugly purple-black mask of tortured flesh. Bogner swallowed hard, laid the sheet back in place, and stepped back.

There was an empty feeling, a foreboding, gut-wrenching, awful awareness that there wasn't a damn thing he could do for Polce Berzin. They had come a long way—but not soon enough. They might have gotten there in time if they had followed their original plan and boarded the train at Zhambyl, or if a bullet hadn't carved a hole in Komenich, or if Polce Berzin hadn't tried to take matters into her own hands. That's the way it was when things came apart at the seams . . . there was always that damned litany of "ifs."

Bogner was still backing away from the bed when he heard Dubchek's voice. Less than five feet from him, the general was glaring at his aide. "I find the lack of discipline in the ranks of your militia regrettable, Major," Dubchek said with a sigh. "I gave specific orders. Under no circumstances were any of the militia reserves to be permitted in either of the two sleeping cars."

"This man is not one of ours," the aide said. "I have never seen him before."

Dubchek's features were suddenly dominated by a thin, mean smile. The aide had drawn his TK and aimed it at Bogner. "Then the offense is more serious than just a mere matter of non-compliance, Major. There has been a serious breach of security. You have failed. You allowed this man to board the train. If he is not one of your men, Major, who is he?"

"Move," Dubchek's aide said. He began prodding Bogner out into the corridor. "It will be a simple matter to dispose of him, General."

Dubchek held up his hand. "One moment, Major. Are you not curious about the man's identity, where he comes from, and why he is here?"

"Yes, General. Most certainly. I intended to interrogate him before—"

"I will save that pleasure for myself," Dubchek said. "It is I who will conduct the interrogation, and I am also the one who will decide his fate. Take him to my compartment and keep him there until I return."

While Bogner watched, Dubchek stepped into the corridor and signaled. Three militiamen entered the room, laid the body of Polce Berzin on the floor, and proceeded to roll it up in the rug. Then they picked the body up and carried it off the train. Dubchek followed.

Bogner was still watching the men struggle up the hill in the snow when he felt the muzzle of the TK in his back. "Move," the major ordered.

When Dubchek returned, he dismissed his aide, removed his greatcoat and tunic, and sat down behind his desk. He appraised Bogner for several moments before he spoke.

"Actually, it serves no purpose for me to know who you are," Dubchek said, "because it is only a matter of time until you also will no longer be with us. Nevertheless, I am curious. Why are you here?"

Bogner waited while the man lit a cigarette and exhaled a thin stream of blue-gray smoke. "If it doesn't matter, why should I go to the trouble of explaining," Bogner said. "I look at it this way. Maybe the fact that I made it this far and left you with unanswered questions gives me some kind of small victory."

"It is a hollow victory," Dubchek said with a sneer, "hardly worth dying for. But as you wish, the grave will be unmarked."

"Since it doesn't matter, suppose you tell me why

Polce Berzin committed suicide," Bogner suggested.

Dubchek picked up a pencil and studied it. "Your question in and of itself is revealing," Dubchek said. "It tells me that you did not know the identity of the dead woman. And it permits me to discard the notion that you might have been her lover—pursuing your passion across three nations."

"What was your first clue?" Bogner asked.

"Did you believe that was the Berzin woman?"

Bogner shrugged. "Like I said, does it matter what I think?"

Dubchek leaned forward. "You are an American, are you not? Americans," he said, "are easy to read. They have the curious habit of being belligerent even when they know they are going to die."

"If that's what you're looking for, how does 'fuck you' sound? Is that American enough for you?"

"You confirm my suspicions," Dubchek said with a smile. "You were sent here to rescue the Berzin woman, correct?"

Bogner laughed. "Same answer, fuck you. But you're wrong. I always heard Abay was a great place to vacation. A great place to get away from it all—nice and quiet. Then, when I saw the train, I got curious. How's that for an answer?"

Dubchek sighed. "I see no harm in telling you what is happening here, my curious American friend. I have heard the American broadcasts before the train left Odessa; within hours after Yefimov's death there was speculation by your people that General Savin engineered the assassination of our President. It is not true. Savin did not arrange Yefimov's death. If not Savin, you ask, then who?

"The answer may come as a surprise to you. Yefimov's death was arranged by Aralov Lavrenti, a Party moderate, who wanted Savin to be blamed for the deed. In one stroke of genius, he eliminated his political arch enemy, Yefimov, and by allowing the Ukrainian people to believe that Savin was responsible for the act, divided the country. Some of my country's people regarded Savin as a hero—others viewed him as little more than a villain, an assassin. But Lavrenti also had to defuse the Party faithful's enthusiasm for the general.

"The people of my country are a passionate and curious lot, my American friend. Loyal members of the Party would have swept Savin into office. But if Savin died, the Party's support would fall to Lavrenti."

Bogner could feel the train begin to move, and Dubchek was momentarily distracted.

"To insure Savin's death, Lavrenti arranged a brilliant and convoluted plot. He kidnapped the daughter of the Deputy Prime Minister and replaced her with one of his agents, who was instructed to see that Savin did not complete his mission.

"Then, when the people of the Ukraine believed that the Berzin woman was guilty of such a vile retaliation, it would hurt the candidacy of Lavrenti's only other viable opponent in the election, the Deputy Prime Minister. It is a dark matter indeed to father an assassin.

"Of course, Lavrenti had to be certain that the woman who killed Savin never had the opportunity to reveal what happened. For that reason alone it was necessary to eliminate her as well. To that end I—how would you say it—arranged her suicide. All very convenient, wouldn't you say?"

"Where is Polce Berzin?"

Dubchek laughed and shrugged his shoulders. "Not that it matters, but she, like the unfortunate woman you saw a few minutes ago, has—how do you Americans say it—gone on to her reward."

Bogner sagged back in his chair and watched the smoke from Dubchek's cigarette layer in patterns over his head.

"So, my American friend, if you did in fact come here to rescue the woman you believed to be the daughter of the Deputy Prime Minister, you are too late—much, much too late."

Bogner could feel the train gathering speed. Already they were entering the high walls of the Tien Shan Pass.

"So what happens now?" Bogner pressed.

"Now, my American friend, I will turn you over to Major Gavirolich, the man you shamed by so brazenly boarding the train. However, for that, I am indebted to you. You have demonstrated his ineptness. Slovenly attention to duty cannot be tolerated. I am afraid I will have to take the appropriate action; disposing of you will no doubt be Major Gavirolich's last official duty."

Datum: Fifteen-Two: The Jinghe Tunnel: 15:03 LT

Rikov Mrachak's reentry into the world of consciousness was accompanied by a gradual awareness of pain. There was a sense of confusion, of being trapped in some kind of ethereal world where everything was out of focus—where time and space were transposed in a commingled puzzle of bewildering parts, none of which had meaning. At the same time there was the pain, a very real pain.

He opened his eyes, searching for some indication of reality—any reality beyond the agony of the throbbing in his right leg. He pushed himself up on his elbows and looked down. His leg was grotesquely twisted to the right just below the knee. There was a smear of blood and the ugly pinkish-white protrusion of bone sticking out of his pants leg.

Piece by tortured piece, the puzzle of time and events began filtering back: the tunnel, the TBU, the Kazakh guards, and finally the recollection and comprehension of the mission.

He tried to move and was rewarded with more of the agonizing and burning pain, a throbbing that gripped and cramped, forcing him to recoil and try to crawl back into his cocoon of escape. Mrachak knew that if he tried again, he would scream out.

It was the uncontrollable, and natural, response—
he had to stem it.

He was sweating, but cold at the same time. With
as little movement as possible, he managed to get
a hand in his pocket, take out his pocket knife, and
begin sawing away at his heavy wool sleeve. When
he finished, he stuffed the piece of fabric in his
mouth to stifle the sound of his involuntary re-
sponses.

Mrachak propped himself on his elbows again
and surveyed his surroundings. He managed to accomplish that much without moving his leg.

Slowly the montage of details began to fall into
place. The Kazakh guard's body lay less than thirty
feet from him. Piece by piece, he remembered—the
man had died in a mini-holocaust, a flash fire, fed
by the fuel of the acetylene torch. It had produced
a flame so intense that it had seared away the flesh
on his face and hands and reduced his clothing to
a charred, unrecognizable travesty.

The torch had burnt itself out and so had the fuel-
soaked soil. The earth was scorched, blackened,
and if possible, even more foul-smelling than before.

Gradually the component of time began to creep
through the confusion and Mrachak began to sense
an element of urgency. He had come all this way
for a purpose. Somehow he had to make order out
of the confusion and pull himself together. He managed to roll over, nearly blacking out with the pain.
Then he waited, his lungs pounding, his heart ham-

mering. He was sweating again and he wanted to scream. There was even the possibility that he had, but there was no sound—only the temptation to plunge back into a world of unconsciousness where the brain would shut out the pain.

Still on his back and with his good leg serving as a kind of fulcrum, Mrachak managed to inch himself into position where he could use the giant coil springs of the TBU as a prop to pull himself to his feet. Each time he gripped a higher coil on the tubular-shaped steel spring to pull himself up, he felt the pain knife its way into his brain.

Finally, he was standing. Weak, trembling, and on the verge of passing out again, he gripped the coil with both hands and refused to look down at what was left of his leg.

The fragments had begun to form a whole. In one sense, he had managed to clear away some of the debris in his muddled thinking: a mission, a train, and the element of time. Somehow it all tied together. There was the dead Kazakh guard—but what about the others. Where were they? Yes. Two more. Then he remembered. He had left them in the stores area; they were bound with primer cord and gagged.

Another fragment, another layer of the mind-boggling fog had dissipated. Stop the train. The demand repeated itself—stop the train. But how? When? Mrachak turned and gripped a rung on the ladder leading up to the platform of the TBU. He was certain the mission involved the TBU.

He knew he would have to pull his way up to the platform, lifting his body, using his good leg, dragging the shattered one. He managed two rungs and his face twisted. His breathing became more difficult—but he knew that if he took the gag out of his mouth he would cry out. By the time he had conquered the third and fourth rungs, he was exhausted. A cold, salty sweat ran down into his eyes. His heartbeat had accelerated until it became a rapid staccato, malleting in his aching chest. His vision clouded and his world had blurred into a frightening web of half images.

Suddenly there was a new threat—something he couldn't identify. He pulled himself up two additional rungs and counted the remaining two. There was a momentary sensation of giddiness as his addled thinking sifted through new data. The sound. What was it? Voices?

The final two rungs seemed to take everything out of him. He pulled himself onto the platform and began crawling toward the control cage. Every inch, every measure of progress became a small victory, an agony of accomplishment. The protruding bone in his leg seemed to be even more evident. The splinters in the rough-hewn plank platform gouged out chunks of flesh, and he was gagging, desperately struggling to suck enough air into his lungs to continue. His focus deserted him and he began to wonder if the crushing sensation in his lungs would feel the same if he was drowning. There was a fleeting image of Ultra Svychi—laughing. Then came the sensation of falling, of arms and legs flailing the air.

The control panel was protected by a cage constructed of heavy steel mesh wiring with a giant two-inch-thick acrylic shield to protect the operator from fragments of rock when the percussive drills bored holes in the granite where the explosives were planted.

Mrachak crawled into the control cage, shook his head, and tried to clear away the confusion. Serafim had instructed him to activate the heating coil first, but the rest of the instructions were gone—clouded—obscured by the sensation of drowning.

What did drowning have to do with it? Was he drowning in chaos? Drowning in confusion? What—what came after that? He tried to sort through the cluttered array of dials, knobs, switches, and indicators—searching feverishly for the preignition switch. Finally, he located it, flipped it into the *on* position, and closed his eyes to shut out the pain.

As the sound of voices grew closer, he opened his eyes and looked down at his leg. He was bleeding again, but his thinking was less addled, less tormented.

The temperature gauge had already climbed out of the blue zone when Mrachak, growing continually weaker, began searching for the explosive cartridges. He found them in a stores crate bolted to the TBU platform, and somehow worked his way around to the four drills located at the corners of a three-inch-thick steel plate mounted on a hydraulic boom at the front of the TBU.

The base plate was equipped with four tungsten carbide drill tips which used a piston to strike the percussive drill rod and create the cavity. By the time Mrachak had wired one explosive cartridge to each drill tip and crawled back into the control cage, he was on the verge of passing out again.

The last thing Rikov Mrachak remembered before he slipped into a world free of pain was hitting the ignition switch on the TBU's control panel and hearing the slumbering V-four configured diesel cough to life.

Chapter Sixteen

Datum: Sixteen-One: Washington: 20:15 LT

It was a chronic symptom of the early days of a Washington winter: cold, monotonous, daylong rains that fell throughout the day and sustained temperatures that did little more than hover at the freezing mark. Then, by late afternoon, the temperature would start to drop and patches of ice would begin to form in the low spots on the blacktop.

Carol Taylor hurried to her car in the Sixteenth Street parking lot, seeking shelter where she could find it, and wishing she had planned something other than another evening in front of the television. For Carol Taylor, her days and nights, like the weather, had become tedious and boring since the day Jeff Rutland died.

At a quarter past four on a Friday afternoon, Carol Taylor was so preoccupied with the drudgery and repetition in her life that she failed to notice the driver of a dark blue BMW sedan just pulling out of the parking lot.

Carol Taylor put her key in the lock, got in, fastened her seat belt, put the key in the ignition, and turned the key.

The white four-year-old Taurus exploded—and Carol Taylor's lonely days and nights were over.

It was just after seven o'clock the same evening when Joy Carpenter, working late in her NBS office, picked up the telephone on the third ring.

"This is Joy," she said.

"Joy Carpenter, are you listening?" The voice was muffled and distorted. She recognized immediately that it was disguised.

"I'm listening," Joy said. "What do you want?" Her hand had already darted across the desk to the voice recorder plugged into the jack on her telephone. The red light went on and Joy checked to make certain the spindle was turning.

Despite her assurance, the caller hesitated. Joy knew the profile of crank callers. The caller could be having second thoughts—the caller wanted to frighten her—the caller was pausing for effect.

"If you've got something to say, say it," Joy bluffed. "I haven't got time for games."

Red Sand

Dozens of such calls came into the network newsroom daily, and there was no reason for Joy to think this call was any different from the others. She took off her earring and shifted the receiver to her other ear.

"Thirty seconds," she said, "and I hang up. The clock is ticking."

"If by chance you haven't had the opportunity to check with your newsroom in the last couple of hours, Ms. Carpenter," the voice droned, "you are probably unaware of the fact that shortly after four o'clock this afternoon, a young woman by the name of Carol Taylor was killed in the parking lot of the First Southern Insurance Company."

"Carol Taylor?" Joy repeated. "Is the name Carol Taylor supposed to mean something to me?" Sure, she knew who Carol Taylor was, but she was doing her best to sound professional, matter-of-fact, the consummate journalist.

The caller bit.

"Does the name Jeff Rutland mean anything to you?" The caller's voice had suddenly become stronger. Now the tone was insistent and demanding.

The mention of Rutland's name sent chills through her. She checked the recorder to make certain she was getting everything on tape. Then she had to make certain her voice was under control before she answered. "Rutland? Are you telling me you know something about—?"

The caller suddenly sounded angry. "Like you,

Ms. Carpenter, I am intolerant of games."

Joy scribbled the word "trace" on a tablet and handed it to one of the writers sitting across from her. She mouthed the word "phone." She saw the young man pick up the receiver and dial the operator.

"That is why I called you, Ms. Carpenter, to tell you just how much I dislike games. Carol Taylor wanted to play games. She wanted to play a dirty little game called blackmail. In fact, she insisted on it. That is why she is dead, Ms. Carpenter, because she insisted on blackmail."

It was a gamble and Joy knew it. "Who gets the information now?" she asked.

There was silence on the other end of the line. She knew it was a question the caller wasn't expecting, a trick she had learned from some of the old hands in the newsroom. Despite the silence she could hear the caller breathing.

"When someone can pass along information like the night you informed Jeff Rutland about the missile shipments from Tarhuna hours before any other network had it, I'm interested," Joy added.

Despite the silence, Joy was convinced she had hit the right button. The caller was weighing his options.

"Suppose you had a customer who wanted to pick up where Jeff left off," she said.

"Not a chance, the store is closed. With Carol Taylor out of the way, the trail from Jeff Rutland goes absolutely nowhere. I like it that way."

"I don't buy it. Why the call if you didn't want to keep the store open?"

There was a silence on the other end of the line.

Joy waited. Finally she said, "Suit yourself." The balance was delicate. She knew that if she continued to press the issue, the caller might become suspicious. If he did, he would hang up. If he hung up, all bets were off. On the other hand, if she left the door open, there was a better than fifty-fifty chance he would be back. Joy Carpenter had been in the business long enough to believe in the old adage "It's a long road that has no turns." When she heard the phone click and the line go dead, she was still willing to bet it wasn't the last time she would hear from the caller.

She hung up and looked across the desk at the young man who'd been attempting to trace the call.

"No luck," he said. "He was calling from a damn phone booth. He's probably gone by now."

"Damn," Joy muttered. She stabbed the rewind button on her recorder and replayed the tape.

By the time Joy Carpenter was able to track down Clancy Packer at the Packard Hills Athletic Club and phone him, she had verified the time and place of Carol Taylor's death and double-checked the information with the media contact, Lieutenant Arnie Davis, at Homicide. Davis was his usual reticent self, prefacing his remarks with the old "at this point everything is preliminary" caveat, but he told her what she needed to know. "It looked like homicide" and the culprit had "probably" used some kind of plastic explosive.

"I suppose you heard about Carol Taylor," Joy began.

"I heard," Packer said. "Miller called me less than ten minutes ago. We're working with the police. They're getting a search warrant for her apartment."

"Clancy," Joy said, clearing her throat. "I think you should know I just got a call from a man who claims he did it."

"Killed Taylor?"

"And Rutland. It's all on tape."

"Are you certain?"

"Listen to the tape. Judge for yourself."

"Where are you?" Packer asked.

"My office. Why?"

"Stay right there. I'm on my way over."

"Better yet, I'll meet you in the parking lot in thirty minutes with the tape," she said.

"Stay right where you—" Packer began, but it was too late. Joy Carpenter didn't hear Packer's warning; she had already hung up.

Datum: Sixteen-Two: The Train: 15:06 LT

Major Asha Gavirolich shoved Bogner into the corridor and began prodding him toward the rear of the car with the muzzle of his 9mm semiautomatic Kontra buried in Bogner's back.

Dubchek's orders had been explicit. "Get rid of

him, Major, and report back when you are finished." Now Gavirolich was scowling, intent on carrying out his orders.

Bogner had been sizing the man up. Gavirolich was shorter than Bogner, a bit heavier, and obviously stronger than a bull. In Bogner's eyes, he conveyed the image of the prototypical Bolshevik. The way Gavirolich was pushing, it was equally obvious the militia major wanted Bogner to try something. Bogner knew the slightest move on his part would give the man the excuse he needed. Gavirolich was the type who would pull the trigger first and ask questions second. Bogner's identity and his reason for being there didn't seem to concern him. If Dubchek wanted him disposed of, that was good enough for Gavirolich.

As they crossed between cars, Bogner put one foot on the grate, slipped on the ice, and fell. It was one of the oldest tricks in the book, but he had banked on Gavirolich falling for it. Bogner had guessed right.

Gavirolich grunted, began shouting at Bogner to get up, and kicked. The kick was his big mistake. For one fleeting second, the militiaman swayed with the moving train—off balance and out of control. It was the opening Bogner needed. Still on his hands and knees, he pivoted, coiled, kicked, caught Gavirolich in his soft belly, and sent him sprawling backwards. Gavirolich's feet went out from under him, and he landed hard, his back slumped against the door of Dubchek's sleeping car. There was only one problem. He was still holding on to the Kontra.

Bogner scrambled to his feet just as Gavirolich managed to squeeze off several rounds. Bogner could hear the 9mm slugs ricocheting off of the steel casing on the door to the next car. He lunged again and took the major out with a shoulder block that sent both of them sprawling. Bogner brought his knee up like a battering ram. Gavirolich caught it in the face, slumped back, momentarily stunned, and Bogner scrambled up the ladder to the top of Dubchek's car. The roof of the car was a glare of ice. Bogner inched his way onto the roof and held on to the ladder until he realized Gavirolich was coming after him. Bogner shimmied backward along the corrugated steel roof plates, holding on to the cup-shaped fresh-air vents. Pellets of sleet were stinging his face and blurring his vision. In the graying twilight he saw Gavirolich's head pop over the roofline. The major swung the Kontra up, locked his other arm in the ladder, braced himself, and used the roof to steady the 9mm.

For Bogner it was now or never. He swung his body around, using the vents for support, kicked, and caught Gavirolich in the side of the head. The militia officer's head snapped back and he wavered for what seemed like an eternity. His death grip on the ladder slipped and he fell.

In the microseconds before he died, Dubchek's aide made one brief, muffled, and final protest. It was wasted, a profane and pointless gesture screamed into the darkness.

Bogner heard the major's body hit the icy grate over the coupling, topple over, and drop beneath the wheels of the next car.

In the end, Gavirolich had died the way most men meet death when they depart life before their allotted time is up: with a scream, an objection—perhaps even a last-minute plea for a reprieve. But no one had heard it. His protest had been drowned out by the cacophony of noises made by the Odessa missile train finally reaching the highest point in the Tien Shan Pass.

Datum: Sixteen-Two: The Jinghe Tunnel: 15:45 LT

Rikov Mrachak's second unwilling return to awareness was accompanied by a mind-numbing pain that all but blotted out his efforts at coherent thought. He was dragging himself into a tormented world of shadows and shapeless images. For some reason he didn't ask himself why—he simply continued the struggle.

Nothing made sense. The visions were fragments, oddly shaped or broken, but always confusing: a montage of dissimilar pieces of something that had no texture or substance.

He rolled over and there was pain. The leg. A useless, appendage, hanging on him like a leech, sucking the blood out of him. He tried to clear his head, gagging on the piece of wet wool he had used to stifle his involuntary cries.

Somehow he managed to get his good leg under him and with the aid of the braces on the control cage, lift himself up until he could crawl into the cockpit of the TBU. He settled into the operator's seat, finding it difficult to focus his glazed eyes on the maze of controls.

He shook his head in another futile attempt to clear away the residue of half images populating the webby aftermath of his unconsciousness. The TBU's control panel looked like a crazy machine, a blinking red-green-white puzzle of confusing commands. Mrachak fumbled with the controls until he activated the power boom, retracted the plate hosting the armed tungston-carbide drills, and slipped the gear lever for both drives into reverse.

It wasn't until the slumbering TBU began inching its way backward that Mrachak saw the two Kazakhs bolt from the shadows in the supply compound. The primer cord restraints had been a good idea at the time, but now they were loose. Neither of the men appeared to be making any effort to stop him until the fat one dropped to one knee, shouldered his Kontra, and squeezed off two quick bursts. Over the din of the TBU's powerful diesel, Mrachak could hear the pinging sound of lead ricocheting off the housing on the base of the two-speed hoist directly behind him. The second burst was closer. The bullets peppered the shield on the operations cab and Mrachak ducked.

The younger of the two guards was scaling the observation tower, going for the alarm. Mrachak swung the telescoped jib around, shoved the ponderous TBU into a forward gear, and used the extendable boom like a lance. It peeled the tiny wooden shack off the observation tower and the young Kazakh with it. Mrachak caught a glimpse of the soldier's face as the man's world splintered around him. He telescoped the jib a second time, rotated the plate with the carbide drills into a horizontal position, and lowered the powered boom like a wrecking ball. The walls and roof of the observation shed—along with the young Kazakh— seemed to atomize.

Mrachak was too late. He had knocked out the phones, but the young soldier had succeeded; the alarm had been activated.

The eerie, rolling *oooh-aaah* sound filled the tunnel and triggered the blinking control lights. Mrachak brought the boom around just as the one remaining Kazakh triggered another burst. This time the little man was on target. Mrachak dropped to the floor of the control cab as the 9mm shells boomeranged off the cage walls. He felt a hot piece of lead bore its way through the fleshy part of his broken leg, and another crease the thin flesh on his temple. Both of the bullets were spent by the time they hit their target.

Mrachak reached up, grabbed the lever on the extendable boom, and swung it around, lowered it, and used it like a battering ram to plow into the storage area. The remaining Kazakh's final defiance was a pointless burst of shells exploding harmlessly in the dirt.

For Mrachak, it was no use. He had begun a hopeless spiral into a disoriented universe of half images and amorphous shadows. His head was spinning and the shrill *oooh-aaah* of the tunnel's alarm system bored into his brain until his only escape was a plunge into madness. He struggled to hold onto the controls. The TBU's control panel had been shattered by the Kazakh's otherwise futile effort to stop him. Part of it had been blown away and all Mrachak could do now was guess. He knew there was a manual override somewhere in the twisted maze of levers, but every move now was a shot in the dark. Vision blurred, he used both hands to pull the giant into reverse, and felt the platform shudder and the TBU protest as the behemoth began to creep backward into the primary tunnel.

Rikov Mrachak had lost track of time. In the labyrinth of his mind, the tangle of connectedness no longer made sense—it bewildered. Reality came and went, as obscure and amorphous as the fleeting images in his nightmares. The dim yellow-white lights used to illuminate the tunnel were no longer adequate. Was it the relentless blaring of the alarm? Was it the pain?

Strangely enough, he recognized what was happening. He knew he was forfeiting, giving up—surrendering. Images of Svychi and Komenich flashed through his mind. Then he recognized himself—but part of him was missing. He decided it was his soul. Either way, the *amerikanski* was on his own.

The TBU now straddled the tracks and Rikov Mrachak used what little strength, what presence of mind he had left to cycle the hydraulic boom until it was fully extended. Then he dropped the drill plate, equipped with the carbide drills and wired with the explosives, into a perpendicular position facing the front of the TBU. Rikov Mrachak leaned into the tangle of controls and shoved all four drive levers forward, and the giant TBU groaned—gradually picking up momentum—lumbering toward its rendezvous with the Odessa missile train.

Datum: Sixteen-Three: The Train: 15:51 LT

Bogner had already decided that if his situation was a game of seven-card stud, he would have folded—he didn't like his hole cards. He was down to two options and neither looked promising. He could jump now as the train lumbered over the summit of the Tien Shan Pass and hope for the best. On the plus side, he had a good idea of where he was and how to get out of there. Or he could wait until the train cleared the last signal and entered the tunnel. Serafim had indicated that with the rash of recent tremors and the possibility of rocks and debris on the tracks, the train would slow to around ten kilometers an hour on the stretch just before the tunnel. After the train entered the tunnel, it picked up speed again.

As far as Bogner was concerned, neither option had much appeal; both included jumping from a moving train, in the cold, in the middle of nowhere. For Bogner, jumping from a moving train ranked right up there with jumping out of an airplane without a parachute.

The train was gathering speed again as it plowed through the treacherous section of track known as Tien Shan Pass. Bogner was numbed by the raw wind and the sleet continued to pelt him. The corrugated metal roof of the sleeping car still glared with ice. His hands and arms ached, and he had lost feeling in his fingers. More than once he had been tempted to just let go.

Suddenly he felt the train begin to slow again. There was the sound of squealing brakes, and the Odessa missile train slowed to a crawl and finally stopped. Bogner pried his fingers loose and pulled himself along the top of Dubchek's sleeping car toward the front. The three shrouded flatcars carrying the missiles separated him from the second locomotive, but he could see that the engineer had stepped down from the first cab and was shining his light on an ice-covered mechanical semaphore signal. The blunted red arm was in the horizontal position and the red light was flashing.

Behind him, toward the rear of the train, he could hear men's voices. When the train stopped they had spilled out of the troop car and milled about in the cold, obviously happy to be temporarily unleashed from their confinement. Bogner knew what it was like, he had been there: infinite hours of playing cards, telling stories, and waiting—endless hours of waiting. Now they had a chance to stretch their legs. They were acting like men who were bored, men who had been confined for too long a time. They were boisterous and raucous; Bogner could hear them laughing.

By the time the order finally came for the men to reboard, Bogner had managed to work himself along the roof and close to the front of the car.

Ahead of him he could hear another exchange, this one between the engineer and someone else.

"There is something wrong," the engineer was saying. He was stabbing the beam of light at the semaphore.

"Someone has merely forgotten to change the signal," the second voice speculated. To Bogner, it sounded like the voice was coming from the cab of one of the locomotives.

"Pay no attention, comrade," the man said. "The work crews have gone for the day. It would not be the first time they have forgotten to raise the red arm to indicate that the track is clear."

"Perhaps something has happened that we don't know about," the engineer suggested. "There may be a problem."

Bogner was counting on the heavy weather and the steady sleet for cover. He pulled himself over to the service ladder, swung his legs over the edge of the car, climbed down, and jumped from the grate to the ground. His legs were stiff from the cold.

When he took a step it was like walking on matchsticks.

He looked back. One militiaman still lingered near the platform at the rear of the troop car. His back was hunched as he braced himself against the weather. He was smoking a cigarette. Bogner, still clad in the makeshift militia uniform supplied by Svychi, ignored the man and started toward the front of the train.

"What is the hold up?" Bogner demanded in Russian.

The engineer cupped his hand over his eyes and squinted through the wind and ice until he saw Bogner's uniform. He gestured toward the semaphore but offered no explanation.

"I told him that the work crews probably forgot to change the signals," a man in the first locomotive cab shouted.

"Another delay will anger General Dubchek," Bogner declared. "We are behind schedule."

The engineer, a small, round man swaddled in a heavy coat and a hat with earflaps, shrugged and started back toward the first cab door. "It will take only a moment to check. We can radiophone ahead."

Bogner didn't wait. He pulled the 9mm Kuskin out from under his bulky coat and pointed it at the engineer. He motioned toward the cab. "I said we are behind schedule. Forget the semaphore. I will take responsibility."

The engineer looked at the Kuskin and tried to

clear his vision. He moved, but not fast enough to suit Bogner, and Bogner prodded him with the barrel of the semiautomatic.

"Look, whatever your name is, you can take your choice," Bogner growled. "You can gamble here or there. Either way you've got big trouble."

The man started to protest, but thought better of it. He gripped the stainless-steel bar beside the cab, hoisted himself up, opened the door, and crawled in. Bogner followed. "Let's roll," he ordered.

The little man's hands were shaking as he took off his gloves, squirmed into his seat, and took the controls. His comrade, quiet now, had backed himself into a corner. His eyes were riveted on Bogner's Kuskin. Bogner heard the generators surge and felt the train lurch. The air compressors hissed as they released the brakes. Finally there was the sound of the wheels grinding against the ice-covered rails as they began to turn. Bogner sagged back against the walls of the cab. Even though every bone in his body ached, he was beginning to regain the feeling in his hands and feet.

"I will report this incident to my supervisor," the engineer grumbled. "You do not have the authority—"

"You do that," Bogner said with a sigh. "I've also got a complaint or two for my supervisor."

R. Karl Largent

**Datum: Sixteen-Four: The Jinghe Tunnel:
16:27 LT**

Rikov Mrachak had maneuvered the giant TBU into the main tunnel with the percussive carbide drills on the shield plate locked in the horizontal position and loaded with explosives. With the TBU now straddling the primary tracks, his task was finished. All that remained was for him to crawl out of the control cage and get back to the construction area in the second tunnel several hundred yards back.

The plan had been a good one. After the collision, all Mrachak had to do was work his way out on the east end of the tunnel. Since he was dressed in militia garb, the Chinese would think he was one of the Kazakh engineers or security guards and eventually allow him to return to his home. The plan, however, had not included the loss of so much blood and a shattered leg that was all but immobilizing him.

Now, when it was time for Rikov Mrachak to seek his sanctuary, he was too weak and too disoriented to do so. Instead of thinking about his escape, he found himself thinking of things out of his past, of the bitter cold of that small village in Afghanistan. Funny, it had been important then, but now he couldn't remember the name.

He remembered his comrade, Serafim Volokitin, and the night he'd spent with the young woman in Kaynar. They had made love even though they could hear the sounds of shells exploding in the distance. Images came and went: the waters of Lake Balkhash, a woman, his mother—and the father that came home to die after the war, his lungs choked with the residue of poison gas. He remembered music, the music that emanated from the opera house in Zhambyl. There were more fleeting images: Svychi, flowers, the red sand earth where he grew up, and the sun on his back.

Finally, though, he let go—of the controls, of the plan, of his memories, and his life. He was being . . . what was the word? "Realistic." Now he knew there would be no escape. No sanctuary. No tomorrow.

Rikov Mrachak slumped back against the wall of the control cab, made certain the explosives were in position, and closed his eyes. The eerie *ooohaaah* warning sirens were the last sound he heard.

Datum: Sixteen-Five: The Train: 16:37 LT

Bogner watched as the rotating beam of the diesel sheared through the heavy storm of sleet to pick out the semaphores. They all gave the same warning. The red arms had all been lowered to the horizontal.

"How far to the tunnel?" Bogner demanded.

"Less than two kilometers." The engineer's voice quivered. "There is still time to stop."

"Keep it rolling," Bogner ordered. He watched the granite walls of the pass move by. He wondered if there was enough feeling in his hands and legs to jump—and if he did, would he make it? He had counted on daylight. He had counted on being able to see where he was jumping. He hadn't counted on the ice.

"One kilometer," the man warned. His voice bordered on panic.

Bogner couldn't wait. He gripped the Kuskin by the barrel, brought it up, then down. Twenty years of ISA training automatically came into play: where to hit a man and how hard to hit him. He crushed the Kuskin against the back of the engineer's skull. The man's arms went limp and he toppled out of his seat. The second maneuver was even more practiced—even more efficient. Bogner wheeled and caught the cowering second engineer across the neck and throat. There was a mushy kind of gurgling sound and the second man sank to his knees sucking for air.

A semaphore flitted by and Bogner lunged for the door, threw it open, held his breath, and jumped. The train had already started into the tunnel. He hit the ground and bounced, his body hurtling into the air. He could feel himself ricochet off of something hard and slam to the ground a second time. There was no control. The rocks gouged out chunks of skin and he felt the earth peel away layers of flesh on his hands and face. He flipped into the air a second time, this time end over end, arms and legs flailing. There was a blow to the back of the head, and another across the mouth. The wind went out of him and his mouth flooded with the salty sweet taste of blood.

His senses kaleidoscoped: the taste of bile, a ringing, crashing sound in his ears, and the distant haunting *oooh-aaah* that had no meaning.

He slammed to the ground—was it the third or three hundredth time?—gasping for air and flirting with the idea of total escape, of never moving, of crawling into a hole and pulling the earth in over him.

Then, the inevitable happened. Slowly the realization came to him—he was alive. And with it came the realization he had survived. The world was spinning and the pain was excruciating, but he could feel the sleet on his face and the ice beneath him. The sensation was important; it proved he was alive.

Then, while Bogner still lay there, he heard the explosion. It was distant, yet at the same time, it was close, very close. His mind, already confused, already bewildered, already off balance, sifted through the raging turmoil of chaos to record the awful chords of shredding metal, of explosion after explosion, of falling rock and debris . . . and even those of hysteria, the hysteria of men dying.

Clouds of dust billowed out from the mouth of the tunnel as the huge cement panels began plummeting to earth creating more dust and more debris. But eventually even that ceased. The eerie drone of the sirens had been silenced and Bogner, in that silence, felt curiously alone.

Chapter Seventeen

Datum: Seventeen-One: Washington: 22:407 LT

Joy Carpenter watched the numbers tick off as
the elevator worked its way toward the NBS lobby.
She had glanced at her watch when it passed the
seventeenth floor, and now she was doing it again.
Bogner had once described her as beautiful, intelligent, and after giving it further thought, impatient—incredibly. She laughed. She wasn't certain
she knew how to judge the first two . . . but Toby
had been right about the "impatient" part. The
truth was, things never happened fast enough for
Joy Carpenter, even when she had time to spare.

The L flashed on the floor indicator above the
door, the elevator came to a halt, and the door

opened. Joy Carpenter crossed the lobby, spoke briefly to the two guards, made a comment about working late, and stepped out into the cold November night. The snow had stopped, but a chill wind whipped an assortment of leaves, papers, and trash around the exit from the revolving door and Joy pushed her hands deeper into her pockets.

Joy Carpenter knew she hadn't been there long when she glanced back at the clock in the lobby. She told Packer she would meet him in the NBS parking lot in thirty minutes because she figured it would take him ten minutes to get dressed and another twenty minutes to drive in from Packard Hills.

She had promised him the tape and now she wished she had taken time to dupe it. Typical, impatient Joy; she hadn't really thought the matter through. If she had given it more thought, she would have realized that Chet Turkoff, the longtime President of the NBS News division, might well have used it in one of the network's glossy new hour-long exposé news programs. That would have meant more air time for Joy.

Even though she knew Packer was on his way, she was still reflecting on her options. She had already decided to go back into the lobby to wait when a dark-colored BMW pulled up to the curb. Cecil Mower stepped out. "Joy," he shouted.

Joy had known Cecil Mower a long time. He was another of those "Washington faces." She had met him at the open house when the new CIA building was christened. She smiled and waved.

"Is the lobby closed?" Mower asked.

Joy nodded.

"Damn," Mower muttered. He started to throw the package he was carrying back in the car. Then he stopped. "Wait a minute; are you coming in tomorrow morning?"

"Bright and early. NBS news at noon, remember?"

"Would you give this package to Chet Turkoff for me?" Mower asked. "It would save me from driving all the way over here tomorrow morning during the rush hour."

Joy had an eight-thirty meeting with Turkoff and she saw no reason not to. She walked out to the car. Mower started to hand her the package, but grabbed her wrist instead. He spun her around, clamped his hand over her mouth, put his hand in her back, and shoved her into the car. Before Joy could recover, Mower had slipped behind the steering wheel, locked the doors, and pulled away from the curb. He drove with one hand, and when she looked down, she realized he was keeping a snub-nosed .38 Special pointed at her with the other.

"I made a mistake," Mower admitted. "I knew the minute I heard your voice that I shouldn't have called you . . . but then, how was I to know how much you knew? Our boy Rutland had a big mouth . . . and he sure as hell had the hots for you. If I fed him something, I could bank on him going to you first."

Red Sand

Joy pinned herself against the door. Mower wheeled the car off Halyard onto Delaware. It was snowing again. "You—you—you killed Rutland," she finally managed to say.

Mower laughed. "Don't tell me you just figured it out, sweetie pie. You knew damn well who was on the other end of the line."

"You give me too much credit," Joy said.

Mower laughed. "Not really. You taped the call, right? By tomorrow morning, your friend Packer would have run that tape through a voice analyzer, voiceprinted me, and my ass would have been buttermilk."

Mower turned off Delaware onto Lake Road.

"I still don't understand," Joy said. "You gave Jeff classified information—but in return for what?"

"Your boy Jeff had all kinds of information, sweetie pie. He had a pipeline right into the White House. Whether you know it or not, Jeff Rutland was wired into some real movers and shakers. We had a tit-for-tat arrangement. He fed me, I fed him. Funny thing, though, old Jeffy never picked up on the fact that any information I was feeding him would have been available within a matter of hours through normal channels."

"What about—"

"What about Rutland and the Taylor woman?"

Joy nodded.

"I arranged that too. A piece of cake. Just in case you haven't noticed, some guys have a helluva time keeping their pants zipped."

"We could work the same kind of deal," Joy said.

Mower shook his head. "No way. I don't play when someone else is holding all the aces. You know who killed Rutland and you know who killed Carol Taylor. That kind of information is bad for my health."

Mower turned toward the entrance to the Washington Navy Yard, but swung onto a side road before they came to the main gate. There was a bend in the Anacostia before the river turned west toward Fort McNair.

Joy was getting nervous. The area was deserted. Mower pulled off to the side of the road, turned off the ignition, opened his door, and walked around to her side of the car. "Joy, baby, I'm afraid this is it. From here on out, Ms. Carpenter, any further questions can be directed to your friends Rutland and Taylor, because, my dear, you're about to join them."

Mower took her by the arm, and steered her toward an abandoned pier cluttered with old barrels and storage containers.

"Not very inventive, I'm afraid, but it's adequate. When your body's found, the authorities will no doubt wonder what you were doing here, and they will of course conduct one of their half-assed investigations."

Joy didn't wait. She twisted away, fell, and rolled. As she did, she caught Mower in the side of the leg. His knees buckled and he slipped in the snow and went to his knees. By the time Mower was able to get to his feet, Joy had scrambled into the maze of storage containers and kicked off her shoes. She couldn't see Mower and she couldn't hear his footsteps in the snow—but she could hear him breathing.

"You're only prolonging the inevitable," Mower shouted. "By now, my dear, you must realize that you are a long, long way from any kind of help."

Joy held her breath. She could hear Mower moving closer but she couldn't see him. She pinned her back against the side of one of the massive shipping containers, and rummaged around in her purse until she came up with a small nail file. It was the closest thing to a weapon she could find.

Mower was edging his way between the containers, and was now less than three feet from her. When he emerged from between the stacks, Joy caught a fleeting glimpse of the gun and lunged. She had gripped the file like a knife and when she brought her arm down, she connected. The file ripped into Mower's face and he managed to get two shots off. Both missed. He staggered, careened backward, dropped the gun, and covered his face with his hands.

Joy, momentarily tempted to run, instead leaped on top of the man. Mower pushed her away and started to get to his feet, but this time she kicked and shoved at the same time. Mower teetered, reached out, and toppled backward toward the edge of the pier. It was too late. In the wet snow and ice, he had nothing to hold onto. Joy stood there, watching his fingers slowly lose their grip on the edge of the pier.

For the next several seconds, Joy Carpenter's world was in slow motion. She could hear him—and she could see him. When he fell, it was into the icy waters of the Anacosta.

For Joy Carpenter, the next few minutes of her life seemed like an eternity. She stood there watching the dark waters swirl in eddies.

Datum: Seventeen-Two: Abay: 17:41 LT

Toby Bogner had made the transition before. It was a journey between two worlds; one was darkness, one was light. One had all the comforts of the womb, the other was reality. Reality was pain and confusion. He knew the opposing worlds well. You vaulted into one; it was sudden and frightening. You had to crawl out of the other, inch by inch, feeling your way back into consciousness.

When he opened his eyes the images were blurred. He tried to move his arms. There was some movement, but it was limited. He tried to figure out where he was—but he was in a fog without definition. Then the central image leaned toward him and came into focus; it was Serafim. He was holding his index finger in front of his mouth.

"You would do well to keep you voice low, my friend. I do not want them to know you are awake."

Bogner tried to comprehend what the man was telling him, but the layer of mind fog was still too thick. He let his eyes ask the question for him.

"First of all, you are safe. The recovery teams brought you back to the provisions store." Serafim's expression did much of the talking. "So far they believe you are the only survivor. Even though you may doubt the truth of what I say, as near as can be determined, nothing is broken. You will be sore for a long time—but nothing is beyond repair. You are in luck. They believe you are one of Dubchek's guards who somehow managed to survive the accident, and they are eager for you to regain consciousness to they can ask you what happened."

Bogner's lips were swollen and his face a mask of cuts and bruises. Despite that he managed to form the word "Mrachak?"

Serafim shook his head. "There has been no sign of him," he admitted. "So far, you are the only known survivor."

Bogner closed his eyes and motioned for Serafim to continue.

The Kazakh lowered his voice. "When we heard the explosion, we rushed to the tunnel. We found you among the boulders and debris at the entrance. When they saw the uniform they naturally assumed that you were one of the militiamen and had managed to somehow escape from the tunnel."

Bogner tried to give order to his confusion of thoughts. "The train . . . ?"

"For the time being, we have no way of knowing for certain. The tunnel is completely sealed off. We don't even know where the explosion occurred. Our

Chinese friends have formed a rescue team and they are attempting to get to the site of the explosion from the east end of the tunnel. Their progress has been very slow and they report that the damage at their end is extensive. If the blast occurred near the center of the tunnel, then they feel certain the tunnel is destroyed and it will take them days, even weeks, to reach the site of the explosion."

Bogner opened his eyes. "Then we did it. . . ." Serafim leaned forward again and cautioned him to whisper. "Yes," he said with a sigh. "We did it."

"So what happens now?" Bogner asked.

"I have volunteered to assist you in your recovery. When you are well enough, we will escape. In the meantime I will say that you have a slight case of amnesia and that your recollections about what happened are vague and disordered."

"We?" Bogner repeated. "You said 'we.' "

Serafim nodded. "Even though Abay is my home and I have spent most of my life here, it is perhaps time for me to discover other worlds. I have a plan. I have contacts. As soon as you are well enough, we will discuss it."

Bogner studied the Kazakh's face for several moments before he began to spiral back into his world of chaos and darkness.

"Sleep, my friend," Serafim said "Our journey begins as soon as you are able."

Red Sand

The piano player in the lounge at the Lockwood
was playing a song Joy cherished.

"I thought I'd give you a couple of days to get your
bearings," Packer said with a smile, "before I sub-
jected you to the old Clancy Packer ISA-approved
interrogation. You look fine, but looks can be de-
ceiving. How are you feeling?"

Joy Carpenter played with her drink and avoided
looking at her old friend. "I'm fine, Clancy. The
bumps and bruises are nothing compared to the
nightmares. When I'm awake, I can concentrate on
other things. When I crawl in bed, that's when the
the whole thing starts haunting me."

Packer took out his pipe and went through the
ritual she had seen so many times before. When he
finished, he lit it and looked at her. "I talked to Oscar Jaffee this afternoon. They've been going
through Mower's files. He had a lot of people
fooled."

When Joy picked up her glass, her hand was
shaking. "What about Toby? Any word?"

Packer shook his head. "As you well know, we've
been getting news reports the past couple of days
from eastern Kazakhstan. From all I hear, that
must have been a helluva explosion. We're hearing
there was a train in that tunnel when the explosion
occurred. The Kazakh News Bureau is saying the
tunnel was completely destroyed. They're saying it

could take them as much as two years to rebuild it."

Joy looked at him. "Toby?"

"You know that's classified information," Packer said.

"It was Toby, wasn't it?"

Packer smiled. "You'll have to ask him."

"Is he all right?"

Packer shrugged and cocked his head to one side, listening to the piano. "What's that song he's playing? Sounds familiar."

"It's by Aleksandr Borodin, the theme from *The Story of Three Loves*."

Packer smiled. "That's it. Borodin. That's where I heard it."